KIRA'S BEST FRIEND

KIRA'S BEST FRIEND

"It's melanoma. Melanoma is the most fatal of skin cancers." Jake's tone was matter-of-fact, but his eyes reflected unreasonable fear. "I'm preparing for the worst."

Kira wasn't going to accept that. "That's stupid. Optimism is more important now."

He let one side of his mouth curve upward. "That's why you're here." He leaned back. "The doctor gave me some literature, and it's pretty grim. I just...feel like it's too late."

"God," Kira whispered, seeing that in his face. He was ready to give up. She wouldn't let him. "How did you know the mole had changed? I rarely look at *my* back."

He looked embarrassed. "Uh, a woman I was dating saw it and said it looked weird." He changed the subject. "The test results will be back tomorrow," he said again. "We'll know for sure then."

Kira's mind raced, mentally rearranging her life to accommodate this sudden, horrific turn of events. She'd sworn to everyone who'd listen that once she left Brook Hollow, she'd never move back. But she hadn't considered this. There'd been a rumor that the schools were thinking about networking. Maybe she could submit a proposal. It would take several months, and she could be with Jake until— Her mind refused to go beyond "until."

ALSO BY NATALIE J. DAMSCHRODER

Sophie's Playboy
The Passion Of Tanner Black
The TreeKeeper

KIRA'S BEST FRIEND

A Brook Hollow Novel

BY

NATALIE J. DAMSCHRODER

AMBER QUILL PRESS, LLC
http://www.amberquill.com

KIRA'S BEST FRIEND
AN AMBER QUILL PRESS BOOK

This book is a work of fiction. All names, characters, locations, and incidents are products of the author's imagination, or have been used fictitiously. Any resemblance to actual persons living or dead, locales, or events is entirely coincidental.

Amber Quill Press, LLC
http://www.amberquill.com

All rights reserved.
No portion of this book may be transmitted or reproduced in any form, or by any means, without permission in writing from the publisher, with the exception of brief excerpts used for the purposes of review.

Copyright © 2005 by Natalie J. Damschroder
ISBN 1-59279-781-4
Cover Art © 2005 Trace Edward Zaber

Layout and Formatting provided by: ElementalAlchemy.com

PUBLISHED IN THE UNITED STATES OF AMERICA

*This book is dedicated to
Jacob Damschroder and McKenna Damschroder,
who were born during its writing and who brightened all our lives, and
to Ezri Damschroder, who was born shortly after and whose
middle name was supposed to be Kira.*

CHAPTER 1

June

"I'm dying."

Kira Macgregor blinked, then swallowed. She fought the urge to say "nuh-uh," because Jake McKenna's voice—the voice of the man who'd been her best friend for twenty-eight years—held no trace of humor. Only one response was possible.

"I'll be right there."

She waited until she hung up the phone before she slid to the floor. She watched her hands, vibrating under the force of her reaction. She'd skipped right over shock and jumped feet-first into abject terror.

Suck it up, Macgregor. Jake needs you. She dragged herself upright and stared at the kitchen table, where she'd been going over her schedule. She wanted to race out the door, but practicality interfered for a moment. Not knowing how long she'd be gone, she had to settle things first.

It took her three hours to wrap up her last job and reschedule her work for the rest of the week and one hour to pack and close up her condo. Then she faced a two-hour drive home to Brook Hollow, Massachusetts. Six hours fighting the lump in her throat. Trying not to imagine what her life would be like without Jake McKenna in it.

She pulled into his driveway at midnight. His living room lights were on, and as soon as she got out of the 4Runner the porch light flashed and the front door opened. Jake stood in the doorway, silhouetted, looking larger than life and as healthy as ever. Kira choked back a sob. She pulled her bag from the back seat and shut the car door. The sound boomed in the small-town quiet. She started moving up the driveway, and by the time she reached the steps she was almost running. Jake met her at the top and she flung herself into his arms.

"Oh, Jake," she whispered, clinging to him. His arms trembled as they wrapped around her, and he pressed his face into her hair. They stood like that for several minutes, until Kira felt strong enough to face whatever he was going to tell her.

"What's happening?" she asked.

Jake shook his head. "Let's go inside. I need a drink."

Kira followed him into the living room and watched while he poured himself a rum and Coke and her a glass of spring water. He added lemon to hers, then joined her on the sofa.

"You know that mole on my back that's been there forever?"

Kira nodded. When she was three she'd thought it was chocolate and tried to bite it off.

"It changed over the last few months. I finally saw the doctor about it. He removed it and sent it for biopsy, but he's pretty sure it's melanoma."

Shock ran through Kira. Long before skin cancer was a general concern, they'd run around in the sun. Kira had burned several times every summer. Jake had burned once, then turned "brown as a berry," as her grandmother always said. He'd continued to tan every year, just from summer activities, but when his mother or Kira tried to get him to use sunscreen, he shrugged off their concerns. "The damage has been done," he always said. "I'm at risk whether I stay indoors three hundred and sixty-five days a year or spend it all outside. I'm not going to live my life paranoid about every little risk."

And now his life may be over.

"What does he mean he's *pretty sure*?" She let anger overcome her despair. "That's a damn careless thing to tell someone. When will the results be back?"

"Tomorrow."

"And then what?"

Jake shrugged. "I don't know, Kira. We didn't discuss anything."

Her anger flamed higher, now at Jake for scaring her based on so little. "If you didn't discuss anything, why do you think you're dying?"

"It's melanoma. Melanoma is the most fatal of skin cancers." His tone was matter-of-fact, but his eyes reflected unreasonable fear. "I'm preparing for the worst."

Kira wasn't going to accept that. "That's stupid. Optimism is more important now."

He let one side of his mouth curve upward. "That's why you're here." He leaned back. "The doctor gave me some literature, and it's pretty grim. I just...feel like it's too late."

"God," Kira whispered, seeing that in his face. He was ready to give up. She wouldn't let him. "How did you know the mole had changed? I rarely look at *my* back."

He looked embarrassed. "Uh, a woman I was dating saw it and said it looked weird." He changed the subject. "The test results will be back tomorrow," he said again. "We'll know for sure then."

Kira's mind raced, mentally rearranging her life to accommodate this sudden, horrific turn of events. She'd sworn to everyone who'd listen that once she left Brook Hollow, she'd never move back. But she hadn't considered this. There'd been a rumor that the schools were thinking about networking. Maybe she could submit a proposal. It would take several months, and she could be with Jake until— Her mind refused to go beyond "until."

"Thank you for coming out here," Jake said, taking her hand. "I was feeling pretty alone." His parents lived in France now, and he was an only child of only children. "I didn't want to call Mom and Dad until I knew for sure. I don't want them to make a wasted trip."

"There's always hope," Kira said.

"Yeah." The despair in his face told a different story. He took a deep breath. "Can you go with me tomorrow? The appointment's at one. They don't do this sort of thing over the phone."

"Of course." Kira scooted closer and tightened her hand on his. "I'll do anything you need, Jake."

The look in his eyes changed. "Anything?"

Kira studied him and saw naked longing and desire. As foreign as those emotions in Jake's eyes were to Kira, in that moment she knew nothing except his soul, and he was all she wanted.

"Anything," she whispered. Then Jake stood, and she wondered what the hell had just happened.

He pulled a photo album from a built-in shelf next to the fireplace. He sat again, and opened the book across both their laps. The first page held one photo, an eight-by-ten picture of the two of them as infants in the hospital, where their mothers had met. Kira wore a pink knit cap, Jake a blue one. They were facing each other, little fists touching.

"I don't think you saw this," he told her. "Mom gave it to me for my last birthday."

Kira had been working and hadn't made it home for their usual joint celebration.

"Our mothers hit it off so well," she said, remembering the stories. "Mine hates that yours is so far away."

"Mom calls Elyse more than she calls me." Jake flipped the page. "Remember this?"

They were in Halloween costumes at age four. Kira had insisted on being a cow, Jake a cowboy. In the photo, Jake held a rope as he tried to lasso a crying Kira.

The documentary continued, mostly large photos of the best or funniest moments of their lives. There were a few smaller pictures of family, but it was mainly a chronicle of their friendship. The friendship that had started at birth and might now be facing the end.

They reminisced for hours, and even managed to laugh, pulling out other photo albums, telling and retelling stories they both knew by heart.

The old grandfather clock over the mantle chimed four times. They sobered then, as if the chiming were a signal of Jake's time left.

"I don't know what to do about the house. Mom and Dad won't want it." He looked at Kira. "Will you take it?"

Kira looked around the house he'd grown up in. She knew it as well as her own, which wasn't a selling point. But to whom else could Jake leave it? Who would want his legacy?

Legacy. Such an elegant word for what was left behind.

"Yes, I'll take it," she said. "But I wish I didn't have to."

"Yeah." For the first time his tone reflected true bitterness. "Me, too."

He stood and began to pace. "You know, Kira, I want to do all the old clichéd things dying people do. Rail at God, ask 'why me?', cry that it isn't fair." His voice rose until he was shouting. "But none of that will make a difference. God still won't care, it will still be me, and it will *never* be fair!" He braced his hands on the mantle and bowed his head between them. Kira saw his shoulders shaking and went to him. He was crying, shuddering with the effort to keep it in.

"Do it, Jake." She slid under his arm and put hers around his waist. "Let go. Rail at God. Cry." And he did. Her body ached with the effort of supporting him while he sobbed. Her eyes and throat burned with her suppressed tears. She would have plenty of time to cry later.

After a long while he excused himself. When he came back, his eyes were still red but he was composed. He pulled her to her feet and wrapped his arms around her again.

"Thank you, Kira." He buried his face in her hair again. "God, I don't know what I would do without you."

I don't know what I will *do without you!* Kira tried to ignore the thought, to fight the panic that assailed her when she contemplated the future. She concentrated, instead, on the heat of Jake's hands at her back.

Her skin burned under his palms. Suddenly, she was aware of the hardness of his chest against her breasts. The scent of musk at his neck. Now their embrace didn't feel like their hundreds of other hugs. She barely had time to wonder why. Then Jake kissed her.

He moved his head slowly, his lips brushing her cheek, then her nose. His breath heated her lips, then his mouth met hers. She shivered at the conflict of his familiar scent and unfamiliar taste.

She pulled back, confused. "Jake?"

"Shh." He dipped his head again, this time the kiss more assured. His lips fit hers perfectly and his tongue, when it slipped between her teeth, seemed to know where it was going.

This is wrong. Kira hushed the voice in her head. This wasn't wrong—it was Jake, and he could be dying. She'd promised him anything. If he needed this to prove he was still alive, she'd give it to him. All of it, if he wanted.

An image filled her mind, of the two of them in a king-sized bed, naked bodies entwined. A whimper escaped her throat. She didn't know if it was a whimper of desire or confusion. Jake pulled her closer, deepening the kiss further.

"Jake?" she managed to ask again when he moved his kisses to her neck. Tingles ran down her arms.

"Please, Kira. I need you."

"Yes, Jake." She dug her fingers into his biceps, exploring the taut muscles she'd barely noticed before. He was so hard—she swept her hand over his chest, down, then up under his shirt to his six-pack abs. He groaned as she traced them, and she reveled in the sensation of a power she'd never had before.

They moved to the bedroom and Jake gently laid her down, leaning over her and giving her a deep, soulful kiss. It reminded Kira of her first time, in college, when she'd felt detached. When her brain had controlled her body.

What the hell is happening? her brain asked now, separating itself from the event, watching with bemusement as their clothes fell to the floor. *This is so—*

"Ooohhh."

Jake's hand closed over her breast and she gasped, stunned at the shock of electricity it sent through her body. She almost heard the switch in her brain when it clicked off. His fingers slid lower, and she moistened. The ache swelled and she turned to him, clinging and eager.

"Oh, babe." He rose over her but paused, stroking a hand through her hair. That single move undid her, and tears slipped down her cheeks. He kissed them, then whispered, "thank you" as he sank into her. She arched against him and he groaned, pulling out, then thrusting deeper, harder.

"Jake," she cried, and it hit her that his name was almost all she'd said for the last half hour.

"Kira." His reply burst out of him, and she could tell he was close. She arched, wanting to go over the edge with him, to avoid the energy of incompletion when he was done. He surprised her, again. He leaned back and pressed himself upward, rubbing against her most sensitive spot. The ache sharpened and focused, and she moved against him, urging him on.

"Kira. Come with me."

"Yes!" was all she could say as she exploded. Jake shouted and thrust one final time, then collapsed over her.

After they'd caught their breath, Jake rolled Kira to her side and spooned behind her. He wrapped one arm around her waist and linked his fingers with hers. Kira stared into the darkness, stunned.

Their relationship had changed, irrevocably. The friendship they'd always had was gone, affected by too many things to count in these last few hours. Something new was taking its place, something that didn't have a chance because he might be dying.

She turned her face into the pillow to stop the fresh tears. Jake tightened his hold on her.

"I love you, Kira."

She froze, not sure she'd heard right. If she had, did he mean it the way she thought he did? She held her breath.

"I always have," he added, his voice soft.

She could feel him waiting for her response. So many thoughts demanded her attention. She had to consider what she wanted, what was best for them. Right now, though, there was only one thing to say.

"I love you, too."

*   *   *

They slept until noon, then Kira showered while Jake cooked breakfast. They didn't mention their dawn tryst, nor did they discuss Jake's declaration of love. They ate bacon and eggs and white toast with real butter and jelly loaded with sugar. Kira couldn't scold him. His diet didn't matter.

"What doctor did you see?" she finally asked.

"Jacobs. With Brook Hollow Family Practice."

"I've never heard of him. What are his credentials?"

Jake shrugged. "Cleveland, Boston, Atlanta. I saw a brochure and was impressed, but I don't remember. He took over Dr. Hall's share of the practice when he retired."

"Will you get a second opinion?" she asked. "See an oncologist?"

"Probably." He mopped up his egg yolk with a piece of folded toast.

"You could come to Boston and stay with me. We've got some excellent doctors there."

"I'm sure you do."

His eyes met hers, and Kira saw censure in them. He thought she was being patronizing. Belittling his beloved small town. Denying it would take them into an old argument she didn't want to start. She changed the subject.

They wandered the house for the next three hours. Finally, it was time to go to the dreaded appointment. It didn't help their nerves that Dr. Jacobs was running late. After half an hour the nurse directed them to another waiting area down the hall.

"What time is it?" Kira leaned over to peer at his wrist. Jake lifted their linked hands so he could see his watch.

"Almost two."

A plumpish, balding man poked his head around an office door. "Jake McKenna? Come in, please."

Kira followed Jake toward the office. "Jake. He's smiling." Something seemed off about that. He was about to discuss the end of a young man's life, and he was greeting them like they were on the golf course. Resentment tightened her face. "Why is he smiling?" she muttered.

"He's a sick bastard," Jake said out of the corner of his mouth. But that wasn't the case at all. Dr. Jacobs practically beamed as they sat in front of his desk.

"Jake, I have good news."

Kira felt his hand tighten around hers and tried not to wince. She held her breath, waiting for the diagnosis.

"It was precancerous."

"What?" Jake looked disbelieving. The doctor looked delighted.

"The mole. It wasn't melanoma. You don't have cancer. You're not dying."

* * *

Jake whooped as they stepped out into the sun. He grabbed Kira and spun her around. When he let go of her, she sank onto a nearby bench, not sure if the nausea was from the spinning or the rush of emotions she'd just gone through.

"Can you believe it? I'm not dying." Jake turned and lifted his arms to the sky and shouted it again. *"I'm not dying!"*

Kira wrapped her own arms around her middle. She sucked in a deep breath, trying to assimilate the new tumble her world had taken. Joy and relief left her lightheaded. She'd barely overcome that reaction when apprehension set in. Where were they going from here? She didn't want things to change. She needed Jake to be her anchor.

"Come on." Jake grabbed her hand and pulled her to her feet. "We need to celebrate."

"How?" Kira broke into a run to keep up with him across the parking lot. "We drank all your booze last night," she joked.

"How else?" Jake winked at her as she slid into the car. "With a sail."

* * *

They'd sailed on North Lake so often that even though it had been years, they worked together like it was yesterday. When the *Mac^2* had reached the center of the lake, they luffed the sail and floated, soaking in the brilliance of the day. Waiting for Jake to mention love again kept Kira from relaxing. She tried to get him to put on sunscreen, but he shook his head.

"There'll be time for that, Keer." He had his eyes closed, his face tilted up to the sun. "One more day isn't going to kill me."

"That's not funny." She studied him, stretched out on deck, his sun-bleached hair fluttering in the light breeze. His nose was perfectly straight. His jaw wasn't quite square, but had a trustworthy strength that matched the rest of him. Kira's eyes drifted the length of his body, taking in the flat stomach and long fingers draped across it, the muscular legs dusted with golden hair. She remembered the feel of that body against her last night, and discomfort crept over her. They were going to have to talk about it, but damned if she knew what to say.

Suddenly Jake rolled onto his side and grabbed her hand. "We have to talk."

"Um." Kira had to clear her throat. "I guess we do."

Jake propped his head on his hand and swept his thumb over her fingers. They tingled, and Kira fought the desire to snatch them away. She wrapped her free arm around her knees.

"I meant what I said." His golden eyes bored into hers. "I love you, Keer. I always have."

Kira felt she should have been surprised, but subconsciously she must have known. And not wanted to know. "I love you, too, Jake." Her throat felt tight, and the words sounded squeezed. "But...."

He sighed and sat up. "But not that way." He shoved his fingers through his hair. "That's enough."

"Jake."

He shook his head and kept staring across the water. "Don't. There's nothing more you have to say. I know it already. I took a risk telling you, but I thought I had good reason." He jerked his head around to her. She shrank from the pain and sorrow she saw there. "So you lied last night."

She shook her head. "No, I didn't. I just didn't mean it the same way." She shifted so they sat side by side. "How I felt didn't matter last night, Jake. You mattered. You still do. You're my best friend." She blinked back tears. "I don't want to lose that."

They were silent for a few minutes, watching the sun begin to sink toward the edge of the world.

"Do you think," Jake finally asked quietly, "you would ever mean it the same way?"

Kira pondered that for a long time. She considered the connection she'd always felt to him, the protectiveness they'd always had for each other. Remembered how it felt to know there was always someone there to celebrate with you, or commiserate when something bad happened. Even thought about how it had been to make love with this man she knew better than anyone. But even the best sex she'd ever had couldn't alter who she was.

"In some ways, Jake," she explained, "we're already like an old married couple. You know exactly how to bring me out of a funk. I could tell you to the minute when you opened the marina, and how exciting it was to fulfill your dreams. But I also know you wear holey underwear for years before buying new, and your favorite meal is scrambled eggs with cheddar and Tabasco. And what the pan looks like after you cook it. There's no discovery to be made."

"And, to help prove your point, I know exactly how you react when you've discovered the last detail. You get bored, and run screaming."

She chuckled, but weakly, hearing the despondence in his voice.

"Oh, Jake, come on." She smoothed his shaggy hair back from his temple. "You don't really love me. I was just there during the scariest moment of your life."

He didn't respond, and Kira felt compelled, for some reason, to keep talking.

"Then there's this town. You love it. You never considered leaving it."

"I went to college."

"And came right back. You thrive in the familiar. Jake McKenna is a big man in this town. You run the Chamber of Commerce, the town council, even the school board."

"Not quite."

She ignored him, focused on hammering her point home. "I need challenge. Stimulation. And I get it in Boston, where something new happens every day. In computing, where I need to constantly upgrade my knowledge and my expertise so I can keep on top of things. We just wouldn't mesh in a daily situation."

Jake sighed and stood. "You're probably right. Forget I ever said anything." He moved to the stern and prepared to return to the marina.

"Of course," Kira murmured, joining him in the routine that was so comfortable.

But she knew things would never be the same.

CHAPTER 2

December

Jake parked at the curb in front of the Macgregors' house and shut off the car. He sat for a minute, taking inventory of the crowded driveway. Brianna's Honda gleamed in the sun, an amusing contrast to her father's disreputable pickup that sat next to it. Elyse's Outback was visible in the open garage, and an unfamiliar Buick stuck its rear out over the sidewalk. Kira's 4Runner was not in sight.

He scanned the street, though he already knew it wasn't there. He didn't even know for sure when—or if—she was coming. He hoped things weren't so bad between them that she'd miss the holidays with her family for the first time, just to avoid him.

For a moment, as he strode up the front walk, he wished Darcy hadn't gone to Texas to be with her folks. He needed her as proof. To show Kira that he'd moved on. To remove the reason for the awkward tone of their relationship.

God, he missed her.

"Jake, come in! What are you knocking for, you silly boy?" Elyse kissed him on the cheek and ushered him into the large kitchen, where everyone inevitably gathered. "I'm so glad you decided to come for dinner. Everyone will be here except for Sophie, who will be here tomorrow." She glanced at her watch. "I hope Kira makes it in time for dinner."

A sharp bark warned Jake a split second before his arms were full of shaggy dog. He laughed and hugged the golden retriever who eagerly licked his face.

"Cory, you rascal." He pushed the dog down and crouched to scratch her ears and ruffle her fur. "I've missed you, pooch. I sure have." Cory was Kira's dog, a gift from Jake when she turned eighteen. A poor substitute, he'd thought, for the captain of the football team, who'd dumped her a week before her birthday. Kira had been thrilled. She'd said a dog who wanted to worship you was much better than a guy who wanted to be worshipped.

What about a guy who worships you? Jake had been afraid to ask the question, then or ever. He shook off the memory.

"Can I help?" He rolled up his sleeves. Elyse shook her head as she bent over the oven.

"No, dear, you just visit. Thank you."

Jake made the rounds of the room, hugging Brianna and backslapping her father, nodding at the distinguished-looking man seated at the kitchen table.

"Jake, this is my friend Bob, Bob Winstein," Brianna introduced them. "He's alone for the holidays, so I invited him to share some of the festivities with us."

Jake accepted a drink from Duncan Macgregor and sat at the table next to Bob. "Welcome." He shook the older man's hand. "Are you new in town?"

"Yes, just in the last month. I met Brianna at the library." Bob's grip was firm, his manner relaxed and attentive. Still, Jake wondered what a guy like him was doing with a twenty-three-year-old woman.

"What is it you do?" He sipped his beer. The guy's name was familiar.

"I own Winstein Development."

"Ah." That explained it. Jake had seen his name in planning commission minutes.

Bob chuckled. "You say that as if you know something about me just from my profession. But I'm not chewing up beautiful farmland on the outskirts of town. The condos at Chestnut Hill don't live up to their high-falutin' name. I'm working on that."

Jake nodded and tried to listen as the man prattled on about his plans to renovate or rebuild existing units and add to the development. Three-quarters of his attention was on the back door. Snow had begun to fall, and he hoped Kira made it before the roads got bad.

"So, Jake." Duncan interrupted Bob's monologue a few minutes later. "I'm hearing rumors that Mayor Kleinfelter's retiring. What's the story?"

Jake tilted his head. "I hadn't heard that rumor." He wasn't lying. The mayor telling him wasn't rumor. It was fact.

Elyse turned from the stove. "Well, if it's true, you know who's getting my vote." She winked at Jake, who smiled back but didn't say anything. He was closer to his dream than he'd ever thought he'd be, and he wasn't going to jinx it.

"How's the plumbing business?" he asked.

Duncan grimaced, but before he opened his mouth Brianna spoke.

"Don't you dare get started, Daddy. I don't want to hear that disgusting story again."

Cory barked and ran to the door. Her tail fanned the room. Jake swallowed. She only got that excited for one person.

He rose and moved to the window that looked out over the front yard. Kira had parked behind his car, and she was pulling a suitcase and a giant red Santa bag out of the back of her truck. The breeze blew her loose curls behind her, and the cold made her cheeks pink. She'd never looked more beautiful.

Before he could move, Duncan and Bob were out the door to help her with her stuff. True to form, she wouldn't relinquish any of it, insisting she could carry it herself. Her voice, as she neared the open door, seemed to invade him. Every hair on his body stood on end, and that old familiar ache started in his chest.

No. He was over her. He had to be. He *was*.

* * *

"Brie, you look great!" Kira hugged her sister and marveled at the changes since she'd last seen her. "You're positively glowing. Don't tell me." She held her sister's shoulders at arm's length. "You've got a man."

Brianna rolled her eyes and stepped to the side. "No, but I'd like you to meet my *friend*, Bob Winstein."

"Oh, hello." Kira blushed, regretting opening her mouth before she noticed the guy. She narrowed her eyes at him as they shook hands. What was this grandfather doing with her baby sister?

"Kira, darlin'!" Her father swept her up into one of his famous bear hugs. "Ohhh, I've missed you, lass."

"Come on, Dad, everyone knows that brogue is fake." He laughed and she hugged her mother, noticing, the way she did when she'd been away for a while, what a contrast her parents were. Her father was giant, robust, his hair the same honey-gold as her own. She'd inherited her pale blue eyes from him, too. Her mother was small and dark and had given neither her coloring nor her size to any of her children.

Finally, Kira bent to hug Cory, who'd been patiently tail-whipping her, waiting her turn for a greeting. "How've you been, old girl?" She buried her face in the fur around the dog's neck. She couldn't avoid Jake any longer. He'd been patiently waiting, but she didn't know how to handle this, not in front of her family.

She lifted her head. "Hi, Jake."

"Hi, Kira."

Awkwardness seemed to fill the room. Kira imagined everyone felt it and stared at them, wondering what had happened. She shook herself and stood, determined no one would know the truth.

She stepped across the room and hugged him, accepting his kiss on the cheek. Hoping she didn't see pain in his eyes.

"Get me a beer, will ya?" She turned to the sink to wash her hands. "What's for dinner, Mom?"

She could feel Jake's eyes on her, sense his skepticism as she tried to act like nothing was different. She had to keep up appearances until they could clear the air. Somehow, she was going to put their friendship back together.

* * *

Dinner was excruciating. Of course, Elyse put them next to each other at the table. Kira could barely smell the aromatic roast beef and garlic mashed potatoes, overwhelmed as the scents were by Jake's unique blend of lake and sunshine, even in December.

Her gaze kept hanging up on his hands, less tanned than usual but still a gorgeous contrast with his white shirtsleeves rolled halfway up his forearms. And his voice, rich and deep and so familiar, rumbled through her in a completely unfamiliar manner.

What the hell was wrong with her? She'd never been so aware of him before. Discomfort she'd expected. Awkwardness, without a doubt. But why this humming physical attraction?

She tried to help her mother clean up after the meal.

"Not on your first night home, you know the rule!" Elyse shooed her out the door. "I have three assistants right here. Jake, you help her unload her Santa bag, there." She waved a towel at them. "Go on, now."

Kira slowly led the way to the living room, where a white pine stood bare, waiting for the annual family tree-trimming. Jake had been involved in her family's traditions forever. So why did it seem so odd to have him here now?

"Are your folks coming home for Christmas?" she asked, trying to dissipate the tension. She knelt next to the tree and opened her bag.

"Yeah, but not until the twenty-third. Dad's lecturing at a conference." He sat on her father's leather recliner and rested his elbows on his knees. "We're all getting together for dinner Christmas Day."

"Of course." *Go ahead, bring it up.* She couldn't find the words and asked another stupid question. "Is the country club ball on the twenty-third?"

"Same as every year." There was impatience in his voice. Since she'd served on the ball committee for seven years, he undoubtedly knew she was stalling.

She pulled a long, flat package from the bag and held it for a moment. The present had seemed perfect for Jake when she finished it three months ago. Now, she was afraid it was completely wrong. She slid it behind the tree.

"Much more in that bag and we won't be able to reach the tree to trim it."

She chuckled, the sound rather thin. "I go overboard every year. I love Christmas."

"Me, too."

Kira froze at the softly murmured words. She didn't know what to say. She wasn't ready to discuss it, but knew that if they weren't going to ruin Christmas for each other, they had to.

"Kira, we need to talk about June."

I know! she wanted to scream. Instead, she sat back on her haunches and smiled ruefully. "It's the elephant in the room, isn't it?"

"Yeah." He glanced over his shoulder. From the sound of things, the kitchen crew was wrapping up. "Let's go for a walk."

Anything to avoid eye contact. "I'll get my coat."

They bundled up against the twenty-degree weather and headed outside. Kira watched her breath fog ahead of her as they walked down the street she'd lived on for almost twenty years.

After two blocks, she finally grabbed her courage with both hands. "I thought we dealt with everything in June, but apparently not, or we wouldn't have gone six months without contact."

Tell her about Darcy, Jake urged himself. It would clear up any doubt Kira had about his feelings. Maybe some of his own, too. But the words wouldn't come.

"I think you're worried about your rejection," he said instead. He felt her wince. "I got over it, Keer." *Tell her*. "I found—"

"I'm not sure I did," she interrupted.

"Did what?"

"Got over it."

Jake's heart leaped, and he stamped it back down. "What do you mean?"

"You're the last person I ever wanted to hurt. You mean more to me than anyone in the world. And it tore me apart to say no to you."

That wasn't the way he remembered it, but the goal here was to *fix* their relationship, not argue it into the cemetery.

"It probably hurt you more than it hurt me," he joked, realizing he'd have to be the one to make emotional sacrifices. He'd ached for her for years; she'd just begun hurting for him. He was used to it, but he had to reassure her or risk losing it all, forever.

He stopped and stuffed his hands in his pockets to avoid pulling her into his arms. Looking at the fear in her eyes, though, he realized that was exactly what they needed. So he wrapped his arms around her back and let her bury her face against his chest. They stood that way for a few minutes. Jake felt every muscle slowly tense as he tried not to make the embrace less friendly, more intimate. *Just habit*, he told his body. He was following old impulses, that was all.

"We okay now?" he asked, knowing they hadn't really addressed the issues. She nodded against him. Foreboding swept through him when her arm moved behind him. Shock followed the cold, wet snow that slipped inside his collar.

"You little—"

Kira took off down the street and he swept a double handful of snow off the wall they'd been standing next to. He squeezed, then let it fly. It hit her square in the back.

"Bullseye!" he yelled, punching a fist in the air, then ducking as a snowball whizzed past his ear. No time to celebrate. Another ball pelted him in the chest when he straightened.

"Double ammo, huh? Well all right, sweetheart, no holds barred!" He let one fly and grinned at her squeal when it broke on top of her head and dusted her face.

They chased each other through the neighborhood, around the block and back into her yard. Breathless and soaked, they tumbled into the kitchen.

Kira pulled off her hat and her curls crackled around her. Her cheeks were flushed, her blue eyes sparkling as she shucked her jacket and hung it on her hook by the back door. Jake's heart contracted, and he feared he'd never be over her, no matter what he did.

Resigned to stuffing his feelings all the way back into the pit he'd housed them in all these years, he sat at the table when Elyse came in to pour hot chocolate from a pan on the stove.

"I kept it warm for you," she said, shaking her head. "I was sure you'd need it. Twenty-eight years old and you act like five. Wouldn't you know it."

"It was fun, Mom, you should try it." Kira sipped her cocoa and sighed. "This is heavenly."

"Of course it is, it's made from scratch."

"Just like always. It's the best, Mrs. Mac." Jake tugged her over for a one-armed hug. He didn't even need to stand. She beamed at him and cupped her hand on his cheek.

"Dear Jake." She looked at her daughter. "And darling Kira. I can't thank you both enough."

"For what?" Kira's raised eyebrows mirrored his surprise.

"For being here, bringing back old times in the best possible way." She slid into the chair next to Jake. "It's good to know that when your father and I are gone, the two of you will take care of each other."

Kira looked scared. "What's going on, Mom? Why are you getting this melancholy?"

Elyse tittered. "Oh, no, honey, it's not melancholy. It's counting my blessings. Sophie goes through ten men a month. Brianna never had one—unless you count Father Time in there, and I don't—but you, Kira, always had Jake."

"Mom, I don't..." Her gaze swung from her mother to Jake, then back. "We're not..."

Elyse smiled the smile of the wise. "Of course not, dear. You misinterpreted." She stood and kissed her daughter on the top of the head. "Finish your chocolate. I'm going to try to boot old Bob out of here so we can have a proper family visit."

Jake drained his cup and stood. "That's my cue." He didn't want to be around to dissect or dismiss Elyse's comments. He wanted to put the whole love fiasco behind him. So he brushed off Elyse's protests, said goodbye to Duncan and Brianna, and walked Bob out to his Buick. And went home to nurse his broken heart. Again.

*   *   *

"So, Brie, what's with old Bob, there?"

Brianna halted halfway up the stairs and turned. "What do you mean? He's a friend."

"Uh-huh." Kira continued past her sister and down the hall to her old bedroom. Her father had dropped her duffel on the bed. She unzipped it and started to unpack. Brianna folded her arms and leaned against the doorjamb.

"What uh-huh? He is."

"Then why bring him home for dinner?"

"He's lonely."

Kira arrowed a look at Brie and carried a handful of underwear to the dresser. "I bet he is. And I'm sure he'd love to have a sweet young thing warm his nights."

Brianna looked about to argue, then came in to sit on the bed. She started pulling Kira's clothes out of the duffel, smoothing them, and piling according to type. "He probably does. I don't know why I invited him home."

"I do."

"Enlighten me, oh great one."

"Mom and Dad are worried about you because you've never had a serious relationship with a guy." Kira pulled wire hangers out of the closet and heaved an exasperated sigh. "Why does Mom put these in here? She knows I hate them."

"You're never home to use them, and she hates to throw them away. They come from the dry cleaners."

"I know." She chucked them into an empty box on the floor of her closet and began hanging dresses. "Anyway, they worry. You don't want them to worry, so you bring home a guy. The fact that he's totally unsuitable and not even remotely your type is irrelevant. You figure they'll be satisfied that at least you're trying."

Brie shook her head. "You should be a psychologist, Keer. You've hit the proverbial nail."

Kira snorted and dumped the empty duffel into the closet. "I wish I could hit my own nails so easily."

"We'll do it for each other. You tell me my perfect mate and where to find him, and I'll tell you yours."

Not sure she wanted to venture down this road, Kira obliged

anyway. "You need a retired Navy SEAL, someone rough, with honor, who wants to settle down. You'll find him in Boston, if you ever venture out of the safe Hollow to visit me."

Brianna laughed so hard she fell backward onto the bed. "Oh, my, you've thought long and hard about that one, haven't you?"

Pleased with herself, Kira flopped onto her stomach and grinned at her sister. "It's all those romance novels I read. I've got Sophie pegged, too."

"Don't tell me, she gets a lion-tamer."

"No, a playboy. She needs a challenge."

"But that's what she dates!"

"Right, so she'll know what to do with the right one when he falls hard for her."

Brianna sobered. "Now you."

"No." Kira lurched back off the bed. "I don't have a perfect mate. I'm married to my career."

"You're trying to be. But you do have one, and he's right here in Brook Hollow."

Kira turned to the dresser and began sorting her toiletries. Please, don't let her sister be going there. She tried to divert her. "He'd better not be, because I need myself a city man. Boston born and bred, preferably."

"That's what you think you want." Brianna caught Kira's eyes in the mirror. "Which makes it all the sadder."

"What?" Kira asked despite herself.

"Jake's your soul mate, Kira. And you'll never find him in Boston."

CHAPTER 3

Kira argued with herself over Brianna's assertions the next day while she helped her mother with the grocery shopping. She didn't believe in soul mates. People had to work hard at relationships, which was another reason she didn't have any.

You and Jake never had to work at it.

That was different. They'd been developing their relationship since birth. And just look what had happened when they turned "romantic." It fell apart, and now they had to work at it.

"Kira, honey, wait here for our number, will you? I'll run down and get the meat." Kira looked at the pink slip of paper her mother had handed her. 101. She looked up at the deli's red digital display. 95. She leaned on the handle of the cart.

She tried to think about the proposals she'd sent out. She checked her answering machine and e-mail daily, but had received no responses. Having no work waiting after the holidays worried her. Maybe she'd better consider the school district network job. The rumor had finally become fact, and she still had time to submit a bid.

"Ninety-six," one of the deli clerks called out.

The thought of leaving Boston sickened her. Wait. No, it didn't. For some reason it actually lifted her spirits to consider coming home for a while. She shuddered. The worst traps were the ones dressed up to look like rewards.

"Ninety-seven."

"Kira, darling!" Her reverie broke under the cloud of Chanel No. 5

and dusty mink that enveloped her. She guessed that somewhere behind it all was Myrna Kleinfelter, the mayor's wife, one of the few women in Brook Hollow who would dare to wear either to the supermarket.

"Ninety-eight."

Kira disengaged herself and took a step back in a search for fresh air. "Mrs. Kleinfelter. How nice to see you. Are you ready for the holidays?"

"Oh, yes! Well, just about. I have a bit more shopping and wrapping to do, but I'll be all done before the tree lighting ceremony in the square tomorrow."

Kira wrinkled her brow. "I thought the tree was lit the day after Thanksgiving."

"Usually it is dear, but we had some difficulty getting the proper tree this year, what with the drought and all."

"Ninety-nine."

Myrna jumped on her three-inch heels and waved a sparkling hand in the air. "Yoo hoo, here I am!" She tiptoed forward, pulling her cart behind her. "I'll see you at the ceremony!" she called over her shoulder.

"One hundred."

Kira inched forward into the space vacated by ninety-eight and waited for her number. She tried to remember if the town had ever lit the tree late any other year, but couldn't think of one. The late ceremony, held on December 22nd, would make the holidays seem rushed. Kira realized she wanted to savor every moment. Maybe she needed a rest.

"One-oh-one."

She straightened. "Right here."

"Kira?"

She turned. A woman her age stood behind her, her brow crumpled in uncertainty.

"Maggie!" Kira hugged her old friend quickly, then held her sleeve while she turned back to the impatient deli clerk.

"One pound of tavern ham, chipped, please." The clerk pulled the ham from the case and Kira hugged Maggie again.

"Maggie, wow! I thought you were in Florida!"

"No." She smiled, but Kira thought she looked sad. "We moved back last month. I'm surprised your mother didn't tell you."

Kira was ashamed to admit she might have. She eyed the infant in the shopping cart's carrier. The little girl—judging by the lace-edged bonnet and blanket—slept peacefully, her lush lashes resting on chubby, rosy cheeks.

"Who's this?" she asked.

"This is Abby." Maggie gently tucked the edge of the blanket under the baby's chin. "She's two months old and sleeps like this all day. When she's not nursing."

Looking at the baby, Kira felt a pang of longing she didn't want to identify. She was only twenty-eight. Her clock wouldn't even start ticking for another four or five years, if ever. But just for an instant, she imagined herself nursing her own child.

She shook off the image and accepted the ham from the clerk. "Two pounds of low-salt Swiss," she told him. "So, Maggie, when can we get together? I'd love to have lunch."

Maggie's face lit up. "That would be wonderful. I'll leave Abby with a sitter, if I can find one, and meet you at Galloway's. How's tomorrow at one? Do you still like late lunches?"

"Definitely."

"Miss, will there be anything else?"

"Oh, yes, a pound of roast beef." She tossed the cheese into the cart and looked around for her mother. "I'm so glad I ran into you. How's John?"

Kira could have sworn fear flitted across Maggie's face. "He's why I'm home." She waved a hand to dismiss the topic. "We'll talk tomorrow. I really need a confidante," she admitted.

Kira grinned. "Just like old times." Maggie Oxford had been her best girl friend growing up. They'd giggled their way through junior high, practiced their model swagger and dismissive looks in high school, and sobbed on each other's shoulders after the disastrous prom night their junior year. Kira regretted she'd let their friendship fall victim to time and distance.

"Not quite like old times. But it'll be good to talk." They hugged, then Kira took her roast beef and maneuvered the cart toward the butcher counter while Maggie waved and headed for produce.

"Mom, you'll never guess who I just ran into."

"Wait." She thumbed her clicker six times, paused, then seven more. "How much was the deli?" Kira read off the tags to her, amused that her mother was still using the old fashioned counter to keep track of her spending. "Mom, that thing must be ancient. Ever heard of a calculator?"

Elyse grimaced. "Your father bought me one for my birthday last year. It had an automatic shut-off, and when I got to talking with Myrtle—you know how she prattles on—it lost everything I'd put into it. This," she waved the piece of red plastic, "won't go away." Kira watched her cross half a dozen items off the list. "So, who did you run into?"

"Maggie Oxford and her baby." She followed her mother down the cereal aisle. "Did you tell me she moved back to town?"

"Of course I did." She checked a label, then replaced the box and pulled off another. "She left her husband for abusing her and came home."

"Abuse!" Kira stared at her mother. "John? I can't believe it." He'd been such a sweet guy in high school. He doted on Maggie.

"Come on, Kira, you live in the big city. You know things happen that seem unbelievable. Especially abuse."

Kira grimaced at the corn flakes her mother put in the cart and retrieved the frosted flakes she'd returned to the shelf. "Still. It's one of those things you think only happens to other people."

"Yeah. Other people like Maggie." Elyse looked at her daughter. "She can probably use a friend."

"She practically said as much. And here I thought we'd be chattering about baby clothes and honeybuns." She felt selfish, thinking about her gadabout lifestyle in Boston compared to the hardships Maggie had apparently gone through.

"First the tree-lighting, now this," she murmured to herself, following her mother to the checkout. "What next?"

* * *

"Jake has a girlfriend."

Kira choked on a piece of shrimp. Brianna pounded her on the back, but Kira ignored her and stared at Sophie. "What did you say?"

Her middle sister glanced up from the fettuccine she was dishing onto her plate. "You didn't know?"

Kira swallowed the bite in her mouth and strove to be more nonchalant. "Obviously. How long have they been dating?"

"Not sure. I just heard."

"Nice girl?" Duncan wiped his mouth with a napkin. "Pass the rolls, please."

Sophie shrugged. "I guess. She's one of those voluptuous women everyone assumes has a vacuum in the skull. Her name matches. 'Darcy Langlais.' She moved to town this summer, supposedly looking for quiet after the chaos of New York." She chewed her broccoli, then swallowed. "I think she was looking for a man, and Jake is the one with the most power. He'll be the next mayor, you know."

Dumbfounded, Kira asked, "How do you know so much? I haven't heard about any of this."

Sophie shrugged. "You live in Boston."

"So do you."

"Well, unlike you, I have friends in Brook Hollow."

"I have friends." Kira heard her defensive tone and winced. "I'm having lunch with one tomorrow."

Her sister snorted. "Yeah, with one you've barely talked to since you left town. Who hasn't lived here more than a month herself. The only friend you have besides family," she waved her fork around the table, "is Jake. And that one's questionable."

Kira set her wine glass down hard. "You don't know what you're talking about."

"Yes, I do. Something happened last summer, and you and Jake practically don't talk anymore. It's true," she insisted to her parents' disbelieving looks. "Ask her."

Suddenly Kira found herself in the exact spot she'd been avoiding since she got home. Heck, since June. Well, too bad. She wasn't giving them more than she wanted to give. But she had to give them something.

"Jake thought he had cancer," she said.

The collective gasp filled the room. Even Sophie looked stunned. Kira swallowed a bite of pasta.

"He had a mole the doctor thought was melanoma. I came home because he thought he was dying. It turned out to be precancerous. Jake and I had a disagreement on the way he should live his life, and things have been a bit tense since then." She kept her gaze on her plate. She hadn't lied, not really. They'd disagreed because he wanted to live his life with *her*.

"Why would the doctor think it was melanoma?" Elyse started the questions.

"He's a jerk who likes to prepare his patients for the worst."

"Cancer doesn't run in his family, does it?" Duncan pointed out.

"It doesn't matter, Dad. Skin cancer is caused by sun damage," Sophie explained. Her gaze narrowed on Kira. "So what happened in this disagreement?"

"I want to know what kind of treatment he's having," Elyse

demanded to the air.

"Mom, he's not having any treatment. It wasn't cancer."

"Then how will he prevent it?"

"The same way the rest of us do. Staying out of the sun would be a good start."

Silence. Duncan and Elyse both chuckled. Sophie said, "Yeah, right." Brianna added, "That'll be the day," and they all went quiet again as the next words of the lyric went through their heads. Kira battled back the wave of remembered fear. Only Sophie seemed unaffected by the moment.

"So what happened?" Sophie prompted again. "What did he say to you to make you stay away so long?"

Kira shook her head. "Nothing important. It was petty."

"You didn't say anything about this last night," Brianna accused.

"Look, we straightened things out. Our friendship is back to normal. In fact," she stood and looked at her watch, "he'll be here any minute to go shopping."

"Shopping?" Brianna shot her a mischievous grin. "He's going shopping with you?"

"We have some last minute gifts to get. You know I always do this." She carried her plate to the sink, rinsed it, and put it in the dishwasher. "It's no big deal."

A knock sounded on the door then, and while Kira got her coat she tried to convince herself the whole exchange had been normal with no undercurrents. But as she greeted Jake and they went out the door, she was painfully aware of the dead silence she'd left behind her.

* * *

Jake reclined the 4Runner's leather seat and wiggled until he was comfortable. "I could sleep in this. Must have cost you a fortune."

"No, just lucky timing and a big down payment. The lease is very reasonable. Toyotas have a great residual." She glanced down and caught him staring at her. "What?"

"Nothing." He closed his eyes against the beauty of her profile. "You just sound so businesslike."

"I *am* a business woman, Jake." She took the turn into the mall parking lot. "No time for a nap, we're here."

"I don't know why I always let you drag me out here." He slid out of the truck and slammed the door. "You don't need my opinion."

"Stop being macho. You love it."

No, I love you. He couldn't say it, and he didn't want to think it. It had been true, all those many years he'd accompanied her on her last-minute buying frenzies. His role was always to carry packages and nod and smile for every choice she made. Things seemed to go faster that way than if he actually offered an opinion. And, contrary to what he'd let her think, he didn't enjoy the shopping. He hated the mall, the crowds aimlessly wandering from store to store, the smoking teenagers. All the fake bargains and smirking sales clerks annoyed him. He'd only gone because it was time with Kira. And, especially after she moved to Boston, he'd treasured every minute they'd spent together. Even shopping.

They stepped into the warm mall from the frigid parking lot and Kira shivered. "Brrr. I don't know if I want to go to the tree lighting tomorrow. It's supposed to be even colder than today."

"C'mon, Keer. It's tradition."

"Well, they're doing it on the wrong day, anyway, so tradition-breaking has a precedent."

They walked down the mall in silence for a while. Kira always wanted to start at the far end and work her way back. Halfway down, she asked, "Why didn't you tell anyone about the mole?"

There were lots of reasons he could give, but the main one was that he didn't want to share that terrifying, amazing night with anyone but her. "I didn't want to listen to the nagging. I figured you'd be bad enough."

She pouted, just a little. "I don't nag."

"Well, you would have, if you'd been around."

She wrinkled her nose. "I probably would have."

"Did you tell anyone?" he asked.

She shook her head. "Not until tonight."

Jake groaned. "Great, just in time for Christmas. Did you tell Sophie?"

"I told the whole family."

Now everyone in town would know. Someone, probably Elyse, would tell his mother. Who would worry, and be all over him from the time they got home until they went back to France.

"If my parents decide to move back to Massachusetts, I blame you."

She laughed. "If you'd use some precautions, you'd have nothing to worry about."

"Nag, nag, nag."

They'd neared the Sears at the end of the mall when she said, quietly, "Sophie says you're dating someone."

He blinked at her. "Why does she think that?"

She shot him an "oh, please" look. "You know Sophie knows everything going on in this town. So, is it true?"

"Yeah, it's true."

"Oh." They passed two more stores. "Why didn't you tell me?"

"I really don't know, Kira."

"Is it because you're still—"

"No." He stopped. "I met her in October. She rented a boat. She seemed great, and I asked her out."

"Can I meet her?" Her tone of voice was the perfect blend of interest and proprietary friendship.

"Eventually. She's in Texas with her family for the holidays."

"Oh. Well, when's she coming back?"

Too soon. Not soon enough. Darcy really wasn't that special to him, merely a distraction from his way-too-old crush on his best friend. He changed the subject. "What are you shopping for, anyway? You already loaded the tree."

"Just little things. Cigars for Dad—"

"He doesn't smoke them."

"For Christmas he does. Underwear for Sophie and Brie..."

He groaned. "Please tell me you're not buying underwear for your mother."

She smiled and patted his arm. "No, hon, I'm buying pajamas for my mother. In Victoria's Secret."

This was why he let her drag him shopping—to share in her sheer delight at doing something for the ones she loved. It was such contrast to her self-centered Boston life, where she lived and worked in relative solitude and called it exciting.

"And me?" he asked.

Her eyes danced and he ruthlessly squashed the urge to kiss her. She focused so hard on getting everyone the perfect gift. She obsessed that no one would like what she'd gotten, which was the reason behind her annual last-minute spree. She always made half the family cry, her gifts were so good.

"You know the drill," she told him. Every year he stuck by her like glue. Every year she managed to buy him "a little something" right under his nose. He always made suggestions, and she always bought the one thing he wanted and didn't tell her about. In the past, he'd seen it as a sign that they were meant for each other. Now he knew better.

Now he knew Kira considered it just another aspect of their boring relationship.

They went into the tobacco shop first, hidden in the exit wing away from all the mainstream stores. Jake admired a carved ivory pipe.

"You wouldn't smoke it," Kira said.

"It would look nice on my desk, though."

"Hm." She paid for her father's cigars and left the store.

In Victoria's Secret, he ignored the thongs she selected for Sophie, and the bikinis for Brie. He helped her select an on-sale flannel-lined satin robe for her mother, then pointed to a corner in the back.

"Did you know they sell men's boxers? I love silk boxers."

She smirked and pushed him toward the cash register. "They're men's boxers for women to wear. Why should you guys have all the comfort?"

He refused to blush. Or to admit he was having fun.

They paused in the food court for a soda, and overheard an older couple arguing about computers. When the woman called the man an old fuddy-duddy because he didn't know what ask.com was, Kira laughed.

"Since when does the senior center have the Internet?" she asked.

"Since August."

"I was joking."

"I wasn't." He pulled the top off his cup and tipped a piece of ice into his mouth. "A few of the residents were complaining about an overdose of bingo. We brainstormed and came up with something for them to do."

Kira's eyes were soft as she looked at him. "We who? When did you get involved in the senior center?"

He tried not to be hurt. He cared about everyone in this town, and helped whenever he was asked. How could she not know that?

"The mayor asked for the council's input," he told her.

"Well, it was a great idea. Did they put up a fight?"

"Why would you think that?" He grinned. She knew as well as he did that any "advance" anyone tried to make in Brook Hollow was met with resistance.

"Oh, silly me." She looked at her watch. "We'd better get a move on."

The game continued. Kira bought perfume for his mother, and dutifully sniffed the Drakkar he sprayed on his wrist. He helped her select argyle socks for his dad, and modeled a fisherman's sweater for her.

"This would look great with a pipe," he mugged, pretending to clamp his teeth on a pipe stem and puff.

"Uh-huh." She barely looked at him. He wondered which gift she'd decided on. This year he was going to guess it for sure. Probably the pipe.

The mall was closing by the time they finished shopping.

"I'm starving," Kira complained, heading for the blue and white pretzel stand. Jake eyed the clerk of the Waldenbooks store, who was searching his keys for the one that would lower the gate.

"Hang on, Keer. I want..."

"Jake!" She gave him a beseeching look. "Please, I'm so hungry. Can't it wait?"

He glanced back at the store, torn between getting the book he'd been waiting for and letting Kira get what she wanted. It occurred to him, as he trudged after her to the pretzel stand, that she always got her way.

"That can't be healthy," he muttered.

"What?"

"You always get what you want," he said.

She looked up at him. "What are you talking about?"

"This." He motioned to the counter, three people ahead of them. "I wanted to go into the bookstore. You wanted a pretzel. Guess what we're getting."

Kira laughed. "This is exactly why last summer went nowhere. You sound like an old married guy, and if I gave in to my impulses, I would argue with you about how many times we went sailing or hiking or rented the testosterone movie instead of the heartwarming one."

Jake didn't want to think about last summer, and the fact that Kira could laugh about it aggravated him more. But he wasn't going to let her be the only mature one, so he bit his tongue and stuffed his hands in his pockets.

Kira offered him a bite of her cinnamon-sugar pretzel on their way out to the car. Jake accepted the peace offering, then shifted her packages to better balance them. "You went overboard this time, Keer."

"No, I didn't." She licked her fingers. Jake stared straight ahead, pretending he was looking for the car. His throat seemed to close when, out of the corner of his eye, he saw her sucking her index finger. *Irritated to aroused in one easy motion*, he thought. *Sure, I'm over her*.

He cleared his throat. "I helped you unload your Santa sack. You bought something for everyone tonight, even though you already had presents for them all. That's going overboard."

"So sue me, I love people. Do you think Maggie will like her present?" She peered into the single bag she carried herself. "I know she'll love the outfit for Abby, and the rattle socks will be fun, but I really wanted to get Maggie something that would make her feel good about herself."

Jake had watched Kira painstakingly select the tiny diamond hummingbird on a filament wire. It represented freedom, she had said.

"I think she'll love it. It's lots better than slipper socks."

Kira punched him on the arm and pressed the button on her remote to unlock the truck. They stowed the packages in the back and Jake looked at his watch. "We've gotta hurry. I'm expecting a call soon."

Kira climbed into the truck. "Isn't it like four a.m. on the continent?"

"Something like that." Jake cleared his throat. "It's Darcy, not Mom and Dad."

"Oh." Kira stopped at the light at the mall exit. "Okay, I'll drop you off and bring you your car tomorrow," she suggested, turning toward his house instead of her own.

"No, I have time."

She shook her head. "This is important. I don't mind."

He felt weird enough talking about another woman with her, so he gave in. For the first time he realized how he always avoided discussing his love life with Kira. No secret why that was.

"I have to be at work early tomorrow," he warned her. "It's been busy in the shop. And I have a Holiday Ball Committee meeting I'll have to drive to."

She grinned. "God forbid the chairman should arrive late. Don't worry, I'll get you there. Brie won't let me oversleep. We have plans for Mom and Dad's gift that we have to take care of tomorrow."

"See you in the morning, then."

He waved her off and went inside to check the answering machine. He found himself half hoping to find he'd missed the call, but the red indicator light glowed steadily.

He tossed his jacket on a chair and settled onto the couch with a beer and the cordless phone. He'd just flipped on the TV when the phone rang.

"Hello?"

"Jake! You're home! I was missing you."

"Me, too." He winced at the lie. "Are you having a good time?"

"Oh, the best. I missed my folks. We've been gallivanting all over town. How about you? What have you been up to?"

"Work, mostly. This is the only time in winter we get much business, except from ice fishermen."

"Will you take me ice fishing next month? When the lake is frozen enough?"

"Really?" Kira hated fishing. He'd never met a woman who voluntarily went. "Are you sure?"

"Sure. My dad and I used to fish all the time, but never through a hole in the ice. I'd love it."

Jake's feelings about this relationship suddenly changed. Finally, a woman who shared his interests. They chatted a little longer about fishing methods, then, after a pause, Darcy's tone changed.

"What are you wearing?"

"Huh?" Jake looked down at himself. "Jeans and a sweater. Oh!" Idiot. He lowered his own voice. "What are *you* wearing?"

She told him.

He chuckled and tried to banish the image of *Kira* in a leather bustier from his mind.

"Ice fishing and leather," he joked. "I just might have found my dream woman."

"You may just have, Jake McKenna." This time, her tone wasn't playful. This time, it was scary. Jake changed the subject. Sure, he wanted a distraction from Kira. He wanted to move on with his life. But he wasn't quite ready for whatever was in Darcy's head.

He might never be.

CHAPTER 4

Kira rolled between satin sheets, letting her limbs slide across the luxurious fabric. In contrast to the cool smoothness, a pair of rough, hot hands stroked her naked body. Heat flared, licking at her fingers and toes, burning deep inside, begging to be stoked. She reached, but the hands were elusive, touching her everywhere she wanted to be touched but, at the same time, as insubstantial as a dream.

"Kira!"

Kira jerked her head up, squinting at the brightness in her room. This wasn't right. She fought the down comforter and wool blanket that had gotten wrapped around her three times.

"Kira!" Brianna shouted again, outside her bedroom door. There was a trio of thumps, then a thud against the wall.

"What!" She struggled to shake off the remnants of the dream, and the disappointment that she was now awake.

"We're late!"

"No kidding," Kira muttered, and finally managed to focus on the clock. "Where are Mom and Dad?" She rubbed a hand across her face and fell back onto the pillow.

Brianna half fell into the room, one hand on the doorknob, the other trying to tug a sock onto her foot. "They just left. We've gotta go *now* if we're going to keep this a secret. You know they'll be all over us from now to Christmas otherwise."

"Great." She lunged out of bed and began yanking on clothes. "I thought you were gonna get me up."

"I was," Brianna called from down the hall. Thump, thump, thump, bang. "I—damn—overslept."

Kira looked out the doorway and saw Brie stomp to adjust her sneaker. "I thought they weren't leaving until later."

"They left early."

Kira cursed as she followed her sister down the stairs and out the door.

"Let's hurry." They climbed into Jake's car and were halfway down the street before Kira realized Brianna was staring at her strangely.

"Why are we driving Jake's car?" she asked when Kira looked at her.

"Because he was late getting home for a phone call. I dropped him off."

"Bummer. I thought it was for something more interesting."

Kira looked at her watch. "Damn it, he's gonna be late for the committee meeting, too."

"We're off to a great start today," Brianna groaned. "I just hope Cassie isn't busy."

Faint hope. The travel agent was deep in discussion with a retired couple about the merits of a "Seven Wonders of the Ancient World" tour versus a French Riviera package. After half an hour they'd tossed both ideas.

"What about Norway?" the wife asked.

Kira groaned and tried to ignore the seconds hand of the wall clock sweeping time away. She'd tried to call Jake at home when they got here, and there'd been no answer. The marina's line was busy. Since then, Cassie, the agent, had had three calls on hold at a time, not only preventing Kira from using the phone, but further delaying the end of her conversation with the couple. Jake was going to kill her.

"Brianna, hi. Sorry to take so long." Finally, Cassie approached them. The words were meaningless but the smile sincere, so Kira let her sister's friend lead them to her desk without complaint. She also curbed her usual desire to take over, and let Brianna handle the transaction.

"What are we doing today?" Cassie pulled a green folder from the stack on her desk and flipped it open, scanning the contents. "Oh, yes, you're paying your balance, and picking up tickets." She glanced up. "Do you have the check?"

Brianna dealt with the details, Kira signed the check, and they rushed back out into the wind.

"I've gotta get this car back to Jake," Kira told her sister, who shook her head.

"We need to hide the packet before Mom and Dad get home. Back to the house."

"Grr." Kira tried not to speed through town. The roads were dry, but an occasional spot of ice lurked dangerously in shadowed corners.

They passed the bank. "Remind me to deposit your checks today," she told Brianna. The three of them were pitching in for their parents' Christmas present, a trip to Las Vegas. They'd been saving all year. If she didn't deposit Sophie and Brianna's share, she'd have a major overdraft situation.

A minute later she screeched to a halt in the driveway and practically pushed Brianna out the door.

"What time's his meeting?" Brianna stuck her head back into the car.

"I don't know! Likely half an hour ago!" Kira flapped her arm at her sister until she shut the door, then roared backward out of the driveway.

She made it to the marina in record time.

"Sorry, Kira, he's gone."

Kira blew her bangs out of her eyes, aware her curls hadn't felt a comb yet today.

"Where is he?" she asked the clerk, who was ringing up a two-hundred dollar gift certificate. Jake would like that.

"He's at the club, at the meeting."

Kira swallowed another curse. "How did he get there?" It wasn't that far, but distance always seemed to double when you were late. If Jake had walked, he'd be really pissed.

But the clerk told her he didn't walk. "I think he ran."

*   *   *

The meeting room at the country club was packed when Kira slipped in the back door. The noise indicated the meeting hadn't started yet. She scanned the room until she found Jake. He stood at the head of the room and looked like he was getting ready to take over. She flinched when his eyes met hers. Pissed was putting it mildly.

"Okay, everyone, let's get started." He rubbed his sleeve across his damp forehead. "This is our last chance to troubleshoot before tomorrow night." The room was quiet by the time he finished speaking, though he'd hardly raised his voice. Kira watched him interact with the committee members, giving a smile of praise here, a quiet look there that said, "almost but not quite good enough." Everyone in the group hung on every word, as if he was giving a speech. *Mayor Kleinfelter, look out,* Kira thought. Jake was heading his way.

"Lance, what's the status of the beverages?"

"Fully stocked."

"Caitlin, the food?"

"The sous chefs are working on pre-prep as we speak."

"Rhonda, how about the reservations? I know we were a little below estimate at the last meeting."

She held up a notebook, showing pages full of names. "Sold out. All but about a dozen are paid, the rest will pay at the door."

Jake whistled. "How'd you do that?"

She smiled and folded her hands on top of her notebook. "I told them they'd be more likely to get a meal with their ticket if they paid in advance."

"And no one wanted a discount for doing that?"

She shook her head. "It's for a good cause."

Kira whistled softly, herself. She'd done Rhonda's job. "Good cause" had never mattered before when it came to prepaid tickets. Each year, Brook Hollow held a holiday dance for a different charity. The country club donated the site and the staff. The band played for free, followed by a volunteer DJ into the wee hours of the night. Local businesses took care of decorations, and tickets paid for the food and drinks. People who paid for advance tickets had *always* expected a discount. But in past years, their charity had always been a "big" cause, with a "big" organization the recipient.

This year the profit was being donated to a cancer fund named for a local child who'd died of leukemia the year before. His family was well known in town and everyone felt Jason's loss. Jake had figured the closer the connection to the charity, the better people felt about donating. He'd obviously been right.

"Well, great. How about decorations? Sandy and Charlie?"

The owners of a floral gift shop and the downtown hardware store gave their reports. Shortly after that they wrapped up the meeting, but Jake let Kira stew in the back for another fifteen minutes. Kira waited patiently. She deserved his anger. He'd given her quite a few dirty looks over the last half hour.

At least it had been unavoidable. Her parents had left early. She'd been counting on Brianna to wake her up, and that dream….

Oh, yes. That dream. She closed her eyes and instantly remembered the familiar feel of those hands on her body. Those hands that had to be attached to someone. But damned if she knew who.

"Kira." Jake's voice snapped her eyes open. He stood close, close enough to kiss, if she wanted to.

She blinked. She didn't want to kiss Jake, for Pete's sake. Ever. And judging by the cold look on his face, he wouldn't ever want to kiss her again, either.

"I'm so sorry," she began.

"Save it," he said. "I'm not in the mood for excuses." He held out a hand.

Stunned, Kira slowly placed his car keys in his palm. Jake had never been like this to her. Never, in all their fights over the years. Not even in June, when she'd rejected him so completely. She couldn't let it be like this.

"Jake, let me explain." He didn't respond, just folded his arms and watched her, stone-faced, while she stumbled through the explanation.

"So that's why I didn't call—well, I tried, but it was busy—and why your car is—"

"Kira."

"What?" She looked up, hopeful that she'd groveled enough and he wasn't going to give her the cold shoulder any more. But his expression hadn't changed, except for a twinkle of satisfaction in his eyes. Eyes that were looking at the clock on the wall.

"You're late for lunch with Maggie," he said.

"Damn!" She was never going to catch up. She leaped off the table she'd been sitting on and ran toward the door, then realized she'd picked up Jake's keys again. She tossed them over her shoulder. "See you later!"

"Not if I see you first."

She really hoped he didn't mean that.

* * *

Jake shook his head as the door drifted closed behind Kira. He let his anger fade and turned to gather his notes. She'd left his keys, which meant she'd either had her sister drive her own car over or she'd be running the three blocks to Galloway's. Served her right, after he'd had to run over here from the marina. Okay, so it was cold outside, and running wasn't that difficult, but when he'd entered the heated meeting room full of bodies, his thermostat had gone haywire. He was still sweating. And he was tired of Kira making him sweat.

He'd never realized before how much he let her get her way all the time. It was starting to grate on his nerves, but he had to blame himself. He'd allowed it. And he needed to stop his old habits, all of them, if he was going to move on.

A flash of pink caught his attention as he tucked a pile of paper into his portfolio. None of his committee notes were on pink paper. He slid it out. It was a note card, the edges cut with some kind of wavy scissors. The back was blank, so he flipped it over. In raised white script the note said "You can *lead* me anywhere, baby." A pair of beckoning eyes was drawn next to Darcy's signature.

He shook his head. What a dichotomy. A woman who ice fished *and* made her own cards. He slid it back into the portfolio and zipped it shut. She must have slipped the card in there before she'd left for Texas, knowing—or hoping, at least—that he'd be missing her. The card should have made him smile. He could only shake his head in frustration that he couldn't feel what he should and stop feeling what he shouldn't.

He left the meeting room and took a detour through the ballroom to check on preparations. The club staff had already set up the round tables for the banquet dinner, and a few were setting them with linens. Not much more would be done before tomorrow morning, but Jake never wanted to take a chance. Some day, he was sure, he'd rely too heavily on someone else and have an unfixable whopper of a mistake. He wasn't going to let that happen.

Jake paused at the main door when a familiar figure stepped in from the hallway.

"Jake, m'boy."

"Mayor."

He shook his mentor's hand. Mayor Kleinfelter had been in charge of Brook Hollow for so long Jake couldn't remember his predecessor. He'd spoken to Jake's civics class in high school, showing such passion for local politics and Brook Hollow that the same passion had ignited in Jake. At the time, he'd decided to be president of the United States.

"How are plans coming for the ball?"

"Fine, sir." Jake outlined a few details for the older man.

"Something we need to talk about, son." He put an arm around Jake's shoulders and led him back into the ballroom. "I'm making an important announcement soon, and it will have direct bearing on you."

"I know, sir. It..."

"Now, we need to talk about your image."

Jake was used to being interrupted by the town's most important citizen. In truth, the mayor interrupted everyone, because he couldn't talk when his wife was around. Overcompensation, everyone figured.

"What about my image?" Jake was squeaky clean, and the whole town knew it. Well, except for a few minor indiscretions as a kid, but those hardly counted. He'd been elected to the town council, and even to the school board though people had questioned his interest as a non-parent. He could do this, too.

"Well, the people feel more comfortable with a married man, Jake. I've heard this right from the horse's mouth. They're afraid a bachelor is too unsettled, might up and leave their town in the lurch." He held up his hands in a gesture too reminiscent of George Bush for Jake's comfort. He folded his arms.

"Are you saying I need to get married to get elected?"

"Well, no, not exactly. Marriage too quickly can be just as bad." He must have seen Jake's skepticism, because he backed off. "I just want you to be careful, is all. I've planted a seed. This is your political career, not mine. Planting a seed is all I can do." He pointed his large index finger at Jake and peered down it. "Marriage."

Then he slapped Jake on the shoulder and sauntered on down the hall toward the main restaurant. Jake shook his head. He was not getting married until he was good and ready, and it would definitely *not* be for Brook Hollow. There were limits even for him how far he would go for this town.

*   *   *

Kira managed to make it to the restaurant before Maggie, and sat at a table by the window trying to catch her breath.

"Kira, honey, so good to see you!"

She looked up as Wilma, the waitress, sat across from her. Kira smiled at her old babysitter.

"You, too, Will. How's Rhonda treating you here?"

"Oh, great. She just opened a 401(k) for us. A gal's gotta plan for her retirement, ya know." She cracked her gum and winked.

"Sure." The woman was hardly more than five years older than Kira. "She must be doing well." She motioned around the full dining room. It reflected rustic New England charm with its rough-hewn beams and hard wood floors. Wilma shrugged.

"Better since Westcott's closed. They were our major competition.

But we got their cook." She grinned and winked again. "So, hon, when ya movin' back to town? I hear the schools are looking to network. Two-year project, they say. Longer, if they need support."

Kira swallowed a smile. The woman projected small town hick but talked like a business tycoon. "Yes, I guess they are. But I'm not leaving Boston. Not yet."

Wilma grinned and Kira frowned. *Where did that "yet" come from?*

Before she could figure it out, Maggie appeared next to the table.

"Hi, Will." She tucked her hair behind one ear and smiled at the woman, who slid out of her seat. "Thanks."

Maggie sat, and Wilma pulled out her pad.

"Drinks?"

"Coffee, please." Kira studied her old friend, who looked worn out. No makeup, shadows under her eyes—and Kira could practically see her ribs through her knit shirt.

Maggie ordered tea and they spent a few moments straightening place settings and chairs and adjusting clothes.

"Where's Abby?" Kira asked, sorry Maggie hadn't brought her.

Maggie's smile shook. "She's home, with my mother. I needed a break."

"I bet." Kira reached across the table and put her hand on her friend's arm. "What's going on? You look like you're *about* to break."

"It's just baby blues." She blinked back tears. "New motherhood, moving, all that stuff. I get a little down sometimes."

Kira sipped the coffee Wilma had brought. "Are you taking anything?"

"No!" Maggie stared at her in horror. "I'm breastfeeding! And besides..." She relaxed and reached for the sugar. "It's normal. I'll get over it in a month or two, once things settle down. Things like my hormones."

"How's your mom doing?"

"Great. She's thrilled to death that Abby's home. She didn't see her right after she was born, because we were in Miami."

Kira nodded. They'd exchanged letters—few and far between, but enough for them to keep tabs on each other. "When did you decide to come home?"

"When John broke my arm."

Shock washed over Kira and she stared at Maggie, not sure what to say. Finally, she asked, "I can't believe he was abusing you!"

"Oh, he wasn't." She stopped and Kira turned to see what she was looking at. Wilma was waving a menu in the air, obviously wanting to take their order.

Kira swept her gaze over the selections in the big menu, then snapped it shut and set it on the table. Maggie took a few moments more, and Kira chafed at every extra instant. She hated the thought of her friend being hurt at the hand of any man, but especially John, who'd always been a guy everyone could count on. And why hadn't she been a better friend? It wouldn't have taken much to stay in better touch, read between the lines, know what was going on.

Finally, Maggie decided and Wilma took their orders for salads and soup.

"So, what happened?" Kira urged.

"John wasn't really abusive. Not even verbally. We were doing great the first five years of our marriage. Then John lost his job."

"Classic beginning," Kira murmured.

"Tell me about it. He got another one right away, but companies seemed to be closing offices left and right. Finally, after a couple of years of job hopping, he went to work for a telecommunications company in their sales department. The big push was for business cellular. He had quotas for the number of businesses he signed up, the number of phones for each business. Bonuses for adding personal accounts. The pressure grew, but the money was great, so he was feeling pretty good about it. We decided to have a baby."

She paused as their salads were set on the table, and fresh pepper ground over them. "I'm so hungry," she said. "Nursing is taking a lot out of me. Mom says I need to eat even more than I did when I was pregnant."

"You must not have eaten much then," Kira noted. "You're really skinny."

Maggie laughed. "Actually, I gained sixty pounds. I lost fifty overnight." She suddenly sobered. "The last ten was harder to lose. John didn't like having a fat wife."

"What!" Kira gasped. "I can't believe—what a jerk!"

Maggie nodded and swallowed a tomato. "I told him that. He apologized, just said his boss wanted to invite us to dinner and I looked pretty sloppy. So I made excuses about not being able to leave the baby. That night kind of started the whole thing."

"Did he start drinking?" Somehow blaming it on alcohol made it more understandable.

But Maggie shook her head. "No, he never did touch alcohol. I don't know if that makes it better or worse. But again the pressure was on. Tom, his boss, started asking him to lie to customers. When they came in to adjust their rate plans to save money, he was to actually sign them up for one that had potential, but would probably cost them more. It went against everything John believed."

"But he had to keep the job, and probably felt there was nowhere else to go," Kira guessed.

"Exactly. The night his boss reamed him out for not playing the game, he came home and started yelling. Abby was too loud, he needed some peace. I hadn't done the dishes, how could he make a sandwich in such a pigsty."

She shook her head. "I still don't know what I could have done differently. I tried soothing him, arguing with him, praising him, badmouthing his boss, nothing worked. He just got angrier."

"You're not blaming yourself, are you?"

"No, of course not, but I wasn't part of the solution, either. Then he grabbed my arm and told me to shut up. I got angry, and tried to jerk away. He twisted, and my arm snapped."

"Oh, my God." Kira felt sick imagining the scene. "What happened?"

"He took me to the hospital, crying the whole way. I had to nurse Abby while I waited for the doctor to set my arm. *That* was no picnic, let me tell you. And John was such a help, so sweet and solicitous, I almost went home with him."

"You didn't, though?"

"I went when he was at work the next day, packed up everything I could, got my neighbor's teenage son to load my car, and drove home."

Kira gaped. "You drove from Florida to Massachusetts with a month-old baby and a broken arm."

"Yep."

"My God, Maggie. No wonder you look so bad."

Her old friend laughed. "Thanks."

"No, you know what I mean." Kira couldn't imagine the exhaustion such a trip would cause. But then she saw the look in Maggie's eyes when she talked about the baby. The twinge in her heart felt oddly like yearning.

"I'm getting some rest, and some perspective. Things'll get better."

Kira sat back so Wilma could set their soup on the table. "Are you working?"

"Funny you should ask that." Maggie jabbed her fork into her salad.

"Jake hired me."

Kira almost choked on a bit of bacon. She didn't know why the idea shocked her so. "Doing what?"

"Counter work, mostly. It's probably temporary, for the holidays, but he might keep me on when his college stock help goes back to school."

Why hadn't Jake told her? They were silent for a minute, eating, and Kira thought back to dinner the other night when Sophie had dropped her bombshell. Could Maggie be Jake's new girlfriend? She could easily picture them together, Jake all protective over the pixie. But no, she realized with relief. Sophie said the woman was voluptuous and from New York. Maggie's chest was certainly larger, due to the nursing, but she couldn't be considered voluptuous. And Florida was a far cry from New York. Not to mention that if it were Maggie, Sophie would definitely know.

"So, what about John? What are you going to do?"

Maggie sighed. "I truly don't know, Kira. I love him. But I refuse to stay with him like this. It's all up to him."

"What if...what if he came home? Got counseling? Found a less stressful job? What would you do?"

"I'd give him a chance."

"Really?" Kira doubted she'd be so forgiving. But Maggie was nodding decisively, though sadly.

"Really. I'd work with him to fix it. Because, like it or not, he's my soul mate. And you can never forget your soul mate."

CHAPTER 5

"Soul mate, schmoul mate." Kira kneaded the bread dough a little too forcefully. Maggie's words kept pounding through her head, running counterpart to Brie's earlier assertion.

"What are you talking about?" Sophie leaned against the counter and bit into a carrot stick.

"Nothing."

"You're muttering to yourself about Jake."

"I am not." Kira glared at her sister. "I'm muttering about John."

Sophie raised her eyebrows. "Who's John?"

"Maggie's husband."

"Ah. How's that working out?"

Kira blew a lock of hair out of her eyes. "How do you think? He broke her arm. But if he straightens up, she'll take him back. He's her *soul mate*." She didn't hide her scorn and expected her sister to snort her own opinion. Instead, she nodded and um-hmmed. Kira dropped the dough into a greased bowl and covered it with a towel. "You agree with that?"

"What, that they're soul mates? Sure. They'd know better than anyone if they are." She handed her sister a glass of water and they sat at the table. "Why, don't you believe in it?"

"What do you think?" Kira wiped flour off her hands with a dish towel and picked up her glass. "It makes no sense."

"Yes, it does. You just want to deny it because you don't want to admit who your soul mate is."

Now Kira snorted. "You, who dates at least ten guys a month, believe in soul mates."

"Sure. What do you think I've been looking for?"

Kira shrugged. "I don't know. A good time?"

Sophie's eyes were sad as she shook her head. "I thought you knew me better than that. Do you really think that little of me?"

Kira stared at Sophie, a little taken aback. "No, I—of course I don't think little of you. That's just the way you are."

Sophie shoved her chair back and stood. She dumped her water into the sink and pivoted to face Kira. "You know, sis, for someone so smart you really are dumb." She aimed a finger at her. "You think I'm be-bopping from man to man because I think it's fun. You probably think Brie's with Bob because she wants a father figure."

"No, I—"

Sophie shook her head. "Look around you, Kira. Look at Mom and Dad. Examine that happiness and understand that's what Brie and I are holding out for. Then wonder why you aren't even looking for it." She stomped out of the room, leaving Kira staring after her without a comeback in her brain.

* * *

Kira huddled in her window seat and stared through the bare black branches of the maple tree to the wet street. Most of the snow had melted, and the weather had warmed in direct opposition to the previous day's forecast. It felt more like March than December, except for the early twilight. She could hear her family shouting back and forth to each other, getting ready to walk downtown for the tree-lighting ceremony at six. Then they'd come home and decorate their own tree. Jake would join them after the final Ball Committee meeting. It would be a comfortable, traditional, heart-warming scene.

But Kira was reluctant to emerge from her sanctuary. She'd been holed up here since Sophie'd taken her to task. The quilt her mother had made when she was a baby barely covered her legs. The pillow she hugged had been her first home ec project. She'd sat on this seat, in this window, hundreds of times. Staring over the yard in just this way.

She was surrounded by the familiar and would normally have been chafing to get away, back to the excitement of Boston. Except Sophie had opened a floodgate of introspection. Kira had spent hours examining her life, something she'd never done before. She'd always accepted herself the way she was, and her life as it came. Now, though,

Boston seemed less exciting and more hectic. Her job less challenging and more tedious. She'd told herself over and over how great it was to hop from job to job, meeting different people, doing different tasks. The truth was, she was bored with it. And that had always been the death knell to anything in her life.

She wasn't satisfied anymore with repeatedly starting things but never getting to follow through. She set up a network, trained the in-house administrator, and moved on. She did her job well enough that the client rarely needed tech support. She'd wished several times that she'd had the opportunity to follow up, work out bugs, try something new.

Something like networking a school district. Three elementary schools, and middle, junior high, and high schools. Six offices to be upgraded and linked, then staff trained and systems debugged. A system that large, more complicated than any she'd done, would definitely have bugs. And tech support was part of the proposal. They wanted a two-year contract. Kira couldn't believe she was considering it. But she was.

Sophie, and Maggie, and Brie and Mom would all claim it was because of Jake. But Kira knew it couldn't be. She still didn't think of him that way, even after last summer and the sizzles she felt now when she was near him. Besides, he had a girlfriend.

Scowling, she threw off the quilt, standing and stomping to her closet to grab a sweatshirt. "I'm not jealous," she muttered, shrugging on the sweatshirt and flipping up the hood. She was growling at her zipper when the knock sounded at the door.

"Keer? You coming?"

"Yeah, Dad. Be right out."

She started to put on lip gloss, then tossed it back onto her dresser. She saw it as the gesture it was, an attempt to feel like she had a romantic life that merited lip gloss. But her love life was emptier than her professional life. She hadn't dated anyone seriously since college. And with her present attitude, no one would *want* to date her.

She joined her family in the foyer and followed them outside, ignoring the festive chatter. She wasn't done wallowing in her own thoughts. She trailed behind the pack as she considered what she really wanted.

She'd told Jake in June that they knew each other like an old married couple and that was boring. What—did she think if she married someone else she'd never get bored? Or that any relationship was doomed with the advent of familiarity? Was she stupid, or nuts? Or trying to protect herself?

Hmm. That was an interesting one. She hunched deeper into her sweatshirt and focused her gaze on the soggy brown leaves under her boots. She felt like those leaves. Once golden, flying high, now their time had passed and they were dull, damp, floppy. Under foot.

"Okay, now you're getting beyond introspection into self pity," she muttered. *Enough*, she told herself. She didn't have to figure it all out now. She hurried to catch up and get on with the festivities.

* * *

Jake searched the crowd around the dias they'd built next to the tree. Mayor Kleinfelter stood on the platform, conversing with an aide about a malfunctioning microphone. Jake could have shown him how to turn it on—again—but his immediate goal was to find Kira.

He didn't know why. He hadn't seen her since yesterday, when she'd tossed his keys at him. His mood had been odd ever since. He felt…adrift. He finally decided it was because he'd ended an obsession and didn't know what to do without it. He was only searching the square out of habit.

He spotted Brie standing on a hill near the Hollow Commons shopping center. Then he saw Sophie, looking chic as always in her red beret and matching coat. Elyse leaned against her husband, her eyes focused on the tree but her attention clearly on the man who held her. Jake felt a pang. He wanted that, what his surrogate parents shared. What his own parents shared. He didn't understand why Kira didn't want it. Did Darcy?

Darcy. He missed her, right? Sure. They'd been together for most of their free time since October. It was only natural that he wished she was here. With him. Searching for Kira.

"Hey, Jake."

Jake turned at the deep voice behind him. Lance, the bartender from the country club, clapped a hand on his shoulder.

"Hi, Lance." He glanced around. "Where's your wife?"

"She's around, talking to someone." He pointed vaguely across the square.

"Everything all right for tomorrow?"

"Sure, man. You know it is. We've got it all under control." Lance nodded toward the tree. "They gonna light that thing sometime tonight?"

Jake shrugged. "If Fritz can find the on switch."

Feedback suddenly shrieked over the crowd, causing a group wince. Mayor Kleinfelter's deep, accented voice boomed.

"Ladies and gentlemen. Welcome to the annual tree-lighting ceremony of Brook Hollow, Massachusetts. A time-honored tradition...."

Jake tuned out the usual speech. It hadn't changed in ten years. His gaze went back to the Macgregors, and now he spotted Kira standing behind her sisters. She wasn't looking at the tree. Even at this distance he could see her chewing her lip as she stared across the square. He wondered what was turning over in her mind.

He recognized that furrowed brow.

Seven years ago, he'd happened across her sitting on the boat dock, frowning into the lake as she dropped bits of bread for the fish. He'd asked what was wrong. She hadn't told him. Two days later his life had fallen apart.

Foreboding swept over him. Was history repeating itself? Seven years ago he'd been gearing up to propose, throwing caution to the wind. He'd bought the ring, prepared his speech, and took her to dinner, ready to open his heart and make Kira think of them as more than friends. Before he could open his mouth, she'd announced she was moving to Boston, killing any hope he'd had.

The floodlights went out and Kira disappeared in the darkness. Jake kept his eyes on the spot where she'd been, and an instant later she was bathed in blue and white light. Her face had smoothed, peace apparent as she gazed at the now-glowing tree. His sense of foreboding deepened. She'd made a decision.

So what? he asked himself. So had he. He was done with her. Done with hoping, dreaming, holding out. He was going to build a life with Darcy. Or at least see if there was one worth building.

The crowd began to disperse and Lance walked with Jake toward the club, where they'd left their cars.

"Hey, Jake, I wanted to tell ya. My wife, Susie? You know, she works at the high school."

"Yeah."

"Well, she told me the district had decided to network the schools. Streamline functions, make it easier to collect stats, share staff in the summer, stuff like that."

"Yeah, the board approved the plan a few weeks ago. They were going to seek proposals from—" He broke off, but Lance continued for him.

"Network administrators. That's what Sue said. So is she gonna submit a proposal?"

"Who?"

"Kira Macgregor."

"I don't know." Jake didn't know what more Lance expected him to say. The man kept glancing at him out of the corner of his eye.

"Do you think she'll come home to do it?"

"I doubt it. She loves Boston, keeps saying how she'd never move back to Brook Hollow."

"You sure?"

He wasn't. In fact, he had an eerie feeling the decision she'd just made had to do with this proposal. She *could* be coming home. For two years. At least. Once that knowledge would have inspired hope in Jake. Now it inspired... frustration.

"See, Jake, my wife is good friends with Darcy Langlais. She jabbers on and on about you when she comes to dinner, you know." Lance hopped over a residual snowbank. Jake followed more slowly, not sure how he was supposed to feel about that. It was like junior high. "So-and-so said she likes you." But Lance had warmed to his topic, walking backward so he could talk right at Jake.

"Anyways, Susie says Darcy would be really hurt if you dumped her to go back to Kira. And, well, she wanted me to feel you out. Casual, she said." He snorted and turned just in time to avoid walking into an SUV. "Like guys know how to 'feel each other out.' That's girl stuff."

"Lance, Kira and I were never together. There's nothing to go back to. We've been friends since we were born. That's all."

Lance snorted again. "Jake, friend, I can't say I want Darcy hurt. But I don't want you hurt, either, and everyone in town knows you and Kira are *it*, man."

Before Jake could correct him again, Lance's wife caught up to them. She grabbed her husband's arm and smiled briefly at Jake.

"Lance, honey, you ready?" she asked a bit breathlessly. She tugged her husband toward their truck. They waved back at Jake, who lifted a hand and moved toward his own car.

Everyone in town knew that, huh? Everyone except Kira.

* * *

"Duncan, where are the girls' ornaments?" Elyse pawed through a pile of tissue paper on the easy chair. "I can't find them."

Kira looked up from her string of popcorn and watched her father lift a flat cardboard box.

"They're right where you put them last year, sweetheart."

Elyse's worried face relaxed and she smiled at her husband. He leaned down and kissed her softly. Kira looked back at her popcorn. For the first time in her life, her parents' affection made her uncomfortable. She didn't need a therapist to know why. Their harmony reflected the emptiness of her own life.

She'd decided, standing in the damp, watching them light the Christmas tree almost a month late, surrounded by brown grass and dirty snow patches, that if no work came up in Boston before January 1, she'd submit a proposal to the school board. And if she got it, she'd move home for two years to do it. And figure out where she wanted to be. She was comfortable with that plan. But it was an awfully lonely plan. Bottom line—she was jealous of her parents.

"Mom, did you ever get restless?" She picked up another handful of popcorn and poked her needle through the kernels, one by one. She shared the bowl with her sisters, one on either side. And still she felt lonely.

Elyse gently fluffed the skirt of a Mrs. Santa Claus and placed it on the mantel. "What do you mean, honey?"

"Oh, like, not sure your life was what you wanted it to be."

"Sure I did. Everyone does."

"Do they?"

"Of course. You think your sisters don't question the choices they made? Wonder what's missing?"

"I don't," Brianna piped up. She didn't look up from tying off the end of her popcorn string. "I love my life."

"Yeah, now," Kira said. "You have rewarding work at the school, plenty of community activities to fill your day, lots of friends. Just wait five more years. You'll wish you had someone special to share it with." Realizing she might be revealing more than she wanted to, she added, "Right, Sophie?"

Sophie shrugged. "I never wondered what's missing. I *know* what is."

"Yeah, you haven't found a playboy you could tame." Brianna stood to loop her garland around the tree.

"What are you talking about?"

Brie winked at her older sister. "Kira has us all figured out. She said you need a challenge, and you'll know what to do when a playboy falls hard for you."

Sophie shook her head and stuck her needle into the orange flower pincushion on the coffee table. "No way. I've had my fill of playboys."

"We'll see," said Kira.

"What did Kira plan for you?" Sophie asked. Brie trilled a laugh.

"A Navy SEAL. 'Someone rough, with honor, who wants to settle down.' But she said I'll find him in Boston."

Elyse smiled at her girls. "Be patient, you three. Your time will come. You won't even guess from what direction."

"Nonsense," Duncan boomed. "I knew from the instant I met you that this is the life we'd lead. And I never had a doubt in my mind, or felt restless for an instant."

Kira's eyebrows shot up at the bitter look her mother threw her father. Her dad got restless every couple of years, and demanded they do something to get out of their rut. But she couldn't figure out why her mother would look *bitter*. Amusedly exasperated, sure. But bitter? She looked at her sisters to see if they'd noticed, but they were busy fighting a tangle around a branch of the tree.

"Mom?"

"Don't worry, Kira. You may be going through a bit of turbulence, but your flight will smooth out soon enough." She dusted off her hands. "Anyone for hot chocolate?"

"I'd love some." The voice was deeper than her sisters'. Kira's heart leapt, and she whirled to see Jake standing in the kitchen doorway. She hadn't heard his car, or the door. She pressed a hand to her chest. She was surprised, that was all. That explained her thumping heart and short breath. She inhaled, then forced a smile.

"You're late." She motioned toward the tree. "It's almost done."

"He's just in time for the most important part," Elyse announced. The heavy sighs and good-natured ribbing didn't fool Kira. Even she loved this moment every year. She lined up next to her sisters in front of the tree, then glanced at Jake, who stood on her right.

"I miss your parents," she said. He looked down at her. "They should be here for this."

"It's okay. They won't expect us to wait."

Elyse handed out their special ornaments. Brianna's was a baby rattle shaped like a barbell, hanging by a ribbon. Her baby picture was taped to the top of the rattle; her high school graduation picture to the bottom. Their mother joked that once Brianna grabbed hold of that rattle at three months old she didn't let go until she was two.

Next was Sophie's—her photos were inside a frame made of Popsicle sticks. She'd painted a football and baseball bat on the top and bottom; on either side were a rough drawing of a doll and a cheerleader's pom-pom. She'd always been a perfect blend of tomboy and little girl.

Kira's and Jake's were the same. They'd made them when they were nine years old, replacing the simple frames their mothers had made. Kira had cut a piece from Jake's favorite shirt, and he'd taken one from hers. They'd wrapped the fabric around pieces of heavy cardboard and glued on stones from the lake, tiny pieces trimmed from the sail of the boat they'd shared that summer, and feathers from a nest they'd found in the woods. In the center of each ornament were identical photos of them hugging at age two. They were squeezing each other so hard Kira's pudgy cheeks made a fish face. And on the bottom left corner of both was a drop of blood. Mingled blood, as they'd become blood-siblings.

Kira stared at the photo for a long time while her mother fussed over her camera. It seemed to symbolize something to her, but what? Eternal friendship, as they'd declared? Or something more?

She looked up at Jake and caught him studying her. Their eyes met and she couldn't break away. It was like that moment in June when he'd asked if she would do anything for him. The world narrowed to him and his lips moved.

"Anything," he whispered.

"Okay, I've got it!"

Kira jumped at her mother's jubilant call and turned to see her waving the camera above her head.

"Everyone say 'cheese'! Put your arm a little higher, Sophie, I can't see the ornament. Okay, go!"

As they put the ornaments on the tree, Elyse snapped the traditional photo. She had a special album devoted to these pictures. She always said she liked to look at her family growing up all at once.

Kira smiled and blinked and struggled to reconcile the traditional scene with her not-so-traditional feelings toward Jake. For just a moment, when he'd mouthed "Anything," she'd felt a joy she'd never known possible.

Which was crazy. She didn't want him. She'd established that a long time ago. And he was over her, he had to be. *He had a girlfriend.*

But Kira felt reckless.

"Jake."

He turned from where he was teasing Brie about her popcorn string and raised his eyebrows. "Yeah?"

She glanced around. Her mother had gone to the kitchen to make the cocoa. Her father was digging under the easy chair for an errant ornament. Sophie and Brie had started arguing about who'd made a particularly ugly paper Santa.

"Can you come outside for a minute?"

"Sure." He followed her to the front porch and shut the door behind them. Kira instantly felt better in the cool air. She took a deep breath.

"Hm, that smells good." She leaned on the rail. Jake sniffed, then leaned next to her.

"Wood smoke, snow, and lake," he said.

"Home," they said together.

Bored, Kira thought, but she wasn't. She felt electrified. Jake's arm touched hers, and his heat seeped through both sweaters.

"Thanks," Jake said, nudging her shoulder.

"For what?"

"Postponing the inevitable lectures, questions, commiserations."

Kira frowned, then understood. "Oh, you mean the cancer."

"Yeah, the cancer."

"What, you're not afraid of my family, are you?" she teased.

"Never."

They stood in silence for a moment, watching the plumes of their breath drift upward.

"This is an odd Christmas," Kira finally confessed.

"How so?"

She shrugged. "Everything's weird. The weather, the town tree. Maggie has a baby and an abusive husband. Your parents aren't here. You've got a girlfriend. Just, nothing is the way it's supposed to be."

She could feel Jake frowning. "Isn't that a good thing? You get bored by the same old, same old, you said. Repeatedly." There was an edge to his voice. Kira sighed.

"I know. I guess I place more value on tradition than I thought." She turned her head and her eyes met his. "On the tried and true."

What am I doing? she yelled inside her head. She knew she was telegraphing something she wasn't sure she wanted Jake to know. Something she wasn't sure she knew herself. If she was playing with him, if she hurt him again, she'd never forgive herself.

She searched his face, sensing a cure for the painful loneliness she'd only recently acknowledged. She turned, almost against her will, and lifted her chin.

CHAPTER 6

Oh, no, Jake thought, stunned by the searching look in her eyes. *Not now.* Her timing sucked. He was over her.

Then why was his mouth meeting hers? Why were flames suddenly licking at his insides, at his skin, while Kira filled his arms, his mouth, his brain?

Oh, God, she felt good. Her breasts were full and heavy against his chest where he pressed her tight against him. Her mouth was sweet, so sweet, her tongue against his lips making him so hot his blood evaporated.

"Kira," he murmured against her mouth.

"Yes," she whispered, and his teeth nipped her lower lip. She gasped and he pulled her up so she rode his thigh. Intense pleasure, so much stronger than last summer, raced through him. Then, his desire had been borne of fear, of the certainty that he'd never have another chance. This time, it was only borne of love.

No! his mind screamed at him, and he tried to cool things down. He didn't know what was in Kira's head, why she was doing this, but he knew it couldn't last. Her words echoed in his head, as they had whenever he started thinking of them together. *No discovery to be made. Already like an old married couple.* But they hadn't anticipated this.

Her mouth clung to his when he eased back. A tiny whimper escaped her, and he felt himself being pulled back in. Her hands pressed against his shoulders, as if to push him away, but clutched him closer at the same time. No, Kira hadn't counted on this, either. This…passion. That was it. They had passion.

Passion that was about to set the front porch on fire. Jake realized his hand was under her sweater, sliding up her side. She moaned in his ear. He wanted her lips back on his.

Something whispered in the back of his mind. Something he didn't want to think about just now. He pressed his mouth against her neck, inhaling the scent that made him feel he was coming home.

The whisper became a shout. Kira may represent home to him—heck, he could even represent home to *her*—but home wasn't what she wanted. Home wasn't enough.

And suddenly, *this* wasn't enough for Jake. A little of Kira was no longer what he wanted. He wanted it all, or nothing. He was not going to allow her to fill his heart, then drain it once more when she left. Never again.

He released her and slid his hand across the moisture on his lower lip. Kira stared at him, her chest heaving as she fought to get her breath.

"Oh, Jake."

He heard so much in those few words. Amazement. Desire. Hope. But he couldn't let her take them down that path. There was too much baggage between them now to go there. And there was Darcy.

Darcy.

He turned away and braced his hands on the wooden rail. "This isn't real." He had to be plain. She hadn't minced words in June. He wouldn't mince them now. "I'm involved with someone else. We're friends, Kira. Friends."

"But—"

"No buts. You're disoriented because the holidays aren't living up to your expectations. I'm a guy. But there isn't anything happening."

"What about June?" she whispered.

June. He studied her flushed face, her sparkling eyes. She swayed on her feet, as off balance after that kiss as he was. But it had to end here. For both their sakes. "You know what about it. You made it very clear it was a pity f—"

"Don't even say it." Her eyes spit fire through the darkness and her shoulders shook. "I never thought you could be such a jerk." She spun and stomped into the house. Jake hung his head.

"Neither did I, Keer. Neither did I."

* * *

December 23rd dawned sunny and warm. Despite the previous evening's hint of snow, the forecast called for highs near sixty degrees through the holiday.

"Great," Kira mumbled, "more weirdness." She reached for her bedside clock radio and silenced the chirpy carol that had followed the news. She let her arm drop over her eyes. "I'm depressed."

"Of course you are. Your wardrobe sucks."

Kira didn't move. "Sophie, please leave me alone."

"Uh-uh. We've got work to do, hon." Hangers squeaked across the rod in the closet. "You don't have a decent thing to wear to the ball tonight. We're going shopping."

"I'm wearing the pink—"

"—strapless monstrosity you wore last year, and you're not." Sophie dropped Kira's robe across her middle. "Get up, shower, and meet us downstairs in fifteen minutes. Brie and I have been looking forward to this all week."

Kira sighed and dragged herself out of bed. "Okay, but I won't have any fun."

"Yes, you will!" Sophie sing-songed out the door.

Deciding it was easier to comply than fight, Kira took a quick shower and dressed in jeans and her favorite sweater from high school. When she got downstairs, she was surprised to see Maggie handing Abby to her mother.

"There are four bottles of breast milk in the cooler bag," she was telling Elyse, "and that should be more than enough. Thank you so much." She kissed the older woman on the cheek. "I'll call."

"No need, we'll be fine." Elyse beamed at the baby, who smiled back. She babbled some baby talk, and Abby cooed. Kira watched the generic affection on her mother's face turn to wistful yearning, and something else. Before Kira could put her finger on it, the older woman looked up with a particular gleam in her eye, and Kira knew what was coming next. She doubted her sisters wanted to hear it any more than she did.

"Okay, I'm ready!" She rushed into the room, snatching up her purse and grabbing Maggie's and Sophie's arms. "See you in a few hours, Mom!" She swept them all out the door.

"Thanks, sis. That was close." Brie feigned wiping sweat from her brow.

"What was close?" Maggie rubbed the arm Kira had just released.

"You okay?" Kira murmured, chagrined. "I'm sorry."

Maggie shook her head. "That's okay. It's the other arm."

She looked at Sophie, who told her, "My mother was about to embark on her favorite soliloquy. 'Why can't my three beautiful, talented, intelligent daughters find men and get married and have babies and make me a happy Grandma?'"

Brie laughed at the way her sister waved her arms. "You look just like her."

Kira unlocked the 4Runner with her remote. "You've heard that a lot, lately, huh?"

They piled into the truck. "Since I'm the only one in town," Brie complained, "she focuses all her energies on me. She fixed me up last month with the nephew of a bridge friend. This guy was uuugg-ly!"

"Oh, you're so superficial, Brie." Sophie shook her head. "He had a healthy bank account, you know."

They laughed, and Kira felt her spirits lift.

An hour later, those same spirits were preparing to dive again. They'd had the bridal salon to themselves, but the cocktail dresses and formal gowns were, not unexpectedly, picked over, leaving them all fighting over the dozen dresses that were left. Well, not quite fighting.

"Can you believe we're all the same size?" Brie said again from the dressing room.

"Yes, Brie," Kira called from the main shop, "it's just as amazing now as it was during the last round of try-ons." She zipped the back of Maggie's dress and looked up at the triple full-length mirror. She whistled. "We may all be the same size, but we don't fill them out the same."

Maggie grimaced and tugged at the sweetheart neckline of the silver sheath. "Yeah, it's fine now, but in two hours it'll be too tight. And tonight, after Abby's emptied me out, it'll bag."

Sophie and Brie stumbled out of the dressing room. Brie kicked at the hem of her full red skirt, which unfortunately made her womanly hips look larger, and Sophie clutched the sagging bodice of her white silk column dress against her lean frame. "Honey, we've all got problems." They lined up in front of the mirror. "Brie, that is a prom dress. Take it off."

Brie pouted. "I like it."

"Here." Kira minced around the clearance rack and lifted a lipstick-red slip dress. "This is more your style, hon."

Brie giggled as Kira tried to bring the dress to her. "Oh, Keer, you can't possibly wear that dancing."

Kira looked down at the mermaid-style skirt that locked her knees together. "No, you're right. But it's got a killer back." She turned and they cat-called at the scoop that plunged to her hips.

"Okay, I guess we've got to trade again." Sophie pointed to a yellow dress balled on top of a rack. "Give me that one, Maggie, please, before Griselda yells at us all." She mock glared at her older sister.

"*I* didn't put that there," Kira protested, trying to hop up the steps to the changing area. "I...whoops!"

She missed the step and fell, collapsing in a heap of laughter. "This is *never* going to work!"

The bells over the front door jingled and they all turned. Kira had never seen the woman who entered. She was what used to be called a "blonde bombshell," with a voluptuous figure and big, flowing hair. She didn't look at the four of them as she went to the counter. Griselda emerged from the back room where she'd been doing paperwork.

"Ah, Darcy, you're here to pick up your dress. Just a minute." She disappeared again.

Something hot filled Kira's chest as she studied the woman who was taking Jake away from her. Her spray-painted purple leggings showed every muscle in the thigh visible to Kira. Her crop sweater stopped just short of exposing skin. Usually, the look made Kira think "tramp," but Darcy managed to stop just short of that label. Her makeup was tasteful, her hair sleek and natural-looking. She looked nothing like Kira.

Kira wanted to mind her own business. She'd meet Darcy soon enough. She wasn't competition. Kira had never wanted Jake. She should be glad he was moving on. But she knew the heat in her chest was jealousy, and a feeling that this woman—any woman—would not be good enough for her best friend. Even if he was acting like a jerk right now.

Before she could consider her actions, Kira was shuffling across the floor. She didn't know what she was going to do when she got there, but she felt a need to make contact.

"Darcy?" The woman turned and Kira held out her hand. It was several moments, however, before she got close enough to shake. Not only did the voluptuous blonde not step to meet her, but she eyed her hand like it was a fish.

"I'm Kira Macgregor. I'm...a friend of Jake's." The woman arched an eyebrow slightly and gazed at her with ice-blue eyes that didn't care.

Kira let her hand drop. "Does he know you're in town?"

Darcy leaned a hip against the glass case. "No. I'm surprising him tonight at the ball. I'd appreciate it if no one told him." She glanced over the room to encompass everyone with her request, but dismissal was just as apparent. Kira resisted her immediate dislike of the woman.

"I hope we get a chance to chat tonight," she said as pleasantly as she could. "I've heard a lot about you." *And I'm determined to learn more.*

"Oh?" Darcy handed a check to Griselda and took her dress. She narrowed her eyes a bit as she looked Kira over. "He hasn't mentioned you." She flipped her transparent dress bag over her shoulder and swept out the door.

"Bitch." Three voices chorused behind Kira. She tried to calm herself before facing her sisters. They'd see more than she wanted them to.

"Did you get a load of her dress?" Sophie pointed to a poster on the wall. "That's her dress. And you can bet your bippy she'll fill it out. I betcha I know why Jake's so into her."

Kira still stared out the door, fighting the drowning emotion she didn't want to acknowledge.

"Kira? You okay?"

Maggie touched her shoulder, and Kira looked at her. Maggie's eyes widened.

"Oh, boy, you're not okay."

Brianna and Sophie rushed over.

"Why? What's going on?" Brianna sounded frustrated that she didn't know. Sophie looked smug as she studied Kira's face.

"Did you finally admit you're in love with Jake?"

Her sister's question jolted Kira out of her daze. She laughed. "Don't be ridiculous." But the protest sounded phony.

"It's not ridiculous," Sophie said. "We keep telling you that you and Jake belong together."

"We don't. We agreed that we don't."

Sophie slapped her hands together. "I knew it. You've talked about it. Last summer, right? The cancer started it."

"But you told him you don't belong together?" Brianna demanded. "Why did you do that? If you talked about it..."

"What cancer?" Maggie chimed in.

Kira sighed and slid to the step below them, then explained about Jake's declaration and what it followed.

"Was it good?" Sophie flashed a wicked grin and waggled her eyebrows.

"I don't even know." Kira shook her head. "It was just weird. Familiar, yet foreign. I *guess* it was good. I...you know." She waved her hand in the universal sign of "you know." They nodded. "I remember thinking it was the best sex I'd ever had." She shrugged. "Not that I've had much, and now I don't even really remember it. It wasn't emotional. Not that kind of emotion," she tried to explain. "Not like last night."

Damn.

"What!"

"What happened last night?"

"Well, um, he kissed me."

"He kissed you?" Brie squealed.

Kira reluctantly nodded. She blinked, and as her lids closed her mind projected a flash image of that kiss. The desire ignited by the merest touch of his lips—she'd never felt that before. Ever. Her body had reacted like a baking soda volcano right after the vinegar is added. How quickly passion turned into anger, though.

"It was a great kiss," she admitted, "then he turned into a jerk. I guess he doesn't feel the same way about me anymore."

"Do you want him to?" Brie asked.

"Back up," Sophie demanded. "What happened *after* last summer?"

Kira shrugged. "Afterward—I mean, after we learned he was okay—he told me he loved me, and I had to tell him I didn't feel that way." All the pain and awkwardness of their discussion on the boat came rushing back, complicated by her loneliness, the passion of his kiss, and her sudden jealousy of Darcy. "I'd done what I'd done because he was dying, and I would have done *anything* to make him feel better. But later...." God, she'd been cruel. How could she have handled it better? Handled it in such a way that things didn't seem so impossible now.

Sophie narrowed her eyes. "You didn't say he'd be boring, did you?" Kira ducked her head, and her sister groaned.

"Well, that was how I felt," she defended herself, lifting her chin. "We know each other too well. Then it was so awkward, knowing he wanted more, that we let six months go by without much contact. Our whole friendship is ruined." She smacked at the big ruffle at the bottom of her dress. "He's got Darcy, and I've got nobody." She sniffed, and felt a tear slip down her left cheek. Horrified, she wiped it away.

Brianna slung her arm around her shoulders.

"Kira, you don't have nobody. You have us." The others nodded, and Kira sniffed.

"I know, but—"

"—it isn't the same," they finished in unison.

"Let me recap." Sophie began ticking off on her fingers. "You don't want forever with Jake. But, you don't want him to be with Darcy. And you don't want to be alone anymore. Close enough?"

Kira sniffled. "Close enough."

Sophie slapped her hands on her knees and stood. "Bottom line—you need a killer dress."

She frowned, not getting the connection. "For what?"

"Either to convince Jake he doesn't want Darcy and buy time to figure out what you want, or to attract another guy to make you not lonely so you'll leave Jake alone."

Kira didn't want to attract another guy. But she wasn't sure of her new-found attraction to Jake, either. "Okay, a killer dress, then." Anything to end this conversation.

Brianna rose and helped her sister and Maggie to their feet. She glanced over her shoulder, then stage-whispered, "This place isn't gonna have it. We've gotta go somewhere else."

They quickly hung all the dresses back on the racks and snuck out the front door.

Four shops and too much time later, they despaired of ever finding appropriate gowns.

"Food. I need replenishment." Brianna sagged onto a bench outside the latest boutique three towns away from Brook Hollow. "Maggie probably needs dairy. Let's get ice cream."

Maggie winced and discreetly adjusted her bra strap. "I really need a ladies' room. Abby would have nursed twice by now."

Kira arched her back against a developing crick and motioned across the street. "I think that café has an ice cream parlor and a good-sized bathroom."

In silent agreement, they trooped over. Kira sent her sisters to order while she accompanied Maggie to the bathroom.

"What about that blue one at La Chanteuse?" Maggie called from behind the stall door.

"Nah. Too clingy." Kira leaned her hips against the sink and listened to the rhythmic suck-squeak of Maggie's pump.

"Clingy is what guys like, isn't it?"

"I'm not trying to get a guy." She didn't need all her friends to suddenly start matchmaking for her. So she was lonely. So she was dissatisfied with her life. Finding just any guy wasn't going to help. She had a bad feeling only Jake could help.

"Hm." Maggie was quiet for a minute. Kira heard a trickle, a shuffle, then the pumping sounds again. "You know, you have an edge over Darcy."

"How so?"

"You know Jake's things."

Kira stifled a giggle. "Well, only that once."

Maggie laughed. "You know what I mean. You know what he goes for. Apparently, for a long time, he went for you. Now combine what you've already got with what he's liked in other women. Then you have the edge."

"I don't know if I want the edge." Kira growled. "I'm so damn confused, I don't know *what* I want."

"Do you know what you don't want?" Maggie asked.

It was unreasonable, but she didn't want Jake to be with Darcy. "I can use what I know he *doesn't* like to try to show him the real Darcy," she offered.

"There you go."

Assuming her impression of the woman was the real one. Kira had to admit it wasn't quite fair to judge her on one thirty-second meeting.

Maggie came out of the stall carrying a full bottle of milk. Kira helped her rinse the pump and watched as Maggie stored the sealed bottle in a tiny cooler. They joined Brianna and Sophie at a booth by the window, where the two younger women were halfway through their sundaes.

"Where's ours?" Kira slid in next to Sophie. Before she'd finished speaking, the counter clerk deposited two more metal bowls on the table. "Thanks." She flashed him her boy-I-love-ice-cream grin and watched in amazement as he blushed and stammered, "You're welcome."

After he'd walked away, Maggie teased her. "You just need to have Jake give you some ice cream, then give him that turned-on smile and he'll be putty in your hands."

Kira snorted. "Yeah, right." She bit through a chunk of cookie dough. "That's enough about me. Let's talk about something else. Have you talked to John?"

"He called last night." Maggie licked her spoon, then dipped it back into her peach ice cream. "He sounded good."

"Any plans?"

Maggie shrugged one shoulder. "He says he's in therapy. Anger management, stress reduction—the therapist is teaching him all these techniques. I think once he comes home things will be much better. He still hasn't quit the job."

Kira touched her wrist. "How's your arm?"

"Fine." Maggie seemed to realize Brianna and Sophie were watching them with interest. She gave them a condensed explanation of what had happened.

"Wow." Brianna shoved her empty bowl away and leaned her forearms on the table. "You're so brave, to leave him, and drive so far alone." She cleared her throat. "I have to admit, I'm surprised you told us. Most women who've…been hurt aren't so forthright."

"Brie works at the women's shelter a few days a month," Kira said.

Maggie nodded. "I'm not ashamed of it," she explained. "It wasn't my fault. I couldn't stop it or fix John's problems. Only he can. When he does, maybe we have a chance again."

"You're so strong," Sophie marveled.

Maggie looked at the half-melted puddle in her bowl and pushed it to the side of the table. "I'm not," she shook her head. "It hurts so much that he can't see Abby. Every day he misses something new." Her voice grew thick. "It's so hard not to forgive him, ask him to come home. I miss him so much." She started to cry, and the other three tried to console her.

But after they'd left the parlor and headed for yet another dress boutique, Kira wondered if *she* was copping out. Maggie was resisting the easy path, but was she, herself, taking the low road? Had her loneliness caused her to focus her attentions on Jake because he was convenient? Was that the real reason for her jealousy? The possibility caused her to lose her enthusiasm for shopping.

Finally, though, the next boutique yielded pay dirt, and they all found the "perfect" dress. Kira wasn't convinced she shouldn't just wear her pink monstrosity again, but shelled out the money her shrinking bank account couldn't afford, anyway. Sometimes you just needed to feel better.

When they got home, the rush of joy she felt when she saw Jake's car added to her confusion. Was it the usual, "best-friend's-here" kind of joy, or something stronger? She didn't know. But her elation only grew as she took the porch steps in one leap.

"Give me your dress," Sophie whispered in the foyer, then snuck up the stairs with it while Kira and Maggie went into the living room, where Jake balanced Abby on his knee and sang the Tigger song to her. Or something that sounded like it, anyway.

"The wonderful thing about Abby, is Abby's a wonderful thing. You're smile's as sweet as a cookie, your laugh a bell when it rings. You're cuddly snuggly wuggly buggly fun fun fun fun fun. But the most wonderful thing about Abby iiiiis... you're my little one!" He ended with a growling tickle into her neck. The baby erupted into giggles that amazed Kira.

"She's so young to be giggling," she said to Maggie, who watched with tears in her eyes.

"She never has before. Like I said...." She looked sad, and Kira wished John had been the first to inspire the giggles. She wrapped her arms tightly around Maggie until her friend took a deep breath and backed away. "I need to use the bathroom," she whispered, wiping her cheeks.

When Kira turned to Jake, he was leaning back on the couch with Abby on his chest. The baby had laid her head down and was sucking on one fist. Kira's heart squeezed with longing. For Jake or the baby—or both—she wasn't certain. And the uncertainty made her angry.

She strode over and sat next to the man who was causing her so many problems. Immediately, she felt like she'd come home. Which was ridiculous, since she *was* home.

"What are you doing here?"

Jake smiled at the fuzzy head he was slowly rubbing. "I have to go get Mom and Dad at the airport. Thought you might want to come."

Kira looked at the clock just as it chimed twice. Not much time to get there and back, and ready for the ball. But she hadn't seen his parents in far too long. They were like another mom and dad to her, and they could spend the drive time catching up.

"Are they coming in to Bradley?" she asked. "Is the flight on time?"

"Yeah, at three. No delays, miracle of miracles."

She thought about Darcy, and how long it would take her to reach competition level. She weighed spending an extra hour alone with Jake—good and bad. Then she watched him nuzzle the baby and felt the longing turn into yearning.

"I'll go."

CHAPTER 7

By the time they were on the road, Kira was cursing herself. Being alone with Jake had become almost unbearable. She tried to analyze the intense awareness that had taken hold of her, even when she was deep in thought.

She was obsessed, she decided. She was aware of every move he made—scratching his chin, tapping his foot to the music, heaving a sigh—because she kept worrying over the issue. Not because she kept reliving their kiss, and wondering what was under it. Not because she was trying to figure out how to let him know she forgave him.

Forgave him for what, though? To be honest—and she was trying very hard to be—she couldn't blame him for his reaction. First she flat-out rejected him. Then she confirmed that rejection. Suddenly, she was throwing herself at him and surely sending signals that would make any man think he was gonna get lucky. Again.

Things felt pretty good between them today, though. Kira didn't want to bring up the kiss and cause tension where there wasn't any. So she kept her mouth shut and just watched Jake shift his long legs under the dash.

"What's wrong?" she finally asked, eyeing his frown.

"Hum?" He half turned his head toward her.

"You're frowning. Anything wrong?"

"Not really." He grunted. "Just lots of town business on my mind."

"Like what? Maybe talking about it will help." *And get my mind off your mouth.*

"Well," he said, scratching his chin again. He always did that when he hadn't shaved. She wondered what he'd do if she reached over and scratched him herself.

"I've got a dispute between McGarvey's downtown and the new book shop. They share the parking lot in back, and McGarvey claims the book shop owner, Karen, isn't doing her share of upkeep."

"What does Karen say?"

Jake grinned. "That she's out there every day picking up cigarette butts his patrons dump because he's too cheap to put an ashtray outside his door."

Kira shook her head. "Sounds like petty stuff to me. Let them work it out together, and if they can't, chain the lot so no one can use it."

"Kira, you know we don't have that authority."

"But I'll bet there are three council members who are on McGarvey's side because they go every night to watch 'The Game,' and three on Karen's side because they're teetotalers, and you're the deciding vote."

"As usual," they chorused.

"What else?" Kira asked as the exit for the airport approached.

Jake glanced at her out the corner of his eye, gauging her reaction to his next, oh-so-casual statement. "The school board has invited bids for their new computer system. It's in the budget and we need to get moving on it."

"Yeah, I heard they were seeking proposals."

Jake ignored the familiar ache in his chest. It was academic. She would never do it. Besides, he didn't care if she did.

"Well?"

"I'm considering it."

His heart stuttered. "You are? But you hate Brook Hollow."

She threw up her hands. "For the last time, I don't hate Brook Hollow. I love Brook Hollow. I hate being bored."

"And Brook Hollow bores you. You've said so many times."

He took a ticket at the short-term parking gate and started searching for a spot. When he looked over at Kira, she was staring out the side window. She didn't answer until he'd parked the car.

"The truth is," she said, "my work has slowed down. I don't have much choice about submitting the proposal."

"But to commit for two years? You'd have to move back to town."

"I know!" She didn't sound happy about it, despite her earlier denials. "I would have to leave Boston." She looked at her watch and opened the door. "Come on, it's almost three."

Jake considered the implications as they crossed the parking lot to the terminal. If Kira was in town, he'd see her a lot more. Which was good if they were just best friends who'd missed each other over the past several years. Bad if they couldn't get over this awkwardness last summer—and last night—had generated. Very bad if he didn't stop reading too much into that kiss. Speaking of which....

He stopped and grabbed Kira's arm, about to confront her about their tiff, try to make amends. But when she frowned up at him, he realized there'd been no real tension between them today and if he mentioned it, there would be. So he just said, "Slow down, will ya?"

Kira laughed. "You men with long legs walk more slowly than anyone else on earth."

Jake slouched into a stroll and grinned up at the sky. "Well, little lady, if ya don't stop and look around once in a while, ya won't see the sky until it falls on ya."

They bantered some more until they got to the security gate and saw the plane had unloaded. Jake spotted his dad's silver head, several inches higher than anyone else's, as soon as he came through the archway. He waved, and his father waved back, then leaned down to say something to the petite woman beside him. Jake felt himself grinning and realized how much he'd missed his parents.

"Jakey, darling!" His mother rushed the last few open yards into his arms. He inhaled her familiar Chantilly scent and lifted her into a big bear hug. As soon as he set her down she was turning to Kira.

"Oh, you two are together! I'm so happy!"

Jake exchanged an alarmed glance with Kira. She quickly turned to his mother.

"I kept him company for the ride down. I couldn't wait to see you guys!" She hugged his mother again, then his father. "It's been way too long! How's France?"

While Fran talked about weather on the continent, Kira scanned the room until she saw a clock, then linked her arm with his mother's and headed toward baggage claim. He and his dad trailed behind.

"So, son, how's life treating you?"

"Can't complain," he replied, with all the things he *could* complain about spinning through his head.

"So, do we get to meet Darcy this week?"

Darcy. "I'm not sure, Dad. She's in Texas with her family."

Luke grunted. "Shame. I was looking forward to meeting this

'perfect woman.'"

Something in the way he said that put Jake's back up. He was about to argue, but his dad stepped forward to grab a garment bag and duffel off the baggage carousel.

"Good thing we hit customs in New York," his mother said, clutching an old-fashioned makeup case and her oversized purse. "If we hurry, we'll have time to get ready for the ball."

The ball. That was why Kira kept looking at the clock. Sheesh, he'd almost forgotten about it! And he chaired the committee! Something was really wrong with his attention span.

"So, Jakey, how did the planning go this year?" his mother asked. "Everything all ready?"

"Seems that way." They crossed single file through the parked cars until they got to his. He opened the trunk to load the bags. When they got in the car, he elaborated. His mother used to chair the committee and he knew she'd missed the planning. She'd asked about it every time they talked.

"The decorations are great. Sandy outdid herself with orchids and lilies. Charlie constructed two arches, one for the entry and one on the dance floor, with mistletoe."

Fran giggled. "I think he's become quite romantic since he remarried."

"The food all arrived on time, and the chefs were hard at work when I stopped earlier. The buffet will be the most elaborate, complete one we've ever had."

"And the music?" his father inquired. He had taught music appreciation at the high school while Jake was growing up, then at a small university before taking a position in France.

"There's a quartet for the meal, then a DJ after for dancing," Jake assured him.

"Good, good. Live music adds elegance to the evening. And the DJ pleases the young people. How's attendance this year?"

"Sold out," he said with a measure of pride. "Rhonda really came through."

"Jason's family will be so pleased," his mother said.

After a moment Kira asked, "How did the conference go, Dad?"

Jake didn't hear the response, because suddenly his world warped. Kira had called his parents Mom and Dad or Fran and Luke interchangeably since they were little kids. It used to make him feel like she was really his sister. But for some reason, this time it was different.

This time, it made him feel like she was his *wife*, and they were heading home with her *in-laws*. He'd dreamed of scenes like this for years but had never confused those dreams with truth.

He finally shook the feeling when his mother asked Kira if she'd met Darcy yet. Kira shot him a look he couldn't interpret.

"Not yet. I hope I do before I return to Boston. If I return."

If she returned. Jake groaned inwardly. She was talking to others about staying. Making it reality. And making his life infinitely harder.

* * *

A few hours later Jake emerged from the country club kitchen and surveyed the ballroom. Every twinkle light was in place, every sprig of mistletoe on the arches fresh. The band played at just the right level, and the early-birds were standing in clusters around the room, enjoying their first glasses of champagne. The bulk of the crowd would be entering any minute.

He took a second to adjust his tie and cuffs and scanned his midnight-black tux for lint. Perfect.

But not perfect. Something was missing, and he had no trouble figuring out what it was. He was alone. No one stood by his side, taking pride in his accomplishment. He had no one to dance with, no one to go home with after a successful evening. And that just sucked.

Get over it, he told himself, and headed for the bar. He was alone tonight, but not forever. Kira would return to Boston—he hoped—and his confusion would pass. Life would go on.

"Everything all right?" he asked Lance, who nodded and handed him a scotch and water.

"Under control, boss."

Jake nodded and turned away, then froze, his movement arrested by the sight of the woman in the doorway.

It was Kira, yet it wasn't Kira. He was used to seeing her in some pink strapless monstrosity she wore every year. It was okay, but not that flattering. But this.... This floored him.

The crimson dress had glittering golden straps that seemed to match her hair—hair that tumbled in soft curls over her shoulders to the tops of her breasts. He hadn't realized it had gotten so long, and it made him focus on the ends. Or maybe it wasn't the hair that drew his attention to her chest. Maybe it was the curve of her breasts. Or the way the dress seemed to slide as she breathed. He tore his gaze away to trail downward. She stepped forward, revealing matching high heels that made her feet look good enough to nibble on, and a slit that went—

Holy God, it went up to her hip! Jake's mouth had gone dry already, but now he felt himself growing hard, right there in the Brook Hollow Country Club. He had to get away. He started to hand his drink back to Lance, then choked when Kira turned around. She had a long scarf thing draped backwards around her neck, and it fell down her back— her *bare* back—to the floor. A tiny train on the bottom of the dress trailed behind her as she walked. *The extra fabric should have been at the top,* Jake thought, trying frantically to get the image of her smooth skin out of his brain. It made him think of June, and the warm satin feel of her under his palms, against his chest. He thought he was going to die.

He'd finally dragged in a lungful of air when Kira disappeared down the hall toward the rest rooms and another woman appeared under the arch. This one wore a black satin gown and had her blond hair pulled back in a twist. He felt like he'd been punched twice when he realized who it was.

The woman smiled at him and started to cross the room. Her dress was less revealing than Kira's, but the way she walked made it look sexier. She dipped her head in a come-hither look and headed straight for him.

"Hello, lover." She slid her hand under his lapel and leaned in to kiss his lips. "Ooh, I guess I bought the right dress." She smirked, and Jake winced. He was still half-hard in reaction to Kira.

He put Kira out of his mind and smiled at Darcy, kissing her again and tucking her next to his side as he guided her across the room.

"When did you get in?" he asked.

"Yesterday. I wanted to surprise you." She set her satin purse on the table and watched while Jake switched a few name cards around.

"You certainly did that. We'll have to squeeze in an extra place setting." He glanced around for a staff person and was caught by Darcy's warm brown eyes gazing up at him. He saw delight that she'd surprised him, satisfaction at what she thought was his reaction to her, and something deeper, more sincere.

"I missed you, Jake." All trace of the siren was gone as she placed her hand on his cheek. "I really missed you."

"Good." He kissed her again, and knew he had to straighten out his head before he hurt this beautiful, vulnerable woman.

* * *

In the ladies' room, Kira checked her makeup and added lipstick where she'd chewed it off on the drive over.

She took a deep breath and looked at herself in the mirror. "All dressed up and no one to knock out," she murmured, adjusting her bodice. She'd insisted on driving over alone, in case she wanted to leave early. She felt like an idiot, chasing a man she could have had free and clear six months ago.

She fought the self-pity threatening to set in and whirled to return to the ballroom. She was going to have fun tonight. Her family and Jake's were seated together, as they always were, and she was just going to enjoy being with them.

Her resolve faltered when she found the table and her families weren't the only ones sitting there. The knockout witch she'd met earlier leaned against Jake, her head tilted toward him and her arm and fingers wrapped around his. Kira gritted her teeth and smiled.

"Well, who have we here?" She winced at her stilted tone, and ached at the happiness on Jake's face.

"Kira, my best friend, this is Darcy, my best girl." He held his arms out toward them as if he expected them to hug or something. Kira bared her teeth.

"Delighted, I'm sure."

Darcy's response was much warmer than it had been in the dress shop. "Kira, it's lovely to meet you." She held out a hand and gently squeezed Kira's. "Jake has told me so much about you."

She was a good actress. Kira would have believed her if she hadn't met her already.

"I hope he's kept our childhood exploits to himself so far." She winked at Jake. "It would really color your opinion."

"So far." Jake tweaked her nose, then held Darcy's chair so she could sit. Kira quivered and felt her face flush. He'd *tweaked her nose*! As if she were a younger sister. Well, she was several hours older than him, and she would not tolerate that kind of treatment.

Unfortunately, there wasn't much she could do. She watched silently while the shrimp appetizer was served. Jake and Darcy showed all the signs of being in the early stages of love. He fed her shrimp and the cherry from her drink. She constantly touched him—stroking his hand, adjusting the flower in his lapel, smoothing a lock of hair off his forehead. Kira's emotions flowed between envy, jealousy, resignation, and loneliness.

"So, Kira," Fran said during a lull in the conversation. "I hear you're bidding on this computer job at the school."

"I haven't decided yet, but it looks like I will."

Elyse's face lit up. "You didn't tell me that, Kira! Oh, you'll be home for two years! I can't wait!"

"No, Mom—" Kira tried to curb her mother's jubilation. She hadn't even bid on it, never mind received the contract. But Elyse was jabbering on and Kira couldn't get her attention.

Luke, sitting to Kira's left, nudged her arm then waggled his fork toward Jake and Darcy.

"So, you gonna stand for this?" he asked her.

Kira pretended confusion. "Stand for what?"

"That woman taking your man."

Kira focused on cutting a bite of chicken. "He chose her, Luke. And he's not my man." She realized she'd made her arguments in the wrong order. Now Luke would think Kira loved Jake, and he'd tell Fran, who'd tell her mother, and they'd all start planning the wedding….

"Honest, Luke, I'm not pining for him. I'm glad he's found someone special."

"Hmph. The only thing special about that woman is her unique ability to fool a man."

Tickled that he saw through the other woman so easily, Kira couldn't help asking, "How do you know she's fooling him?"

"Broad says she likes ice fishing. No woman who likes ice fishing has three-inch fingernails."

A chuckle popped through Kira's lips at the terms he used. She couldn't remember the refined, rather proper music appreciation teacher ever calling a woman a "broad" before.

As she watched, Darcy tossed her head back and laughed at something Jake said. When he turned to answer his mother, Darcy aimed a glare at Brianna, who raised her eyebrows and shoulders in a "who, me?" pose.

What was that all about? Kira felt out of the loop, but since Brie was on the other side of the table, next to Darcy, she'd have to find out later.

"So, Darcy, tell us what you do." Kira reached for her wine glass.

"I'm a realtor."

"Oh, how interesting." Kira looked down at her plate and speared a piece of potato. The silence at the table made her look up. Her parents were both frowning at her. Sophie was pursing her lips, and Bri was hiding behind her napkin. Darcy and Jake looked expectant.

"What?"

"Is that it?" Jake said.

"Well, yeah." Kira shrugged. "It would be rude to ask if she's sold anything yet, and none of my business which houses are on her list. I'm just being polite."

Now Jake was frowning, too, but he turned away from Kira and laid his hand along the base of Darcy's neck.

"Tell them about that family you took out last week. The ones with the cat?"

Darcy smiled. "Oh, yeah. This family took their cat to every house I showed them. Let her run around loose. They said if Pepper didn't like it, they couldn't buy it. I found a darling Cape that was exactly what they were looking for, but the owners had a dog and Pepper caught one whiff and headed straight for the door."

Everyone laughed, and Kira fought the unwise urge to best her in storytelling. Luckily, the waiter deposited a dessert goblet full of chocolate mousse in front of her and she filled her mouth instead.

Halfway through dessert, the mayor stood and cleared his throat into the mike. Since this speech, like the Christmas tree lighting speech, hadn't changed in ten years, Kira tuned him out and took the opportunity to watch Jake.

She realized he was paler than normal, which hopefully indicated he was avoiding the sun. She'd have expected the lack of tan to fade his streaked hair, and eliminate the gleam in his golden eyes. Dim him somewhat. But he looked just as good to her now as he always had.

Maybe better. She suddenly recalled the sensation of his long fingers stroking over her back. She shivered, and felt her nipples tighten against the bodice of her dress.

Last year, despite their physical distance, he'd been the center of her world. Their friendship had anchored everything, had been the yardstick by which she measured success. If Jake was happy for her, she went up a rung on the ladder. If he was lukewarm about a decision, she rethought. Their love for each other, nurtured from the cradle, had been the purest form, unsullied by jealousy or sibling rivalry.

Or so she'd thought. Jake had told her in June that he loved her as a woman, that he had for a long time. And in her panic, she'd responded wrong and tossed her well-ordered but challenging life in the blender.

It was ironic, really, that she'd professed for so long to having a fear of boredom, then structured her life so tightly. And even more so that when that order unraveled, so did she.

Slowly she became aware of a difference in the mayor's speech. She focused in time to hear him announce his retirement. Stunned, she exchanged incredulous looks with everyone at the table. Everyone except Jake. Her eyes narrowed. Why hadn't he told her this?

"It has been my honor to serve this town for over twenty years, in many capacities and with full devotion to the good of the people. Now, it is time to turn my attentions to my long-suffering wife—" He held out a hand toward Myrna, who tossed her beehive hairdo and toasted him with a martini glass. "—and my own passions, fishing and perseverating."

The crowd murmured a bit at the unfamiliar word. Kira figured he'd gotten it from his psychologist son and didn't know what it really meant. But based on the murmurs Kira could hear, the attendees figured it meant talk a lot.

"I will be stepping graciously aside at the end of my term next year. Of course, any qualifying candidate can run, but I think most of you will be satisfied with the man I intend to endorse."

He cleared his throat and shuffled his index cards, referring to them for the first time. "This man has also served our community well for the past ten years. He began his political career in student government, running for and obtaining the presidency of almost every class."

Kira knew immediately who he was talking about. She had backed Jake every year, running his campaign and sweet-talking the boys into voting for him and not Sweater-Sally Piscopo. The two years Sally had won, Kira and Jake had fought about something stupid enough to forget, but important enough that she swung votes in the other direction.

"After college, he returned to Brook Hollow to run the family business..."

Well, not quite. He'd bought the marina from Joe Davis, who'd retired to Florida.

"...and stepped in where others could not, taking a leadership role on the Chamber of Commerce, the town council, and the school board. Since his election to the latter, standardized test scores have increased forty percent..."

Which was more a testimony to Brianna and other teachers who breathed new life into the curriculum than to Jake, who only recognized a need and let them fill it.

"...and, last but not least, the Annual Benefit Ball has raised record amounts of money every year since he began chairing the committee."

Clapping followed his echoing praise, and Kira saw Jake's mother slide a finger across her cheek. She rolled her eyes, then chastised herself. The mayor may have exaggerated, but she knew Jake would serve the town well as his successor. This was his big dream come true. She should be thrilled for him. She couldn't figure out why this announcement made her feel grumpy.

She looked across the table to where he sat, implacable, one hand holding Darcy's against his thigh, the other arm hooked over the back of his chair. As if he didn't know what was coming. If he acted astonished, Kira was going to barf on the fancy white linen tablecloth.

"Without further ado, I would like to introduce my favored candidate for Mayor of Brook Hollow, Massachusetts. Our friend, our son, our own All-American, Jake McKenna!"

A standing ovation rocked the room and Mayor Kleinfelter motioned for Jake to approach the podium. Kira folded her arms and tried not to grumble. The truth was, she was happy for him. It was what he had worked toward all these years. So she clapped along with the crowd, and smiled when he did. She'd deal with her feelings in private.

What Jake said when he reached the microphone didn't surprise her. It was all him.

"While I appreciate Mayor Kleinfelter's endorsement, and acknowledge his desire to make this announcement at a community event, I must shun the spotlight in favor of a much more important cause." He nodded to the back of the room and a slide flashed onto the screen behind him. The boy in the photo looked about ten, laughing, the joy on his face a stark counterpoint to his bald head.

"In 1999, this town lost one of its truest assets. Jason Dean was just eleven when he succumbed to leukemia, after a valiant battle in which he never lost his optimism or his humor."

Kira's chest felt tight as she watched the slides flash from Jason to Emily, to other children she didn't know. The scenes illustrated both how lucky she was, and how empty her life, since she had no one to share it with.

"Tonight, we honor Jason, and all the other children who've fought his fight, and who have yet to face battle. Proceeds from the Holiday Ball will go to the Jason Dean Foundation, which is dedicated to keeping the joy in these children's lives, helping them find happiness in the midst of tragedy."

Sniffles sounded all over the room. It wasn't Jake's words, Kira thought as she dug in her evening bag for a tissue, so much as his delivery. The emotions, she knew, were sincere, stemming from his own cancer scare. He could identify with Jason, and all the other kids, in a way few in the audience could. Pride and love shoved aside all the other petty feelings she'd been harboring all day.

This was what Christmas was about.

She discreetly wiped her nose and watched Jake present the foundation chairperson with a check. The photographer for the local paper took a few photos, then Jake stepped back, ending the formal portion of the evening.

On cue, the DJ turned up the music. An oldies tune led some couples to the dance floor. Kira rose to go tell Jake how wonderful his speech had been and found she couldn't get within six feet of him.

It was just as well. She didn't need to be near him when she was overflowing with holiday sentimentality. He'd probably laugh at her.

She found Maggie on the far side of the room, sitting at her table with a sleeping Abby. A man sat next to her, and Kira was surprised she'd brought a date. Then the man lifted his head and smiled tentatively at her.

It was John. She caught Maggie's eye and saw hope, happiness, and fear. The hope and happiness she understood. The fear made her heart ache.

"John." She gave him a hug when he stood, then sat next to Maggie. She gently touched Abby's silky hair where it peeked above the sling Maggie wore. "She's been good. I haven't heard a peep."

"She's been sleeping." John couldn't take his eyes off the baby. "I can't believe how big she's gotten."

The line was almost a cliché, but Kira could see the anguish he couldn't hide. But she didn't know how to ease either his or Maggie's pain. "They do grow fast," was the best she could come up with.

"So, how long are you staying in town?" she asked after a long silence. "Will you be here to watch the snowflake drop at New Year's?"

John looked at Maggie. "Well, I hope, um, plan to be. I've moved back for good."

Before Kira could react to that, she felt an unusual heat on her left side. Immediately after, Jake sat next to her and nodded at Maggie's husband.

"John." His tone was stern, and Kira realized he knew Maggie's story. Had he come over to protect her? Them?

"Hi, Jake. Great party." John's smile faltered and Kira felt sorry for him. He seemed to be trying so hard.

"Thanks."

No one said anything, and Kira realized Maggie hadn't spoken since she'd sat down. She leaned toward her. "Are you all right?" she whispered. Maggie nodded, but didn't look up from the baby. "Do you want to come to my house tonight?"

Maggie's startled gaze lifted to Kira's. "Oh, no! Everything's fine." She glanced at the guys, who were still engaged in "conversation," and whispered back, "He says he's been sober since I left. And he quit his job. He told me he realized he didn't have to prove anything, he only had to change himself. So he finished his counseling series and came home."

"That's great." Kira didn't get to comment further because John turned back, resolve clear in his manner. "Maggie, hon, we can leave any time you're ready."

"Okay." Kira relaxed when she saw the serenity on Maggie's face. She suspected the worst was past for them. They stood and said their goodbyes, and suddenly she was alone with Jake.

Her left side still burned, more at her shoulder and knee, where he was closer to her. He shifted and his knee brushed hers. Kira could hear the rustle of fabric rubbing, even over the music. Then her back started to feel hot, and she realized Jake had put his hand on her chair.

"...dance?"

The roar in Kira's ears subsided and she figured out what he'd said. She nodded and turned her head, finding herself inches from his face.

CHAPTER 8

Kira swallowed hard and backed up an inch. Jake must have leaned closer so he didn't have to shout. She could see the copper flecks that gave his eyes the gleam. Without intending to, she raised a finger to trace the circles under his eyes.

"You haven't been sleeping," she said. He shook his head and she felt his fingers brush the nape of her neck.

"Too much to dwell on." His hand slid down her shoulder, then her arm, to her hand. He lifted it. "So, do you want to dance?"

Kira did, badly, but managed to croak, "Where's Darcy?"

"Holding court with my parents." He motioned with his head as they rose. "Charming them, I think."

"I'm sure." But for the moment Kira was beyond jealousy. After all, he was about to dance with her, not Darcy.

Then she realized the song playing was Chubby Checker and the Fat Boys' "Yo, Twist." Great. The perfect best friend song. Oh, well, what had she expected, with his girlfriend mere feet away?

When they got to the dance floor she began to follow the song, swiveling her hips and arms. But her long dress threatened to trip her, so she lifted the skirt and let one leg hang out.

Jake's gaze seemed to focus on her thigh. Kira felt an unworthy satisfaction and shifted the skirt higher. His Adam's apple bobbed. She made sure her breasts bounced. His cheeks turned pink and heat rushed through her, no longer confined to her left side but coursing through her body.

The song changed and they stopped dancing for a moment.

"You picked me up from off the floor..."

Without discussion Jake held up his arms and Kira drifted into them, closing her eyes as his scent surrounded her.

"Hm. Lake and sunshine."

"What?"

She didn't realize she'd said it out loud until he murmured the question in her ear.

"You smell like lake and sunshine," she told him.

"Oh." He adjusted his grip on her hand. "Is that a good thing?"

"Yes. Definitely."

He leaned back far enough to see her face. She tried to drop her smile, afraid it was far too womanly for a "best friends" dance. But he noticed.

"Kira, what are you doing?"

She moved a little closer and sighed when her breasts brushed his chest. "I don't know, Jake. If I said I was confused, it wouldn't begin to cover my feelings right now."

She laid her head on his shoulder and he automatically wrapped his arm a little tighter around her waist. She slowly slid her inside foot forward and pressed with her hips. He was definitely reacting to her.

The realization made her instantly wet. Oh, God, she wanted to feel him against her again. Inside her. She wanted to be his.

A cool hand on her shoulder doused her arousal.

"May I cut in?"

*　　*　　*

Again Jake was caught off guard by his reaction to Kira, coupled with Darcy's arrival. This time it would be even more difficult to hide. He held Darcy half an arm's length away and fought to control his desire. That was tough to do when he couldn't tear his eyes off Kira's retreating back. The back he couldn't stop thinking about.

"Jake."

Darcy's tone slashed through the haze.

"Yeah." He looked down at her. Her mouth looked tight, her eyes drilling into his.

"What's the deal?"

Jake pondered a dozen responses to that question, but knew none would be the right one. "What deal are you referring to?"

"I cut short the holidays with my family, lost money on my traded ticket, and bought an expensive dress I'll never wear again just so I could watch you ogle another woman?"

Oh. That deal. Jake felt his life beginning to crumble and reached to hold it together.

"Darcy, you know I wouldn't do that to you. I was concerned about Kira. She's...having some financial problems."

"Oh." Darcy glanced over her shoulder, then turned back with that smug smile again. "Is she, now?"

"We don't need to talk about her. Let's talk about us."

"Okay." She let go of his hand and slid her arm under his, clasping her hands behind his back. "Let's talk about us. I'm ready to move our relationship up a step."

Alarm sizzled along his nerves. "Which step is the next one?"

She giggled. "Well, for us, I think it's the Big Step."

He didn't want to hear this. Not now. Maybe in six months. But not this month, when he was in transition between "loving Kira helplessly" and "completely over Kira." He tried to head her off.

"Darcy, you know, my parents are staying with me for the next few weeks. Dad's off school until mid-January. They wouldn't approve...."

"Oh, posh. They're not as conservative as you think. But we wouldn't have to do anything immediately. I could move in after they leave, then—" She stopped and shook her head. "I'm getting ahead of myself. Jake? Will you—"

The country club banquet manager stepped up to them.

"Excuse me, Jake."

Relief unfroze his muscles and he turned to the man. Darcy graciously agreed to wait while he took care of a minor catering crisis. When he exited the kitchen after settling the dispute, he saw Darcy talking to Lance and his wife at the bar, so he slipped down the hallway toward the lounges.

He had to find Kira. He didn't know why she was suddenly coming on to him, but he had to stop her. She'd told him they didn't have a future. Now she had to tell herself.

He caught her coming out of the ladies' room and grabbed her arm, fighting the urge to caress it.

"We need to talk." He pulled her behind him further down the hall to the offices.

"Jake. Four-inch heels, here." She stumbled.

"Sorry." He let go. *Better off not touching her, anyway,* he told himself. The door to the central office was unlocked, and he flipped on a table lamp as they entered.

"What do we need to talk about?" Kira wandered to the center of the room, then draped herself over a chair and tilted her head, resting her chin against her fingers. Her leg was exposed by the dress's slit almost all the way to her....

Jake cleared his throat and perched on the arm of an upholstered chair.

"Us. Or rather, Darcy and me. Or all three of us." He blew out and braced his hands on his thighs. "I need to clear the air."

"Okay."

Okay. How? What could he say without hurting her? His mind flashed back to June, and how quickly she'd rejected him. Avoiding his pain hadn't been foremost in her mind then. He wouldn't worry about hers now.

"I'm in love with Darcy." Well, that was a bit of an exaggeration. Hell, a huge lie. But he could be, if he tried hard and if Kira left him alone.

"I know."

He stared at her, shock blanking his mind. "You know?"

She nodded. "You can tell just by looking at you."

You could? He must be a better actor than he thought. "So, why?"

"Why what?"

She wasn't giving him an inch. "Why are you coming on to me?"

She rolled to her feet and paced, then leaned her hips on the secretary's desk. When she folded her arms under her breasts, they swelled above the top of her dress. Jake felt his throat close up.

"I'm lonely, Jake." She rushed to continue, as if she was afraid he'd get the wrong idea. "I don't mean I'm using you to fill a void." She began to pace again and waved her arms as her speech picked up speed. "It's just that I'm realizing there is a void, and I've been attributing it to missing our friendship, but it's more than that, it's babies and a home and a partner and something more fulfilling than what I have and the most fulfilling part of my life has always been...." She stopped abruptly and turned to him, bracing her hands behind her on the desk. "You."

He frowned at her, hating the hope and fear battling in him. "I don't get it. You didn't want me in June. But now you do?"

"I don't know." Her voice was low, and she shrugged her shoulders. Jake imagined hearing it in a darkened bedroom. His blood pumped faster. He could not act on this arousal. *Darcy*, he reminded himself. He channeled the arousal into anger.

"I can't believe it. You'd chance ruining our friendship *and* my relationship, plus hurting an innocent woman, but you 'don't know?'"

"The holidays have really bothered me this year," she tried to explain. "I'm unsettled. And I'm learning more about myself. That I need structure even though I say I don't want it, for example. I'm in turmoil, Jake, and you've been my anchor my whole life. For some reason, my subconscious seems to be turning me toward you."

"You're really something." He bounced his right leg faster and faster. He was going to explode if he didn't do something. "I loved you for years, Kira, and you couldn't care less. I was your *anchor*," he spat. "And what were you to me? A comet. Passing through on your annual orbit." He stood and shoved his hand through his hair, then stalked around the room, energy pouring through him, urging him to action. "I take months to get over you, and when I finally do you come around."

"Jake, I—"

"I can't, Kira. I can't switch back and forth at your whim." He passed the dark windows and turned the corner next to the desk. His pacing brought him in front of Kira.

"I'm sorry, Jake," she whispered, her voice breaking.

"It hurts, Kira," he murmured as he looked down at her. But he didn't know what hurt most.

"I know."

"There are other people involved." For the life of him, he couldn't remember who.

"I know."

"I can't handle another rejection." But part of him was screaming that he could handle the potential of one, and if he didn't go after what he needed now, he'd never get it.

"I know."

A single tear slid down Kira's cheek. All the protective, possessive passion Jake had ever felt for her solidified into one giant ball, and something broke inside his chest.

His arms wrapped around her, tugging her the last few inches to him. His mouth landed on hers, clinging, absorbing, and he felt his whole being sink into her. She tasted dark, like the richest chocolate, and he could smell her desire.

Passion roared through him. He had to stop. He couldn't stop. He couldn't think. His hands took control when his brain failed. One slid into the slit of her skirt to cup her bare behind. Her skin was so smooth, so warm. He pressed her closer, against him, and groaned when she arched. Her own hands were under his jacket, had slipped under his shirt, and were tracing electric patterns across his back.

"God, Kira. I...."

"Yes, Jake. Please." She sobbed the words, put her mouth on his neck. He hissed at the heat of her tongue on his skin. So much heat.

Her breast had come free of her bodice, and he caressed it, reveling in the wonder of its feel. He didn't remember her nipples being so hard, her reaction being so intense. His body threatened to burst the seams of his trousers, but before he could do anything about it, Kira's hand was on him, stroking.

"Baby, we can't."

"Please, Jake."

That was the end of Jake's resistance. He laid her back on the mercifully empty desk and pulled her dress aside as she fumbled with his zipper. His mouth was on her breast, his hips already surging, his body burning with the need to bury himself inside her, to take him home.

A voice passing the doorway cut through the frenzy and he started to pull back. *Wrong place, wrong time, wrong woman.* But as he straightened, the part of him that could chip rock brushed her moist center, and she cried out and arched at the contact.

The sight of her electrified him. She was passion itself. His ultimate fantasy, open to him, eager, her mouth swollen, her nipples puckered. She writhed on the desk and reached for him. Her hot hand pulled him back in, and he was lost.

In seconds he felt the pleasure building, and he wasn't even completely inside her.

"Kira." He groaned her name, not sure if it was protest or entreaty.

"Ohhhhhhh, Jake." She pulled at his hips, surging to meet him, to take him deeper. "God. Now. Harder." He responded and she clutched the desk, holding herself in place. Her mouth opened and he swooped down to capture her scream as she came.

Only after he'd followed her over the peak, then slowly, throbbingly down the other side, did he comprehend what they'd done.

CHAPTER 9

Kira knew as soon as Jake became still that it was all over. He'd hate her now. Probably himself, too. But she couldn't regret it. This time was so different. Passion was the focus, rather than fear. And she knew, sometime after Jake had lost control but before he'd sent her soaring, that her life would never be the same.

She loved him.

And he loved another woman.

Well, he said he did. She still didn't like Darcy, but he seemed happy with her, and she, herself, was no good for him. She'd selfishly attended to her own needs, let him fill those he could, and went about her life assuming he'd always be there for her. Now, when his attention began to focus elsewhere, she "changed her mind" and tried to get it back. She suddenly felt dirty and mean. Selfish and rotten. She had to get out of here.

"Oh, Kira," Jake whispered next to her ear, and her heart ached. She knew what she had to do. She gently pushed him to the side and sat up, adjusting her dress and hoping they hadn't pulled a Lewinski.

"Thank you, Jake." She turned and watched him tuck his shirt into his pants. She tried not to let her love and despair show. "That was a good—" She swallowed against the lump in her throat. "Um, goodbye. Be happy, okay?"

He looked like she'd just kicked a hole in the side of his boat. "What are you saying?"

"I'm saying...well, I don't know what I'm saying. You love Darcy, which should make this a mistake." She waved a hand at the desk. "But I don't regret it. So it has to be a goodbye."

"No, Kira, I—"

"Shh." She kissed her fingers and pressed them to his lips. "Goodbye."

She slipped out the door and turned to the ladies' room for the third time that night. Luckily, no one was in the hall and she made it in time to repair the damage before being seen. Her hair was beyond help, so she just shook the curls and let it hang. She rubbed her eyelids and cheeks where her makeup had smudged and wiped off the remnants of her lipstick. The dress had miraculously escaped damage.

She washed her hands, rubbing the silky soap slowly between her fingers. Every cell seemed sensitized. It took no effort to remember Jake's palms on her skin, what he felt like inside her. She could even—just—remember the power of her climax. When she reached for a paper towel she saw the smile on her face. Oh, it had been good. No one had ever made love to her like that before, with complete abandon. No one had brought her such pleasure. Even the desk had felt like a feather bed. Everything had been perfect.

The thought wiped the smile off her face. Perfect. Too perfect. *Skin to skin perfect.*

Fear washed through her. She'd just said goodbye to Jake. She'd thrown their relationship out the window and handed him over to witch-woman. Her head told her that was what she had to do. Her heart whimpered in pain, but didn't argue with her head.

Her soul cracked.

*　　*　　*

Jake tried to pull himself together after Kira left. He finished tucking in his shirt and checked his pants for spots. He buttoned his jacket, which he hadn't taken off. He'd never been so aroused that he didn't remove his jacket. He would have smiled, except for Darcy.

Damned Darcy. He should never have gotten involved with her. His heart belonged to Kira. It always had, and now it always would. Darcy didn't deserve to be dumped, but she didn't deserve to be second choice, either. He had to break it off.

But as he strode down the hall to the ballroom, he heard the unmistakable crooning of Nat King Cole singing "The Christmas Song." He realized he couldn't dump her two days before Christmas. The thought of enduring the next three days with her and Kira, pretending nothing had happened…. God, he'd cheated on a woman. He never thought he'd be so low. How could he keep Darcy from finding out?

He hoped he didn't smell like Kira.

He found Darcy still hanging around the bar. Actually, hanging *on* it, a whisky sour in her right hand, her left clutching the rail so she wouldn't fall over.

"Darcy." He put his hands on her shoulders and tried to raise her. "How many of these have you had?" He hadn't been paying attention during dinner, or after. He pulled the drink from her and handed it to Lance, who dumped it into the tiny sink.

"Well, les see." She managed to straighten and began to tick on her fingers. "One before dinner. One at dinner. But then!" Her floppy hand slapped against Jake's chest and her head lolled as she looked up at him. "Then I had a glass of wine." Her mouth pouted into a closed "o." "I can't remember. Hmm. Lance, did I have two or three glasses of wine?"

Lance shrugged at Jake, who didn't like the situation but couldn't really blame the bartender.

"After the wine, I asked the waitress to get me another of *these*!" She held up her empty hand, then frowned at it. "Where'd it go?"

"It's gone." She began to slide downward and Jake gripped her arm. "Come on, Darce. Let's get you home."

"Oh, yes," she purred, turning so her torso leaned on his. She tilted her face upward, smiling at him but with her eyes closed. "Les do go home. I *need* you, Jake."

"You need a bed," he mumbled, then lowered her into the nearest chair. "Darcy." He crouched and held her chin to make sure she was focused on his face. "I need to wrap things up. You stay *right here*—" He pointed at the chair. "—until I come back. Got it?"

"Got it." She snapped a salute and almost fell onto the floor.

"Damn it." Jake scanned the crowd, but couldn't see anyone he could leave Darcy with. His parents and Kira's were out of reach. He wasn't sure what had transpired at the dinner table, but he'd caught Brianna's snicker and couldn't trust her or Sophie. Kira was heading his way, though she wasn't looking at them. But there was no way he could ask her to watch over his girlfriend. Not after they'd just…well, just.

With relief he heard Susie's voice behind him. He turned to see her kissing her husband's cheek.

"Susie."

She eyed him coolly. He couldn't blame her, even if she didn't know what had just happened.

"I want to take Darcy home, but need to wrap a few things up. Can you sit with her a minute?"

"Of course." She glared at him as if Darcy's condition was his fault. He refused to feel guilty for *that*, at least. She was a grown woman and knew when she'd had too much to drink. But he felt enough other guilt to cover this, too.

After he'd checked with all key personnel, back-slapped the mayor and a few major business owners, and said goodbye to his parents and Kira's, he made his way over to Darcy. Susie looked exasperated.

"She's half asleep, Jake. I tried to get her coffee, but the waiters don't seem to be passing it anymore."

"It's okay, Suz. Thanks for your help."

"Take care of her."

It was a definite warning. "I will."

He managed to get Darcy on her feet, and they shuffled to the coat check. Putting her coat on without dropping her was enough of a challenge that he tossed his own coat over his shoulder rather than don it. The cold air when they stepped outside roused Darcy. She chattered all the way across the parking lot.

"And my dad and his sister have opened this restaurant, and the food is so *good*! I might open one right here. This town needs a McDonald's. I mean, where can you get a good hamburger on a Saturday night?"

"Your dad opened a McDonald's?"

She glowered at him. "No, silly, a Dawson's."

Jake had never heard of it. "Why Dawson's?"

"It's only the best Tex-Mex on the planet. Which planet are you from? Which planet?" She looked up at the sky and stumbled. "Mercury-Venus-Earth-Mars. My very excellent mother just served us nine pancakes. Or pizzas. Or pumpkins. No, pumpkins aren't served. They're carved."

Jake sighed and stuffed her into the car. He wished this damned long night was over. He tuned Darcy out and tried to figure out a way to end their relationship now without being a complete heel. He figured he'd at least try to keep her away from his family—until she mentioned how Elyse had kindly invited her to their open house the next night.

Damn. "You don't have to go," he told her, flipping on his turn signal although there were no other cars in sight.

"Of course I'm going to go! I can't insult her by not going. Besides, where else would I be when my main man is there? It's a networking opportunity, anyway. You gotta go. Boy, I gotta go!" She crossed her legs and giggled.

Jake groaned and pressed his fingers against his throbbing temple. Darcy kept up her stream of consciousness monologue until he pulled into the driveway of her condo.

"Hee heeeeeeee!" Her giggle reached new heights as they tried to climb the steps made of rough-hewn logs. Darcy kept catching her heel in the hem of her dress. The tearing sound made Jake cringe, but he doubted Darcy would care.

"Darcy, give me your key."

"You already have the key," she said huskily, tilting her head up again in what she must have thought was a sexy pose. "The key to my heart." She ruined the sentiment with that glass-shattering giggle. Jake swallowed his frustration and dug into her tiny purse himself. He could barely get his hand inside it, and of course the key was at the bottom.

"Oh, hell," he grumbled when he dropped the purse. But he had the key.

"Oh, don't be like that, Jakey." Darcy bent to get the purse and fell against the door he'd just unlocked. "Oops!" She toppled into the hallway but somehow managed to right herself. Jake steered her down the hall to her bedroom and helped her sit on the bed. He slipped her coat off her shoulders, her shoes off her feet, and her legs under the satin comforter.

"Come in here with me, Jakey baby." Her murmur faded as her eyes drifted closed. The last word ended in a snore. Jake sighed in relief and snuck out the door. God, he wanted to get home. He fervently desired the ability to sleep for three days, tactfully and without recrimination end the relationship with Darcy, and see just how deep Kira's feelings actually ran.

He turned his car around and headed for his house. Kira had admitted she was lonely, that he was her anchor and she felt adrift. But their lovemaking was more than that. He knew it was. It wasn't something he'd felt in his body, or thought in his mind. It was…a connection they'd made with their souls.

"Oh, man," he groaned. It was way too late at night to get so philosophical. Hell, it was way too late in *life*. Kira could turn another one-hundred-and-eighty degrees and tell him it was an experiment that failed. She could flee to her beloved Boston and shun the town he didn't want to leave.

But for the first time he had real hope.

* * *

Kira hadn't seen Jake leave, but she didn't need to look around to know he wasn't at the ball anymore. She'd felt him go, as if a door had closed in her heart to match the one closing behind him.

"Stupid, Kira." She slumped in her chair, leaning sideways against the backrest. She had only had one drink, but felt like she had a three-martini hangover. Her body throbbed, her heart ached, and her mind kept poking at the bruises. She'd really screwed up this time.

"Kira, darling. Aren't you having a good time?" Elyse sat next to her and fanned her face with a napkin. "Wasn't it a great ball?"

"Sure. It was great." She eyed the dance floor, where the die-hards swayed to the last song of the evening. Sophie was out there with an old high school friend. Brie danced with Bob. Kira would have been worried if she hadn't known this was the first time they'd danced tonight. But she wouldn't have known *that* if Brie hadn't told her. Since she'd spent much of the night either in the ladies' room or boinking her best friend.

She cringed at the thought and looked at her mother. The older woman's eyes glowed. She looked fifteen years younger in the faint light. Kira wondered what of those fifteen years she would have changed.

"What do you think of Darcy?" Kira asked her.

Elyse shrugged. "Not much. She's okay. Not right for Jake, though."

"He seemed enamored."

"It'll pass."

Kira hated to hope she was right. She was finished with this roller coaster. Jake wanted her, she didn't want him. She might want him, but he's done with her. She *really* wanted him, he had her. But he didn't want her.

She couldn't blame him. He deserved so much better than what she'd given him over the past few years. The more she thought about it, the more she realized how much she'd taken and how little he'd gotten in return.

She felt herself sliding deeper and deeper into a self-pitying funk. Not where she wanted to be during the holidays. But when she thought about facing Jake tomorrow for the Macgregors' annual open house, then on Christmas Day for dinner at his house, she wanted to hide under her covers for three days, then skip back to Boston and forget today had ever happened.

The DJ faded the last song into some generic classical background music and lifted his microphone.

"I'm sorry to say, that's all we have for tonight, folks. Before I close, I have one final announcement. Tonight Jake McKenna presented the Jason Dean Foundation with a check. Since that presentation, one thousand additional dollars have been donated to help these children find happiness in the midst of tragedy." Kira's eyes misted when he repeated Jake's words. She suffered, knowing it was her fault he wasn't here to hear this.

"I need to go home," she told her mother, exasperated with herself. Elyse eyed her with the knowing expression of a mother.

"What happened tonight, dear?"

"Nothing, why?" She strove to sound light and unconcerned. Her mother snorted and went back to fanning herself.

"Nothing, my patootie. Something's wrong." Her eyes locked on Kira's. "Do you want to talk about it?"

Kira shook her head, then laid it on her arm on the back of the chair in front of her. She absently watched the stragglers gathering belongings and taking last sips of drinks. "I wouldn't know what to say."

"You know I'm here when you do."

"I know."

"Okay, let's go home."

They stood and headed for the foyer. Suddenly, home sounded pretty good to Kira.

*   *   *

December 24th dawned bright and clear. And cold. And snowy. Kira woke up early and grinned at the sunlight sparkling on the whitened lawn. She'd left her window open a crack last night and now inhaled pure winter.

"Thirty-six, if not lower." She bounced out of bed and hummed a Christmas carol as she gathered her clothes and beat the rest of the family into the bathroom. By the time anyone else was up, she was frying bacon and flipping pancakes.

"Smells good," Brianna complimented as she came into the kitchen.

She went to the cupboard that held the plates and began setting the table.

"Have a good time last night?" Kira asked, hoping she'd be able to keep conversation off her own evening's activities.

"Sure," Brianna said. "Most of the night."

"I saw you dancing with Bob, after all. Is he coming tonight?"

Brie shuddered as she returned to the drawer for silverware. "Bob's finished. Don't say 'I told you so,' but he 'exposed' himself to me last night."

"Yep," Sophie confirmed as she hobbled into the kitchen. "He waved the little white flag, all right."

"Sophie!" Brianna chided. Her sister lifted a hand to her head and moaned.

Unlike her sisters, Sophie hadn't dressed and Kira giggled at her rumpled flannel nightgown and feathered mules. "Stop giggling. Why aren't you two hung over?"

"Maybe because we didn't drink," Brianna said.

Sophie yawned and slumped at the table. Brianna nudged her arms and stuck a plate in front of her. "I didn't drink much." She pushed the plate forward and laid her head on the table. "It was the dancing. My feet are killing me."

"Your feet are killing you because of the slippers," Kira told her. "You don't have to glam up for us."

Sophie peered under the table, then shrugged. "Hey, did you guys notice the tension between Mom and Dad last night?"

Brie nodded and carried glasses to the table. "How could we miss it?"

Kira turned back to her bacon. What tension? If she admitted she didn't know, they'd try to find out why. But what tension?

"What do you think it is?" she asked casually.

"Maybe Daddy's having an affair," Brianna murmured, darting glances at the door, keeping watch for the couple in question.

"Mom would never stand for it," Sophie declared.

"Stand for what?" Elyse glided into the kitchen, her old cotton robe belted tightly over her white Victorian nightgown.

Kira glared at Brianna for not seeing her. "Pecan pancakes!" She set the platter on the table and let everyone ooh and ah enough for the question to go unanswered. "Where's Dad?"

"He's showering. He said to start without us."

"Maybe our Christmas present should have been a second

bathroom," Kira joked.

"Yeah, but then what would he complain about?"

"Pass the butter, please."

They filled their plates, then their mouths. Kira swallowed, then turned to her mother.

"Did you talk to Fran about Jake's mole?" she asked.

Elyse shook her head. "I didn't have a chance. Too much going on at the ball, and I didn't want to ruin her night. You know she'll be as scared as if she'd known then."

"Why is it your responsibility to tell her?" Sophie asked. "It should be Jake's. He's not a child. We don't have to tattle on him."

"I did consider that," her mother said. "But I would want to know if it were one of you girls. I'd be angrier at my friend for not telling me. She has a right to know."

Sophie shrugged and turned her attention back to her plate. They ate in silence for a minute. Kira had almost finished her breakfast and thought she'd escape without an inquisition when Sophie's coffee kicked in.

"So, what did everyone think of the Divine Darcy?"

Hoping to keep the attention off her, Kira turned to Brianna. "Yeah, what was that all about at the table?"

"All what?" Her manner was too casual, and was ruined when her pancakes dropped off her fork.

"You know, the glare Darcy threw at you? The 'who, me?' look you gave her back? If you were ten, I'd have thought you kicked her."

"I don't know what you're talking about." Her nose tilted in the air.

Elyse watched her daughters interestedly. "Why would you do anything, Brianna? Don't you like Darcy?"

"Ha!"

The outburst came from all three daughters, and Elyse raised one eyebrow. "Do tell, my dears. Why the antipathy?"

Kira looked at her plate. Her sisters had no reservations.

"Darcy is a bitch. You should have seen her at the dress shop." Sophie stabbed a piece of pancake.

Brianna lifted her nose in the air. "'He never mentioned *you*. And by all means, kiss my hem.'"

"Ice fishing, my fat—"

"That piece of ice slid into her cleavage on its own. I could never have bumped the waiter with that degree of accuracy."

"All she wants is to get into Jake's pants. And he can't want more than that from her—"

"I don't think he even wants that. Did you see how far he held her from him on the dance floor?"

Kira watched her mother's face darken with each word her sisters uttered. She sure didn't want to be on the end of the blistering lecture that was coming. She tried to shrink into her chair and kept her gaze on her own coffee cup.

"I did not raise you two to be so uncharitable. Jake is like a brother to you. Darcy is his choice. She is likely to be joining us for the festivities, and you will both be civil to her."

Oh, God. It had been hard enough to consider facing Jake for the next few days. Now there was the possibility Darcy would be with him. Kira fought the continuing urge to run home to Boston. She had the feeling she'd be fighting that urge until she actually went back.

"Mom, you don't understand." Brianna's tone came awfully close to whining.

"Oh, I certainly do. I raised you better than that. However, I understand where you're coming from. The woman is after the primest catch in Brook Hollow, and we don't like our Jake being the prey."

"Something like that." Sophie stirred sugar into her third cup of coffee. "Speaking of…was anyone surprised by Kleinfelter's announcement last night?"

"A bit. I expected him to wait at least until after the holidays." Elyse shook her head. "It's not like Jake will have opposition."

"He might."

The others turned to stare at Sophie.

"Oh, all right, he won't."

"Were you really considering it, Sophie?" Kira asked. She acknowledged the pang in her heart as it prepared to divide loyalties.

Her sister tilted her head and raised one shoulder. "Not really, not against Jake. I wouldn't stand a chance. If he wanted to wait a few years, though…."

"I never knew you were interested in politics," Brie said.

"You haven't even lived here for a while," Kira added, trying to say it nicely.

Elyse patted Sophie's hand. "I would have voted for you, darling."

"Thanks, Mom." She sighed and stood to bring her dishes to the sink. "I didn't really want the job. But I want *something* more than what I'm doing."

Kira felt better hearing someone else voice the same feelings she'd been having. But she couldn't resist asking, "What are you doing, anyway?" Sophie tossed a hand towel at her.

"Now, girls." Their mother stepped between them. "Let's do the dishes, since Kira cooked. Kira, you sit at the table and make a list. There's a lot to do today before the open house."

They fell into familiar routines, and Kira reveled in the camaraderie and gentle teasing. Her earlier good mood revived. *This* was what the holidays were all about. She convinced herself that Jake wouldn't bring Darcy to the open house. They had too much history, she decided. He wouldn't want to hurt her that way, even if he believed what she'd said last night.

She even managed to forget their unprotected sex. Well, the unprotected part. She couldn't change what was done. She rubbed harder at the silver punch bowl she was polishing. There was no reason to worry. Her time of the month was all wrong. Well, kind of wrong. Maybe a few days off. Nothing to worry about.

She set the bowl on the linen-and-lace covered dining room table and smiled at the gleam. Perfect.

Just like tonight was going to be.

CHAPTER 10

Perfect.

Kira stood in a corner of the living room where she could clearly see the front door. She'd stopped what she was doing half a dozen times to see who was coming in. After Bob, the Kleinfelters, Maggie and John, and Maggie's mom and the baby came in, Kira had tried to stay busy. But she'd almost spilled ginger ale on the white tablecloth when her parents' new next door neighbors arrived, and had burned her hand on the baking pan of chicken wings when a group of her father's coworkers sneaked through the back way.

She gave the food-and-drink supervision over to Sophie and began mingling. She still couldn't keep her attention off the front door, but at least she wasn't hurting herself or making a mess.

She was laughing at a lame joke her father's best friend had told when the door opened again and her "perfect" night came to an end. Darcy's expectant face came through, looking fresh and sweet in front of Jake's rugged countenance.

Kira watched Jake look around as he shut the door, his eyes scanning the room as he took Darcy's wool coat. He was taking off his own leather jacket when he spotted Kira. She froze, struck by the message in his eyes. He was pleading for something, but she didn't know what. Forgiveness? Freedom? Understanding? She nodded. Whatever it was, she had to give it. He deserved no less, after all the years she did nothing but take from him.

Darcy was already making the rounds. A few more groups of

people entered behind Jake, many of them Brook Hollow business owners. Darcy smiled and shook hands, nodding and winking, and Kira thought she already looked like a politician's wife. Was the woman campaigning? On Christmas Eve? When the candidate was a shoo-in? Kira suppressed a giggle.

"What are you laughing at?"

The murmured voice at her ear sent shivers rippling down Kira's arms and deep into her gut. She battled back memories of the night before and clutched her glass to keep from pressing her hand against her stomach.

"Darcy's fitting right in," she commented without turning around.

"For now."

"What does that mean?"

The mayor requested Jake's attention before he could answer, then started a mild debate on the threat of superstores to local business, and Kira was able to slip away.

Darcy caught up to her a bit later in the kitchen, where Kira was scraping dishes over a trash bag.

"I thought I'd find you here," the other woman said, gazing pointedly at the bag in front of Kira.

"Hi, Darcy." Kira was determined to be nice. Jake might marry this woman, and she wanted to keep his friendship. No matter how much it grated, she'd be nice. "I'm glad you could come." She tried not to grit her teeth.

"Yes, well, I don't have family in town, so it gave me something to do." She paused, then added, "It was nice of your mother to invite me."

"She hates for anyone to be alone," Kira said, straightening. She cocked her head at Darcy. "What did bring you to Brook Hollow, if not family? Especially from a city like New York, and when your family is in Texas."

Darcy shrugged and looked around the unusually messy kitchen. "I was passing through on my way to Vermont, taking the scenic route, and I liked it. I needed a change of pace. New York is, well, you know." She flapped a hand. Kira murmured something that could pass for assent and began stacking the scraped dishes in the dishwasher.

"So has it lived up to your expectations?"

"Oh, yes. Especially Jake." Her tone firmed. "He's a dream come true, you know."

"I know," Kira almost whispered. She kept her back to Darcy, but the woman went on, each word like a barb in Kira's heart.

"I get the small town values and safety, ideal for raising a child, with the excitement of politics and the distinction of being the wife of the mayor."

Kira froze as Darcy tittered unconvincingly. "Oh, well, that's going a bit beyond things. But not too far." She paused as if waiting for Kira to say something. When she didn't, Darcy went on. "Jake said you'll be returning to Boston after the holidays?"

Kira finally turned. "Yes, probably early next week. Why?"

"Oh, just wondering. He'll have this campaign to concentrate on, you know."

And Kira would interfere? She wouldn't let the woman get away with that.

"What's your point?"

Darcy seemed taken aback by her directness. "Well, he seems distracted by your...problems. He mentioned them. I just want to make sure he can focus on what's important."

Kira folded her arms. "I've been Jake's campaign manager for all of his winning campaigns, Darcy. I don't think my problems, whatever they are, will get in the way of this one."

"But you are going back to Boston."

The devil got into her. She was fed up with this woman's interference. "Actually, Darcy, I'm submitting a proposal for the school district's networking. If I get it, I'll be here for two years. At least."

Kira walked out of the room then, satisfied that she'd left Darcy looking like she'd just sucked a lemon.

* * *

Jake began to worry when he couldn't find Darcy or Kira. He tried to escape the main party, but couldn't get past the dining room. Someone kept nabbing him, congratulating him on his announcement, asking about Darcy, complaining about some inconsequential thing. Was this what being mayor was going to be like? If so, he didn't want the job.

"Jake!" The chairperson of the school board approached, smiling widely. "I'm so glad for Fritz's endorsement." She rested a hand on Jake's upper arm. "No one could do a better job."

"Thanks, Candace." Okay, he did want the job. It wasn't the constant attention or the power he craved, although he didn't hate that part. He liked knowing this was what he was born for, that everyone recognized it. He liked being relied on for his opinion, his ability to find a solution.

Well, a solution for everyone else's problems, anyway. He saw Kira charge out of the kitchen and up the stairs and tried to follow her. Candace had his ear, though, and wouldn't relinquish it. He gave in to the inevitable, but kept one eye on the stairway.

The other eye caught Darcy emerging from the kitchen a few moments later. She looked thunderous, until the owner of the local grocery store paused next to her. She turned on her smile and began schmoozing again. Jake's heart sank, though, when he realized Darcy and Kira had been talking. No wonder Kira had gone upstairs.

By the time she came back down, the crowd had thinned and Darcy had attached herself to Jake's left arm. His smile had grown more and more forced and, much like last night, he fought his desires. These desires ran more toward breaking off fake three-inch fingernails and outlawing high-pitched laughs, however.

During his vigil at the stairs, too, he'd seen his mother and Elyse sequester themselves in a nook. Their discussion was too intense, his mother's face too shocked, for them to be discussing anything other than Jake's mole. He was in for quite a lecture later.

Kira paused in the doorway and Jake allowed her to distract him. None of the departing guests was likely to notice that he watched her, and if they did, they were so used to seeing friendship between them he doubted they'd sense more.

Within a few minutes only family was left.

"Jake, baby, come sit." Darcy commandeered the couch and pulled him down next to her while the Macgregors filled in around them. Jake grit his teeth again and wondered what had made him believe he could keep his distance until he broke up with Darcy. The woman was acting like he was a crown prince and she his intended bride. She'd even dressed royally, in a purple crushed velvet jacket over a fluffy blouse. He much preferred Kira's ivory silk sweater and the red bow she'd pinned to it. He especially liked the v-neck of the sweater....

"Oh, what a relief." Elyse dropped into an overstuffed chair and eased off her shoes. Jake smiled as Duncan sat on the ottoman next to her and began to rub her feet. "Oohh, Duncan, that's wonderful."

"It was a wonderful party. You deserve some pampering."

Jake's parents returned from taking trash to the bins out back. Jake shifted on the couch to make room for his mother. Darcy beamed and snuggled even closer. He wondered how he could convey that this was a family time and ask her to go home without being unpardonably rude, something his mother would never forgive.

"Brrr." His father rubbed his hands together, then took a seat on the hearth near the gently crackling fire. "It turned cold again. Smells like more snow coming."

"Good." Sophie grinned up from her position on the floor. "I want to go sledding tomorrow."

"Me, too," Brianna said, "but on what? All our sleds are gone."

"We could use high school cafeteria trays, like we used to," Sophie suggested.

"Absolutely not," Jake said.

Brianna rolled her eyes. "Cardboard boxes?"

Kira shook her head and leaned against the wall near the tree. Her folded arms plumped her breasts, emphasizing her cleavage in the v of her sweater. Jake had to take a sip of his whiskey to ease his dry throat, but he couldn't look away.

"They get too soggy," she said. "How about the tarps dad uses for leaves?"

"That might work," Sophie mused. "We can cut them up—"

"Or not," Duncan interjected.

"Or fold and tape them." Sophie smiled at her father, who winked, then pulled Kira down on one knee.

"I remember when you kids used to slide on your butts and nothing else," Duncan slung one arm around his daughter's shoulders and squeezed. "Those were the days."

"Yeah, Dad, but we wore nylon snow suits back then. We'll try the tarps." Kira kissed his nose and stood, then resettled herself on her knees near the Christmas tree. Jake wondered if he could find a way to sit next to her.

"We have some news," Jake's father said after it was clear the sledding topic was exhausted. Jake looked from his father to his mother.

"You're pregnant," he joked, then wondered why Kira turned green. Darcy tucked her hand around his arm, and he tore his gaze from the woman he'd rather be with.

"Don't be ridiculous," his mother said, slapping him gently on the shoulder. She shifted forward on the couch. "It's much more logical, really."

Elyse gasped and sat upright, pulling her feet from her husband's hands. "You're moving back!"

Fran beamed. "Yes, we are."

Stunned, Jake stared at her, then at his father, who sat looking smug.

"When? How? How did you keep this a secret? Why?" He couldn't get more coherent than that.

"We weren't at a seminar, son." Luke quirked a smile. "Who holds an international conference two days before Christmas? No, we were packing. All our stuff is being shipped back here next week. We're done with France, and moving home."

A dozen questions pounded through Jake's head, but now wasn't really the time to ask them. He felt displaced. They'd surely want their house back. They wouldn't kick him out right away, of course, but he didn't really want to live with his parents again. And, ick, they'd be sleeping in the bed where he'd first made love with Kira.

Darcy grinned up at him. "Now I can find you your own house," she said, reminding him with a wink of the hints she'd made yesterday about living together. He barely refrained from groaning. His life was getting more complicated by the minute.

The four older adults began talking all at once about how wonderful it was going to be. Jake wanted no part of that conversation, and was relieved when Sophie asked him about his campaign.

"What are your stands on the issues, Jake?" Her eyes twinkled at him.

"What issues?" Kira teased. "This is Brook Hollow. The only issue is whether or not to stock the lake next summer, and you know there's only one position to take."

"I'll stock the lake if environmental conditions call for it," Jake said, "or if the fishermen and women need more fish."

They laughed, and Darcy's high pitch scratched across his composure. He wondered how bad it would be to break up with her tonight. He couldn't stand another day of this. But then Kira jumped up and grabbed a Santa hat from the tree.

"Okay, everyone! Time for the final Christmas Eve tradition." The grandfather clock over the mantle began to chime midnight as she donned her hat and plucked another one off a low branch. "Whose turn is it to play elf?"

Darcy's brow creased. "Presents? I didn't…."

Kira smiled…compassionately? "Don't worry, Darce. It's just one gift for each person. We open the rest tomorrow. Don't feel left out." She looked around with a mock frown. "Now, I'll ask again, whose turn is it to play elf?"

"I think it's Brie's," Fran said, starting the game.

"No, it's Luke's," Elyse played along.

Kira grinned at her family. She clearly loved this tradition, despite her proclaimed lack of interest in them.

Finally it was Sophie's turn. She sighed heavily. "This is so stupid." She was shouted down. "Okay, okay!" She rolled her eyes to the ceiling and adopted a fake storybook tone of voice. "Oh, goodness. It must be Daddy's. Or is it Mommy's? Oh, no!" She slapped one hand to her cheek. The laughter at her antics almost drowned out her last line. "It must be…"

"Jake's!" Everyone yelled it. Jake smiled and stood, basking in the feel of belonging, the connection tradition gave them, the warmth of the love in the room. They played this game every year, and he always took it as a sign he and Kira belonged together. Last year he'd been trying to fight that feeling. Tonight it burned stronger than ever.

"I guess it's me again," he murmured as he pulled the floppy double-pom-pommed hat from Kira's hand. Her eyes were so blue, so dewy, he quickly turned away and slipped the hat onto his head. It still fit, like the well-worn seat of his boat or the leather jacket he'd worn since high school.

Kira ignored him and bent to pick up a gift. "Sophie." She handed it to Jake, who took two steps across the room and dropped the soft package onto her head.

"Hey!" She pretended to bite his leg and he danced away, knocking into the end table.

"This worked better when we were ten," he commented, one hand still steadying the lamp. "We fit better."

"Brianna." Kira ignored him and held out another gift.

Jake dutifully handed out the rest of the packages, then sat back next to Darcy. She grinned at him.

"I have a gift, Jake. Isn't that sweet?" Her Texas drawl slid into the comment and he realized how rarely she let that happen. It meant she was having a genuine moment, he realized. This was the Darcy he'd been attracted to.

No, he realized, he couldn't break up with her tonight. He sighed and fingered the bow on his package. Maybe tomorrow. Early, before everyone else showed up.

"Your turn." He looked up. Sophie was holding out a handful of straws. Jake plucked a dark blue one and looked at the number on the tab on the bottom. Three. He opened his package third. He watched

Darcy nibble her lower lip before selecting a pink straw.

"One!" she squealed, actually bouncing in her seat. This woman had too many faces. Jake knew that if he hadn't already decided to break up with her, he would have made that decision tonight. Unpredictable women were dangerous.

"Okay, Darcy, go ahead." Sophie had finished the drawing and everyone was looking expectantly at the invader. Jake felt a rush of warmth for these people who'd uncomplainingly included Darcy in their traditions, despite their collective dislike for her. No one had said so, but he could tell.

They watched Darcy carefully peel the wrapping away, then slide the top off the small box.

"A CD!" she exclaimed. She flipped it over. She was a good enough actress that Jake figured only he saw her face fall when she saw the artist.

"Yanni. How...soothing." She looked around the room. "Thank you."

"Me next!" Brianna wasn't quite so delicate with her wrapping. The paper was off the shirt box in seconds, and she ran her hands over the cashmere scarf inside.

"Oh, it's lovely, Jake!"

"I thought it would look good with your camel coat," he said. Brie rubbed it against her cheek and he noted the pale blue did match her eyes, as he'd hoped.

He turned to his present, knowing by the name on the tag what it was. Duncan always gave him a fishing lure. He admired it and they moved on. Elyse exclaimed over the sweater Luke and Fran had brought from France. Duncan sniffed his cigars, Sophie tried on the tall leather boots from Brianna, and his parents ooh'd and ah'd over the gift basket Elyse had made them.

"I thought once you got back to the continent you'd appreciate the American stuff you're always complaining you can't get." She smiled. "I'm glad that won't be the case."

Finally, Kira prepared to open hers. Jake yawned and checked his watch. Luckily, no young children would be waking them in five hours, but he was bushed. He still had to get Darcy home and try to avoid her attempts to get him to commit.

Suddenly he recognized the package Kira was about to open. "Wait!" he shouted, holding out a hand like he could physically stop her. Everyone stared at him. Kira frowned.

"What?"

"Not that one." It was too private. He'd intended to leave it at home and give it to her alone tomorrow. One of his parents must have scooped it up when they gathered the presents. They liked to have them all in one place, even though they only opened one on Christmas Eve and half of them would be dragged home for tomorrow.

"Open something else," he said.

Kira looked down at the heavy box and the half-torn tapestry print paper. Part of her wanted to be ornery and finish opening it, but that was the part that was worn out and sick of watching Darcy clutch at Jake. She didn't want to give in to childishness, so she smoothed the tape back onto the bottom of the package and chose something else.

She dutifully drooled over the Swiss chocolates from Jake's mom and dad, then was grateful when everyone immediately stood.

"Noon tomorrow?" Fran asked, and everyone groaned.

"I'll be lucky to be up by noon, Mom K," Sophie voiced all their sentiments.

"All right, we'll make it two. Eat a light breakfast— turkey dinner at two-thirty!"

Plans made, they all went their separate ways, amid hugs and kisses and promises of more good stuff tomorrow. Kira lingered as she gathered up wrapping paper and threw it in the fireplace. She'd thought everyone had left the room and started when hands closed over her shoulders.

"I'm sorry about the present," Jake murmured into her hair. Kira stared into the fire and tried not to relax back into his chest.

"Where's Darcy?"

"In the car. I forgot my lure." He held it up so she could see it. "I just wanted you to understand that I didn't want anyone else to see your gift."

She turned around. "Why?"

"You'll know when you open it." His face was solemn, gorgeous with the firelight and Christmas tree lights flickering over it. Kira's heart ached at what she'd missed all these years. What she'd wasted and was now throwing away.

"When can I open it?" Though she didn't care.

"Tomorrow. Keer," he began, and Kira panicked. She didn't want to talk about what she heard approaching in his voice.

"Good night, Jake." She lifted on tiptoe and kissed his rough cheek. "See you tomorrow. Merry Christmas." She would have gone upstairs except she still had to turn off the tree and bank the fire.

She stood still, silently begging Jake to let go of her arm where it burned under his fingers. He looked reluctant, but finally whispered, "Good night," and left.

Kira sighed and collapsed onto the couch, watching the flames die in the fireplace as their fuel became spent.

Tonight had been one of the hardest nights she'd ever lived through, emotionally. And tomorrow would be just as bad. Maybe worse, because there'd be fewer people to act as buffer. And without a doubt Darcy would be there. Ugh.

Merry Christmas.

CHAPTER 11

Kira exchanged gifts with her family after they'd all gotten out of bed and eaten the traditional breakfast. They gathered in their robes in the living room and took turns opening the presents after the yearly argument between Sophie, who wanted to open them all at once, and Brie, who liked to go slow and savor the experience.

Kira once again donned the Santa hat and distributed the presents. She felt a very child-like satisfaction at the size of her pile.

They went around the circle five or six times, giving orders on which present to open next. Kira exclaimed over the subscription to a trade magazine her parents gave her every year, the impractical earrings from Sophie, the journal and perfume from Brie.

"Is this a hint?" she asked her. Brie grinned cheekily. "To help you attract that man who isn't Jake," she teased.

To Kira's relief, everyone seemed to love their presents, both the ones she'd agonized over and the last-minute fun ones she'd bought at the mall with Jake. Finally, it was time for the Big Gift. Kira deliberately waited until everything else was done.

"Merry Christmas and thank you, everyone." Elyse stood and adjusted the belt of her new robe. "I get first dibs on the shower." She looked down at her husband. "Duncan, get your hand off me. I swear the man has never touched satin before."

The girls froze, not sure whether their mother was joking. Their father seemed unaffected. He slid his palm toward the hem of the robe. "It's been years, my sweet. You might want to save this for special occasions."

Elyse went "phfft" and headed for the stairs. Kira jumped up and reached for a large envelope that had gone unnoticed, propped on the side of the tree.

"Hey, what's this?" She waited until her mother turned. "It says 'For Duncan and Elyse, from Santa. No two people ever deserved anything more.'" Kira tried to look innocent as she held out the envelope. "I guess it's for you." She sat cross-legged on the floor between her sisters. Elyse sank back onto the couch, staring in puzzlement at the white envelope, then at her husband.

"What are you up to?" she asked him. "You already gave me the beautiful sapphire necklace." But Duncan shook his head.

"Not me," he said. "I'm in the dark."

Their mother squinted at her daughters, then slowly unsealed the flap and pulled out several items. She flipped open the plane ticket holder and frowned. Her husband selected a brochure for the Flamingo hotel from the pile on her lap.

"Hot damn! The Flamingo!" He sifted through the paperwork. "Rental car. Gift certificate for Gatsby's restaurant. Plane tickets. Hotel reservation. Lysie, darling, they've given us a vacation!"

Tears filled Kira's eyes when she saw the glitter of them in her mother's. She hadn't heard her father call her mother Lysie in years. She clutched her sisters' hands and grinned at them. They'd made the right choice.

But suddenly Kira realized her mother was staring at the items on her lap, and her tears didn't look like tears of joy.

"What on earth made you girls do this?"

Something twanged in Kira's chest. What was wrong? That was annoyance, not delight, in her mother's voice. "You've always wanted to go to Vegas," she explained. "We decided to make it possible. Look, there's even a money order for your gambling money. It's not a lot, but—"

"Who told you we wanted to go to Vegas?" her mother demanded.

"Well, you guys talk about it all the time. Dad always wanted to see the Strip. And he never gambled, so he wanted to try—"

She broke off as her mother stood up, dumping their gift on the floor.

"Your *father* always wanted to go to Vegas! *He* talked about it all the time. I never said anything because I didn't want to ruin his fantasy. I certainly would have spoken up if I had known you girls would do *this*!" She gestured at the floor. "I have never in my life wanted to go to Vegas."

Kira still felt confused. "But, Mom." She didn't get any further. Elyse turned on Duncan.

"I am tired of catering to your every whim. Of doing things for everyone else, and not fulfilling my own needs. Never restless, my sweet patootie." She poked a finger at his chest. "You get restless every two years, like clockwork. And we always do something to 'get out of the rut.' Day trips to places you read about and decide we should visit. Motorcycle rentals. Fly fishing. Building your God damned workshop!" She stomped her foot.

Kira knew her chin was sagging, but couldn't snap her mouth shut. She'd never seen her mother like this. She'd always acted like serving others—within reason—was the be-all and end-all of her existence. That if Duncan was happy, she was happy. Kira had never noticed anything indicating restlessness in her *mother*.

Until lately. She remembered the look on her mother's face when they were decorating the tree, and Kira had asked if she'd ever felt restless. And the other look a day later, the one Kira couldn't identify, when she had Abby in her arms.

Sheesh. Was her mother having a midlife crisis?

"Elyse," Duncan started, rising and moving to soothe his wife. Elyse backed up and pointed a finger at him.

"I'm not finished. Every time you get restless, we do something you think is fun. Well, now *I'm* restless. I need to do something fun. But I *do not want to go to Vegas*!" She swept up everything that had been in the envelope and stomped up the stairs.

Kira, Sophie, and Brianna stared after her. Brie moved to get up, but Kira stopped her. Their father slumped on the sofa, his eyes closed, his hands dangling limp from his knees.

"Dad," Kira started, not really sure what she was going to say. But he stopped her.

"It's okay, girls. I know I've been taking your mother for granted." He gazed up the stairs, his face sagging and making him look ten years older. "I've been trying to make it up to her in little ways." Now he grinned a sad little grin and ran his hand over his face. "I guess she needed something bigger."

"But you didn't know I did."

They looked up to see Elyse coming down the stairs a bit more sedately than she'd climbed them. She stopped at the end of the couch, not close enough to touch her husband. Kira noticed her hands were still in fists, though she was clearly trying to stay composed.

"Duncan, you can't know how I feel if I don't tell you. None of you can." She bent and kissed each of her daughters on the forehead, lingering over Kira's. Her cool hand on the side of Kira's face made her feel five years old again, and safe.

"I'm sorry, dears. You worked so hard on this gift, and spent so much money. I love that you wanted to give us something special."

Duncan stood and looked at his wife, his gaze pleading. "You know I'm completely dedicated to you, Elyse."

"I know." Her tone softened a fraction. "And I've been completely devoted to you. But when did we ever discuss *my* dream vacation? When did we ever talk about my interests, minor as they are, instead of plumbing and football or our family?" She held up the sheaf of papers she still clutched in her left hand. "I need some space. Some time away. I'm trading these in and getting my own vacation. And I'm not telling you where."

She turned to her daughters, still sitting like children on the floor, and bent to touch Kira's curls. "It's not your fault, girls. Believe me." She straightened again. "Now, let's go to the McKennas, and I don't want to discuss this again today. Let's have a nice, traditional Christmas."

"Traditional, my ass," Kira grumbled, watching her parents leave the room. Once again her perception of her world was incorrect. Her parents hadn't always had the perfect marriage, and it appeared they still didn't. She didn't know what that meant for her, except that her world had tilted a few more degrees.

* * *

Brianna and Sophie crept into Kira's room while their parents were dressing.

"One of you should be in the shower," Kira told them. She didn't look up from her dresser, where she was putting away presents and trying to decide what to wear to Jake's.

"They can wait." Sophie's hurt manifested in anger. She paced, while Brie curled up on the bed. "Can you believe this? Poor Mom. Giving her whole life to Dad and not getting any fulfillment in return!"

Brie bit her lip and Kira heard her sniffle. "Well, what about Daddy? Mom admitted she never told Dad she was unhappy."

Kira stopped what she was doing and sat next to her sister on the bed.

"It really doesn't have anything to do with us," she said. "They'll work through it."

"But Mom basically gave herself up for us. Endured so many years unhappy."

"No, she didn't, hon." Kira smoothed the younger woman's hair. "She did what she wanted to do. She made the choices. She could have said something to Daddy a long time ago."

"Then why the outburst?" Sophie demanded. She whirled on them and pointed at the door. "Why is she running out now?"

"Sophie, calm down," Kira soothed. "They'll hear you. And don't say you don't care. *We* care." Brianna nodded.

"Empty nest." The more she thought about it, the more that fit. "Mom has been struggling with us leaving for the past couple of years. She still meddles, and worries too much. I think she's reached crisis point and this is the camel's straw."

Sophie pursed her lips and narrowed her eyes at the ceiling. "I think you might be right."

Brie hugged Kira. "It makes perfect sense. No wonder you're the oldest. You're so wise."

"No, I'm wise because I'm the oldest. The question is, what do we do now?"

"Nothing," Sophie stated. "She's doing it. We just leave her alone to choose her vacation, do something just for herself for once."

"Should we be more attentive?"

Kira pondered her sister's question. "No, because she'll think we're doing that so she'll go back to being her old self. Let's just leave her alone, like Sophie said."

"Well, it's not like I bring my laundry over or anything," Brie griped as they went out the door.

The sweater dress Kira wanted to wear drooped from her hand. She felt an awful lot like that. Limp. And she still had to face Jake and Darcy.

She already had a headache.

* * *

Jake had a headache.

His mother was fussing around as if the Pope was coming to dinner instead of friends who'd been here a thousand times before. His father had slipped and pulled his back trying to chop firewood in the snowy back yard.

And he couldn't get a hold of Darcy.

She'd gotten away from him the night before, accepting a ride home from his parents, who'd already loaded all the presents into his car. Jake had reluctantly kissed her goodbye and thanked his father for taking Darcy home. He'd thought about calling or going to her condo, but it had been so late he decided to wait until morning.

This morning he'd called her first thing, before his parents got up, but only got her answering machine. Three calls later, still nothing. Everyone else would be here any minute, and he didn't know what to do about Darcy.

"Hey, Mom?"

She didn't pause in her kitchen busywork. "Mm-hm?"

"Did you say anything to Darcy about today?"

"Of course, dear. I invited her for dinner. Poor thing is all alone, no reason she should be that way on Christmas Day."

"Did she say she was coming?"

"I'm sure she did."

Jake snitched a carrot stick from a tray. Maybe she'd made other plans and wouldn't come.

The doorbell rang.

Sighing in relief, Jake checked his watch and headed for the doorway. Maybe there was still time to break it off before the rest of the gang got here.

"I'll get it." Fran put a hand against Jake's chest to stop him and turned him toward the back door. "We need more wood stacked by the back door. Don't worry, I'll entertain your guest."

"But—"

"Go, Jake."

Jake went, cursing himself for a coward the whole way.

* * *

A short time later, the Macgregors invaded Jake's little house en masse. Kira kept her expression neutral when she saw Darcy lounging on the sofa with an eggnog in her hand. Kira was surprised she didn't greet them at the door, like a proper mistress of the house. Of course, Fran did that, so maybe Darcy was deferring to "her" future mother-in-law.

"It smells wonderful in here!" Elyse sniffed, then gathered her family's coats and disappeared briefly down the hall to deposit them in the bedroom. She reappeared and followed the other women into the kitchen, where Fran promptly put them all to work.

Darcy stayed in the living room, Kira noticed. She gathered bowls and utensils while Sophie mashed potatoes and Brie referred to a list and pulled things from the oven as they finished cooking. Elyse laid hot plates and mats on the dining room table, which was already set, and Luke stood at one end of the counter, carving the turkey.

Jake was nowhere to be seen, and Kira wondered if he was entertaining Darcy while everyone else worked. *I shouldn't be such a shrew.* She arranged warm rolls in a Longaberger basket. Darcy was a guest, not a relative. But she was the only one not helping. Besides Jake. Kira's back ached from tension by the time he appeared.

"Wood's all stacked," he announced, rubbing his hands together as he entered the kitchen through the back door.

"Jake, did you do all that without a coat?"

Kira hid a smile. Fran sounded just like her mother. She even looked like her, brandishing a knife in Jake's direction. Jake caught her eye and they shared their amusement. It was a bit disconcerting to realize their connection was intact despite the events of the last few days.

"You're the one who sent me out there," Jake protested.

"But not without a coat. You'll catch your death."

"Oh, Ma, I'm fine. See?" Fran squealed when he put his cold hands on the back of her neck.

"You naughty boy!" Jake dodged the fist she shook at him, then gave her a smack on the cheek. She kissed him back.

Cheered now that she knew Jake hadn't been with Darcy for the last half hour, Kira willingly ferried full platters and bowls to the dining room. She was even able to ignore Darcy when she entered the room ten seconds after the last item had been placed on the table.

"Can I help?" she asked, though it was clear she couldn't. Fran was turning off the oven and checking the stove burners. The dishwasher began to hum when Brianna closed the door. Sophie hung a towel on the rack, and Kira wiped the last drip off the island counter top and tossed the sponge in the sink.

"Thanks anyway," Fran said, taking Darcy's arm and leading her to the dining room. "You can help clean up after we eat."

Kira snickered. Yeah, right. In her dreams, Darcy would do all the clean-up. She doubted the woman would lift a finger.

* * *

"So, son, Mayor Kleinfelter told me he was a bit concerned about scandal during your campaign."

Jake kept his head down and hoped he could get out of discussing this. So far, every conversation had gotten derailed by another. It was inevitable with so many people at the table. But no one came to his rescue, so he responded. "No campaign is free of the threat of scandal, Dad. But come on, what could he possibly be concerned about?"

"He seems to think you have a better chance if you're married."

For several seconds Jake just stared at his father and felt the flush creep up the back of his neck. Water would have boiled if there had been any in his glass. How dare his father bring this up in front of Darcy? He tried to think of something to say but she beat him to it.

"I don't think Mayor Kleinfelter has to worry," Darcy said coyly.

Jake left his hand limp when she folded her fingers around it. He ate his last mouthful of stuffing and leaned back. The action forced her to let go, so she smiled at him.

"Actually, Fritz talked to me a few days ago," he interjected before Darcy could elaborate. "He's afraid if the town thinks I could leave, they won't elect me." He looked right at Darcy. "If I married a woman who wasn't local, they'd be more concerned."

"He's right. There was Joe Coluck, who moved to Pennsylvania because his wife got homesick." Everyone nodded at Elyse's remarks. "And Karina Joy, she followed her husband to Wyoming. Or was it Utah?"

"It was Arizona, actually, and because I sold their house recently, I can tell you they left town because of his job." Her tone grew haughty and her nose actually lifted in the air. "Which would not be the case with us. I have committed to this town, and of course there can be no doubt about Jake."

Silence greeted her statement. Darcy seemed to deflate. At least she had the grace to be embarrassed at implying they'd be marrying. He felt sorry for her when he saw the look on her face. Not sorry enough not to break up with her, though. If he thought he could get away with it, he'd do it now.

"Anyone know if the Patriots' running back will play on Sunday?" Sophie finally broke the silence.

Jake's breath whooshed out. He sent a grateful look at Sophie, who winked back. He hated walking this tightrope.

"Pie, anyone?" Fran rose and began to gather plates. Everyone jumped up to pitch in, and Jake noticed Darcy reluctantly picked up a couple of bowls and brought them to the kitchen.

"Pie now, or later?" Fran asked again. The collective groan prompted her to chirp, "Later, then. Let's do presents!" They trooped into the living room and chaos ensued for the next hour.

Most of the gifts had been unwrapped by the time Kira gave hers to Jake. She placed the long flat package he'd watched her slide behind the tree a few days ago on his lap and handed him a smaller, heavy one.

Jake leaned forward and began to open the square package. It felt padded, and he wondered which of his hints Kira had picked up on. He went slowly, using the large object on his lap as an excuse for putting space between him and Darcy, who'd been glued to his side all afternoon.

"You sneak." The padding was a decoy, cotton batting wrapped around a book. The latest Clive Cussler, he noted.

"How did you do that? The one thing I didn't mention. The thing I wanted most. How?"

"I'm a witch." Kira grinned from her spot on the floor, where she sat on her knees. She was clearly delighted with herself. "I think that's twelve in a row now."

"You won't get me next year," he cautioned.

"Jake, open this one." Darcy, clearly annoyed at being excluded, wiggled the item in Jake's lap. He tried not to roll his eyes, wishing for the fiftieth time she'd answered one of his phone calls.

"All right." He flipped it over and back again, savoring the anticipation. This was his last gift, and promised to be the most rewarding. Darcy nudged him with her toe.

"Open it already."

Kira's glare was full of daggers, but Darcy didn't even look at her. Jake had to relax his jaw. He concentrated on the package.

A few inches of smooth wood protected by more cotton batting emerged from beneath the paper. Teak, from the looks of it. Expensive.

He worked from the narrow end to the wide, recognizing the distinctive shape of an oar. He'd commented last June that he needed a new set of oars for the dinghy, but why only one?

The answer came when the paddle end emerged from its wrappings. By now everyone's eyes were on Jake and Kira and the paddle.

Finally, he pulled off the last bit of cotton and rolled the oar on his lap. The paddle was elaborately carved with an image of North Lake, a sunset, and *Mac^2* floating on the calm water. His throat swelled and he couldn't talk.

"Remember?" Kira murmured, rising to lean closer. "We talked about doing this when you first launched her." She stroked her fingertips over the boat. "You wanted to immortalize her, but in a way that left details to the imagination. That would recall all the best things about being on North Lake."

"I remember."

His husky voice zinged straight to Kira's abdomen. She cleared her throat and pointed to the oar. She couldn't meet his eyes. She knew the love she'd see there. It had been there all her life, though she hadn't recognized it, and she couldn't bear to recognize it now, when she didn't deserve it.

"I tried to get the basics—"

"You did this?" Jake interrupted. She couldn't help herself. She glanced up and nearly moaned at the look on his face. It almost made a roomful of people disappear. But she was acutely conscious of the hatred radiating from his girlfriend.

Kira stood and dusted off the seat of the jeans she'd worn instead of her ivory dress. She was glad she had. She felt much more secure in her habitual jeans than she did all dressed up.

"It took me three years and six oars, but yeah, I did it."

"Six oars?"

Kira laughed at the horror on Jake's face. "I started with pine, silly. By the time I got to teak, I had a handle on it. No pun intended.

"Now, I think we're ready for pie!" She herded everyone back to the dining room.

Chatter had given her a headache by the time they were ready to leave. Kira was gathering coats when she overheard Jake and his mother at the end of the hall.

"Mom, why do we have to do this now?"

"I couldn't hold it in any longer. I'm so hurt, Jake, that you wouldn't tell me."

"I didn't want to worry you. It didn't matter until the results were back."

"There was no reason not to tell us after that."

"Yes, there was, Mother."

Kira held her breath while she waited for his reason. Was it her? That he hadn't wanted to think about the whole incident? Her rejection? Were the events that night and day as entwined in his mind as hers? Or was she being selfish to imagine he dwelled on her that much?

Oh, no, would he tell his mother what she'd done?

"It doesn't matter," he finally said. "It's over. I don't have a tumor. You know now. Let's drop it, okay?"

Kira heard the soft slap that was Fran's motherly pat on Jake's cheek.

"Okay, darling. I'll drop it for now. Let's talk about Darcy, instead."

No way. Kira cleared her throat as she gathered coats, then deliberately dropped a purse on the floor with a thud. Soft footsteps went down the hall, then Jake came into the room.

"I didn't give you your present," he said, closing the door. Kira wished he hadn't done that. She didn't want to be alone with him, in this room where they'd made love. She hadn't thought about it until now, until his presence.

"You don't have to," she tried, but he moved toward her, trapping her behind the bed.

Jake pulled the box she'd started to open last night from his pocket. He did it so slowly she wondered if he was reluctant to give it to her.

"What's wrong?" she asked.

He shrugged. "I hadn't intended to give you this until your thirtieth birthday. It's not quite done. But after what's been happening, I think we both need to remember the little things."

The phrase rang a bell in Kira's mind, but she couldn't connect it to anything. She took the box as he held it out. The paper she'd started to remove the night before came off easily in one sheet. She lifted the lid. It took several seconds to register what the innocuous item was. When she understood, she sank onto the bed, overwhelmed.

"Oh, Jake," she said, blinking back tears. "You made it. You made my remembrance book."

He lifted the battered leather book from the box. "It's nothing like carving wood, but it took a while."

She sank onto the bed and slid the album from his hands, caressing the cover. "You started this when we were ten."

It had been the summer following the creation of their memory frame Christmas ornaments. They'd been drifting on the lake, lying on their backs on a wooden raft. Kira had started talking about all the little memories they could forget, like finding the bird's nest with the empty eggs or skipping stones. *Those* they would remember, because they had the memory frames. But there were so many more, she said.

"We could keep a scrapbook," Jake had suggested. His mother had a scrapbook of all his event programs and newspaper clippings and report cards—anything that had his name on it.

"What about the things we can't keep in a scrapbook?" she asked, very concerned about losing her memory. "Sticks and stones can't go in a scrapbook. Feelings can't go in a scrapbook. Like the way my heart flips when the sun is about to set and the whole sky is glowing copper. You can't save food, either, or even flowers for very long." She took a deep breath. "Remember the Queen Anne's lace?"

She remembered it now, when she opened the book and the first page held a perfectly preserved blossom head. One single flower on the cluster was deep red, in contrast to the white ones surrounding it.

"Timmy O'Malley," she said, blinking back more tears. "The history play. I was in the chorus, and he said I'd always be one of a crowd."

"Do you remember what I said?" Jake asked.

Of course she did. He'd told her she was like that red flower. One of a crowd, maybe. But deeply unique. He'd always had a knack for making her feel like she was special enough to conquer the world.

"Jake, is this whole thing...." She didn't know how to ask if it was a testament to his love for her.

"Shh. No. Turn the page."

She did, and laughed when she saw how Jake had gotten around the limitations of a flat-paged book. Sticks and stones lay in hollows he'd formed from several pages.

She turned another page, and another hollow showed a golden dragon, tiny and exquisitely formed from gold. It had crystal eyes and claws and its gaze held hers, clear and cold.

"It looks like it's going to walk off the page," she said, brushing one finger over the spread wings. "I can't believe you remembered Pumpkin."

"How could I forget? For two years all you talked about was finding Pumpkin, as if you'd lost this twenty-foot dragon on the playground. You irritated the hell out of me with your search parties and your treats that never lured a dragon but sure delighted the neighborhood dogs."

Kira laughed again. "Yet you found him, and put him in my book."

"Of course."

His tone tried to be light, but Kira heard the conviction behind it. Her misgivings grew. Jake had said this book wasn't a tribute, yet everything she saw as she turned the pages highlighted the man he'd been growing into, the man she should be in love with, the man who was probably going to marry another woman.

The last page was a photo, the only traditional item in the book. It was a glowing copper sunset over North Lake, the kind she'd tried to evoke on the oar she'd carved. The kind she'd lamented forgetting eighteen years ago.

Her heart flipped.

Everything in her cried out to reach for Jake. He sat close enough on the bed that she could smell him, feel his heat. Remember.

But Darcy was only a short distance away. Whatever Jake's intentions, today she was his girlfriend, one who had definite plans for more. What they'd done two nights ago was more than enough deceit.

Kira cleared her throat and stood. "It's gorgeous, Jake. I love it." She kissed him on the cheek. "Thank you. For the little things."

Before he could respond, she gathered her stuff and said, "They're going to be waiting for me. For these, anyway." She held up the coats and started for the door.

"Kira, wait." He caught up to her and reached out.

She paused, not moving for fear of dislodging the fingers Jake had placed against her jaw. His eyes held hers intently, sending her another of those messages. Did she dare hope that what she saw was real, not wishful thinking? Could he be that brave? Was it possible he'd leave Darcy for her, for a potential return to the pit of heartache she'd always given him?

She saw in his eyes the answer she desperately sought, but he didn't voice it. "Soon," was all he said.

Feeling lighter, happier, and melting inside from the sentiment represented by the book he'd given her, Kira even had a hug for Darcy on her way out.

Christmas was nearly over. And maybe, hopefully, so was Jake's relationship with the witch-woman.

CHAPTER 12

Much to Jake's surprise, Darcy helped clean up the living room and kitchen after the Macgregors had left. Granted, not much was left to do, and she refused to take anything outside, "into that frigid nightmare," but it was more than he'd expected.

When the clock chimed seven, he offered to drive Darcy home. It would be a good opportunity to break it off, he thought, except that her car would still be in his driveway.

"No, dear, you have things to work out with your parents. You can walk me to my car, though."

"What things?" Jake asked when they got outside.

"Hmm?" Darcy hugged herself inside her down coat and shrank deeper into her scarf. "Things?"

"What things do I have to work out with my parents?"

Darcy paused next to her Miata. "You know, who's going to live where, when they're taking over the house, stuff like that."

"There's nothing to work out. They're home for good, as of now. I'll have to find my own place, but there's no rush."

Darcy let go of herself and placed her mittened hands on either side of his head. Jake frowned even as she kissed him. How was she going to drive potentially icy roads in that summer car with two-inch-thick mittens on?

"In that case, I have a proposition for you."

Uh, oh. He retreated a few steps.

"You don't need to settle for less than perfect, and you can get out from under your parents' feet right away. You can move in with me."

This was it. She'd batted the ball straight back at him, and his court was shrinking. He wished he'd prepared better for this moment. "No."

She raised her eyebrows at him and hugged herself against the cold. "No?"

"No, we're not going to live together." Well, he'd never claimed to have finesse. He took a deep breath. "In fact—"

Darcy shivered. "Can we continue this tomorrow? I'm freezing."

"I really want to talk about it now," he said, but she shook her head and moved away. Jake leaned into the car as she slid into the driver's seat. For a moment her face hardened. Her cheekbones burned a little redder than the cold had made them, and her eyes glittered.

"No, Jake. Not tonight. Think about what I said. We'll talk about it tomorrow." She pulled off her mittens and shut the door as Jake stepped back. He frowned at her when she kissed her fingers and waggled them at him. He should have insisted. *Coward*, he thought, watching the Miata's lights disappear down the street.

Yeah, well, sometimes cowards lived to fight another day. He'd deal with it tomorrow. For sure. There was no reason to let it go any longer.

Especially after the signal he'd given Kira tonight. He trudged up the porch steps. He knew she'd gotten it when he saw the hope on her face. Heaven help him if he'd given her that hope falsely.

He went through the front door and from freezer to oven. The fire his dad had built roared in the little fireplace. Jake went to the hearth and picked up the poker, crouching. The heat reminded him of how he'd felt at the ball with Kira. Of her passion, both when they made love and earlier, when she'd called him her anchor. He stabbed at the pile of blazing wood. An anchor and a comet. They couldn't even be considered opposites. How could they ever make it work?

He wouldn't settle for a friendship like they'd had for the last ten years, since college began. He couldn't be mayor of Brook Hollow and live with his computer-genius wife in Boston, nor could he expect her to administer to her Fortune 500 clients from here. An anchor would drag down a comet, douse the fire that made it what it was.

An apt analogy, Jake considered, staring at the now-manageable fire. The fire worked, too. Was perhaps even more apt. He loved the water, more than most anything else. Water puts out fire, he thought. Kills the passion. He didn't want to kill Kira's passion.

"Long day, huh son?" Luke pressed through the swinging door from the kitchen and slumped onto the couch. "Thanks for fixing my fire."

"No problem." Jake didn't move, just kept staring at the flames now flickering behind the safety of the fire screen. He didn't remember closing it.

"How about sharing a Christmas brandy?"

"Sure." Jake rose and moved to the tiny bar in the corner of the room. He unstoppered the crystal decanter they used only at Christmas and poured two snifters, then joined his father on the couch.

"Merry Christmas, Dad."

"Merry Christmas, son."

They sipped in silence. Jake savored the burn of the fine brandy and silently thanked his father for hitting on the one thing that would ease his tension.

"Is our moving home a problem for you?" Luke asked.

"No, of course not." Jake wouldn't have admitted it if it was. Too many people were going to be happy the McKennas were home. He was one of them. It was a minor inconvenience, and he was glad to have it. He told his father that.

"Good. I'd hate to cause friction with Darcy," he said, looking sideways at his son. "How does she feel about us living with you?"

Jake chuckled wryly. "Darcy offered to let me move in with her."

"Humph." Luke reached down and pulled the recliner lever on his side of the sofa. He shifted until he was in the perfect comfort zone. "I don't want to advise you, Jake."

"Since when?" He couldn't stop a smile, though. His father was like any other, sure he could lead his child down the right path. But often his greater wisdom helped Jake at least see the path, even if it wasn't the same one his father saw.

"It just doesn't seem like Darcy's the right woman for you."

"You're right."

"Now, I can't say she's not a nice woman." Luke held up a hand and continued talking to the fire. "She seems to be, at least on the outside. But she also seems to think folks in this town are stupid. I can't tell you how many complained to me about her phony schmoozing last night."

"I know, Dad. I'm breaking up with her tomorrow."

His father was silent for a minute. Jake wondered if he'd lost his momentum and had to regroup.

"Well, I think that's best. Don't want the poor thing to be hurt, of course, but hurt her now or hurt her later, not much difference."

"I tried to do it tonight," Jake admitted. "She put me off."

"Just like a woman."

They stared into the fire for a few minutes more.

"Where's Mom?" Jake finally asked.

Luke smiled at him. "You sure you want to know? She's pretty het up about the cancer thing."

"I sure am," came her voice from behind them. "And we're going to talk about it right now, Jake." Fran marched into the room and set herself on a chair. The pinched look on her face fought the anti-aging effects of the Christmas tree lights.

Jake sighed and laid his head on the back of the couch, preparing for more of the same lecture he'd gotten in the hall.

"Jake, you are our only son. And I can't tell you what to do anymore. All I can do is appeal to your love and sense of responsibility."

Jake frowned up at the ceiling. What did that mean? Did she want him to say he'd stay out of the sun? Eat healthy, cancer-fighting foods? Up his intake of antioxidants? Or did she mean they were getting old and he'd have to take care of them?

"Part of the reason we came home was that we were missing so much of your life. Yours, and Kira's, and her sisters. We missed our friends."

Jake looked over at her now. This was far from what he'd expected. Her voice thickened and she blinked hard, but didn't move otherwise.

"This situation illustrates how far removed we were from it all. If we'd been here, you would have told us. We could have shared it with you, supported you, instead of letting you face it alone." She slid forward until she was barely sitting on the chair. Her hand, looking older, more frail, reached out and Jake cradled it in his palm. "Promise us, Jakey, that you'll talk to us next time something big like this happens. Don't leave us out of your life."

Jake sat up and hugged her. His earlier resistance had faded and now he only wanted to make her feel better. "Don't worry, I won't. I promise I won't."

"It tears me apart to think of you here alone, scared, facing the results of that test."

"I wasn't alone, Mom," he tried to reassure her. "Kira was with me."

She froze on his shoulder. Sniffed. Pulled back. "Oh?"

Uh, oh. Jake quickly lifted her hands from his shoulders and set them back in her own lap. When he stood, she followed him.

"Kira was here? In June? Why was she here in June?"

He heard a grunt as his father pulled himself out of his chair to trail behind them into the kitchen.

"I called her. She came." He pulled an almost empty carton of orange juice from the refrigerator and opened it. "That's all." He took a swallow of the sweet juice straight from the carton. His mother didn't notice.

"That's all?" Fran's eyes were large and round, and as delighted as if she'd found a grandchild in her Christmas stocking. "The girl drives hours to be with you for the scariest moment of your life, and that's all? That's not all, Jake. She feels more for you than you realize. And it's not surprising, really, given your history. She—"

"Mom."

The quiet word stopped her mid-babble.

"There isn't anything between me and Kira that wasn't there before." He hoped the lie wouldn't count against him later. He just didn't want his mother and Elyse making wedding plans before he proposed. Before he even broke up with Darcy.

"Kira and I have been friends for twenty-eight years. Of course she came when I needed her. Of course she was the one I called when my parents were an ocean away." He chugged the rest of the juice and dropped the carton into the trash.

"But, Jake—"

"No buts, Mom. I'll see you in the morning." He kissed her on the cheek and slapped his father's shoulder. The old man's eyes twinkled and his lips twitched, but he said nothing.

"You're going to bed? It's not even eight-thirty."

"Night, Mom."

She was still talking to him when he shut his bedroom door.

* * *

The next morning Jake untangled himself from his sheets and dragged into the shower before the sun was even up. He hadn't slept much at all, and didn't expect to get any more rest. He might as well set the stage for his breakup with Darcy.

How to do it, he wondered as he lathered his hair. Take her somewhere public? No, that was too obvious. Guys always tried to avoid a scene. He couldn't do it here unless he wanted to give his parents a show, so he had to get to her before she showed up. He'd just go to her condo, he decided, maybe bring some breakfast. Whole grain bagels. He remembered she was on a diet. She'd said something about fiber being the new best thing.

He dried off and pulled on a pair of jeans and a sweater. His parents were still sleeping when he left, so he jotted a quick note and attached it to the refrigerator.

He took his time getting bagels and fat-free cream cheese, but it was still only seven-thirty when he got to Darcy's. He waited until he saw a light in her front window, then waited fifteen minutes more. By then it was completely light out and Darcy would hopefully have finished her first cup of coffee.

He rang the bell and had counted to six when the door opened. Darcy was attractively rumpled, still in her bathrobe, and Jake wished he'd waited longer. The robe was silk, and semi-sheer except for strategic satin pockets, lapels, and belt. He didn't know why she'd wear that in the winter, when she was alone in the house.

"Well, hello, big guy." Darcy leaned seductively on the door and crooked her finger at him. "Come in."

She stretched up and tried to kiss him as he passed. He allowed a peck on his lips but pulled quickly away and handed her the bagels.

"Breakfast. Let's go in the kitchen." The kitchen felt less intimate to him than the living room.

When he got there, though, Darcy pressed herself to his back and rubbed against him.

"Oh, I missed you, baby." She slithered around his side and twined her fingers in his hair. "I'm so glad you came over."

Her lips locked onto Jake's and he barely avoided jerking violently away. He couldn't believe he'd ever found this woman attractive enough to sleep with her. Had she always been this aggressive? Or had it appealed to him before, when he wanted something to lose his mind in? He managed to break her hold without making it obvious.

"Darcy, we have to talk."

"Okay, Jakey-baby." She slid onto a stool and let her robe fall open across her legs. "It's about moving in here, I presume."

Jake looked around the rather small condo. She'd decorated it tastefully, but in her own taste. It didn't resemble his. He didn't really care for daisies, which were her theme in the kitchen, or the color salmon, which accented her drab beige living room. He couldn't imagine living comfortably here under any circumstances.

"There's plenty of room for your stuff," Darcy said, obviously misinterpreting his look. "It's bigger than it seems."

Jake wondered why she was pretending he hadn't already told her no.

"Darcy, I'm not moving in with you. No, don't pout," he directed when her lower lip started to slide out. "It's more than that. I can't…have that kind of relationship with you anymore."

He cursed the cowardice that had him couching his rejection. It was only going to cause problems.

"What kind of relationship did you have in mind?" She'd raised one eyebrow and looked up at him from under her lashes. It was a triumphant kitty look. Like one who'd gotten her way but was going to pretend to beg for it.

She still didn't get it. "No kind."

Finally, her attitude changed. She sat up straight and yanked her robe over her legs. Her eyes flashed some of that fire Jake had been thinking about last night.

"What do you mean, no kind?"

He didn't like the cold anger in her voice. He was in for a fight.

"Darcy, just listen for a minute." He knew the placating tone he'd used as he sat on the stool next to her was the wrong one. But she simply looked at him over her shoulder, much the way his mother eyed dirt that dared to get into the foyer.

"You're a sweet, warm, loving woman." He cringed at the fib, but she didn't respond. "It's just that, that's not enough for me."

No, wrong tack. She'd want to *be* enough, no matter what it took.

"What do you need, Jake? I mean, beyond a perfect political wife with a double D chest?" She was angling said chest higher, as if she thought it would change his mind. "What more can I possibly give you? I thought I'd been doing pretty damn well."

"Darcy, I'm not after the perfect political wife. I don't even see this mayoral race as politics. It's just a job."

Darcy slid off her stool. "Just a job, huh?" She fingered an arrangement of holly and snow-dusted fruit on the island next to them. "So, if it's just a job, you don't care if you get it or not."

Uh, oh. Jake didn't know what to say. If he agreed with that, he'd be lying. If he disagreed, they'd be back to politics and Darcy's perceived ability to schmooze his way into office. He had to avoid that angle.

"This is not about the job, Darcy. It's about me. Us."

"Not us."

"No," he sighed. "Not us. You obviously want more than I do from 'us,'" he tried. He thought about saying he wasn't ready to settle down, but that would insult her and set her up for more pain later. Assuming she felt anything real for him in the first place, that is.

"I just want to make you happy, Jake. You want to be mayor," she offered, beginning to pace and looking like any campaign manager from any president movie. Except for the robe. "I can help make you mayor. You want a wife and mother for your children. I can be a wife and mother."

Well, that one was a bit hard to imagine, Jake thought. But before he could say anything she began another argument.

"You need another breadwinner? I just got a six thousand dollar commission. Homemaker? Look around."

"Darcy," he interrupted, before she could get to policy- and baby-maker. "It's not about you. I'm in love with someone else."

She froze. Not only in motion; her whole face stopped moving. Anger didn't even cover it now, Jake thought.

"Who?"

"It doesn't matter. She—"

"Oh, it always matters, Jake." Her eyes glittered as she neared him, one fist on her hip, the other hand pointing at him. "I have a right to know who's been in your bed when you've been avoiding mine."

Jake didn't know if she was fishing or more intuitive than he'd given her credit for. "I'm not telling you who she is, Darcy."

"You don't need to. I sensed the tension between the two of you this week." She spun away and paced into the living room, as if the kitchen wasn't big enough now. Her sleeves flapped as she threw up her hands. "I've heard all about precious Kira for the past three months. How you met in the hospital—as if infants could meet, for God's sake. How she's been your best friend your whole life. How I'd better measure up, get Kira's approval, or it'd be over."

"I never—"

She turned on him. "You didn't have to, Jake. It was all I heard. I ignored it because I thought I was the winner. I guess I shouldn't have been so complacent."

He didn't want to ask what she would have done if she'd thought there was competition.

"I don't suppose anything I say can change your mind."

"No." He tried to sound regretful, but didn't pull it off.

Darcy traced one finger over the groove in the edge of her tall lacquer end table. Something shifted, and she sighed. Relief swept through Jake.

"I don't know what to say."

"You don't have to say anything, Darcy. I'm sorry...." He stopped because she was moving away from him, toward a bag on a chair on the far side of the room. She pulled something from the bag and straightened but didn't turn.

"I'll let you go, Jake. I don't have a choice. But I suggest you leave your little tart alone for a while."

"You can't—"

She cut him off for the umpteenth time. "I can." She turned and held out the box she'd taken from the bag. "You'd be well advised to leave things alone until next week. Until I can use this."

He stepped closer and squinted at the box. When he realized what it was, his heart fell without resistance straight to the bottom of hell.

It was a pregnancy test kit.

CHAPTER 13

Kira endured Jake's silence for the week between Christmas and New Year's, but barely. He didn't call or drop by. She didn't run into him in town. Sophie, who had returned to Boston the day after Christmas, had no new gossip. Even Maggie knew nothing.

"I'm not working there anymore," she told Kira one afternoon as they lunched in Maggie's new duplex apartment. "He let all his holiday help go. There won't be much business until spring, now."

Kira nudged her chicken salad with her fork. "I know. I'm being childish, anyway. I should just go over there."

Maggie stretched to peer into the bassinet on the other side of the kitchen. Abby slept peacefully on, a rhythmic sucking noise testifying to her contentment.

"I don't think you should." Maggie rested her chin on her fist and studied Kira, considering. "He's the one with a girlfriend. If you want your relationship to be resolved, he has to take care of that part first."

"You're right," Kira admitted. She marveled at the changes in Maggie. "Listen to you, so decisive and opinionated. A week ago you were still meek and uncertain. What's happened?"

Maggie shrugged but couldn't look anything but pleased with herself. "John has really changed, Kira. He's like the man I married, but better. More mature. He's found a good job locally and is so much more relaxed than before."

"Then why isn't he here with you?"

"Good question." Maggie wiped her mouth with her napkin and sat back in her chair. "The only thing standing between us is his guilt. He can't forgive himself for hurting me."

That made sense. "How will you work through that?"

"I won't. I forgave him. Now he has to forgive himself, and until he realizes our marriage is on hold, he won't. And he won't be living with us." The front door opened as she finished speaking.

"Hello?" A man's voice echoed down the hall. Kira raised an eyebrow at Maggie, who tilted her head sheepishly.

"Well, he does have a key."

John entered the kitchen, carrying a briefcase that clashed with his jeans and fisherman's sweater. "Hi, Keer. I didn't know you were here."

"Hi, John." Kira swallowed the last bite of her salad and took her plate to the sink. "I'm about ready to leave. I'll get out of your way."

"That's okay," John protested. "We don't have any plans." He set the briefcase next to the counter and leaned next to the tiny telephone table. When Kira finished rinsing her plate and turned around, Maggie was snuggled under John's shoulder, one hand on his abdomen. Except for the shadows under John's eyes that testified to his continuing pain, the couple looked like they had in high school.

Kira turned back to the sink to give them their private moment. Hope flickered in her chest. If Maggie and John could get through something so harmful to their marriage, maybe she and Jake could still get their friendship out of the fire. Or have it be reborn as something magical, like the Phoenix.

She washed the rest of the dishes in the sink while Maggie and John chatted behind her. She didn't realize she was so lost in thought until John said, "...does it, Kira?"

"I'm sorry, I didn't hear you." She folded the dish towel and resumed her seat at the table. "Does what?"

"It doesn't seem like Jake to disappear for a week."

"Has he disappeared?" Alarm swept through her. She thought he'd only been avoiding *her*.

"No one's seen him. Not at the shop, or in town. He missed a council meeting. That never happened before. His car's in the driveway, but he never answers the phone."

"How do you know all this?" Kira asked.

"My boss is on the town council, too. He's been talking about it."

Terror very reminiscent of what she'd felt in June struggled to get a grip in Kira's heart. She fought it with logic. Jake could have decided to take a vacation, to get away from his problems for a while. It might be coincidence that no one had seen him or called when he happened to be home. None of those explanations accounted for the council meeting, though. Jake had the biggest sense of civic responsibility Kira had ever seen.

"What about his parents?" She knew Fran and Elyse, at least, had talked. "Has anyone asked them?"

John shrugged. "Don't know."

Kira stood. She had to find out. "I'd better go. Thanks for lunch." She kissed her friend, ignoring her worried gaze, and waved at John as she sped out the door.

It took only minutes to get to Jake's house. Sure enough, his car was in the driveway. She didn't stop to think, just dashed up the steps and rang the bell.

Jake opened the door almost instantly, as if he'd been waiting for someone. Kira braced one hand on the door jamb and waited for the darkness to recede from her peripheral vision. When equilibrium returned, she looked up at her best friend and almost passed out again.

No man had ever looked at her that way, like she was his reason for living. Not even Jake. She'd never seen his eyes burn like molten gold, actually reach for her even though his hands gripped the door jamb.

"I was worried about you," she managed to force past the dryness in her throat.

"Were you?" He murmured it, as if conversation was superfluous.

His hand reached for hers, and he tugged her into the house and shut the door behind her. His gentleness was belied by the tautness of his muscles. Kira's pulse quickened and she wondered what it would be like to release the leashed power she sensed in him.

Oh, boy, she thought, moving away to try to regain her bearings again. That wasn't what she'd come here for.

"Yes, I was," she finally said. "No one's seen you in days."

"I know." Lightening quick, his mood changed. He shoved up the sleeves of his shirt and crossed the living room. "I've been holed up in here waiting. I don't know if she's deliberately torturing me, or what. I'm about ready to storm her condo and demand answers." He stomped out of the room and Kira followed him to the kitchen.

"Who? Answers about what?"

Jake yanked the refrigerator door open and grabbed a bottle of beer. He cocked it at Kira, who shook her head. The door shut on its own, and he pressed his forehead on his arm against the freezer door.

"Oh, Kira, I've messed everything up. I don't know what I'm going to do."

Years of practice in consolation had Kira next to him immediately. She ran her hand over his back and tried not to enjoy the ridges of muscle under his knit shirt.

"Everything will work out, Jake. Sometimes it takes time, but it always works out." She doubted her own words, but didn't know what else to say. "What can I do?" she asked, knowing it was a futile question.

The phone rang, but neither moved.

"Do you want me to get it?" she asked on the third ring.

He moved suddenly, jerking upright and then trudging across the room. "Thanks anyway."

Kira registered the irony in his voice but didn't understand it.

"Hello."

She watched thunder take over Jake's face. She guessed it wasn't a sales call.

"Yeah. Well, what was it? Okay." He didn't move, but suddenly the storm was gone, replaced by cold emptiness. Kira felt fear seeping in again.

"I guess we have some decisions to make," Jake said. The shriek that came over the line told Kira it was Darcy on the other end. Coldness invaded her own heart. Nothing good could be coming from that shriek.

"No, that's not what I mean, Darcy. Of course not. It's only an option if you want it to be. No. No. Look, you brought it up, not me. I wasn't even thinking that. I can't. Listen, I have company. I'll call you later."

He hung up, then slumped to the floor, his back against the desk. His hands hung limply where he rested his wrists on his knees. Kira crouched and rescued the beer bottle before it hit the tile floor.

"Jake, hon, what is it? What's going on?"

He looked at her with eyes so bleak she was sure someone had died. Nothing else could make him look that way. But when he opened his mouth, she almost wished that was what had happened.

"Darcy's pregnant."

* * *

The implications didn't penetrate right away. Kira waited, as if Jake would supply a punchline and punctuate it with a kiss. When the bleakness didn't go away, when he didn't take it back, the coldness that had crept in when he was on the phone spread, seeping not only into her extremities but into her soul.

She'd never expected this.

In her fantasies over the past week Jake had broken up with Darcy and come immediately to Kira. They'd made love again—and again, and again—and apologized. They'd communicated all their feelings, hopes, desires. All the clichéd stuff Kira usually hated.

Then, somewhere along the line, there had been a big wedding in the town's only Catholic church, followed by glimpses of red-haired babies and golden-eyed toddlers. In one two-a.m. dream, Kira had even seen Jake as an old man, rocking on his front porch. She'd awakened at peace, until she realized it was a dream.

"What are you going to do?" she finally managed to ask. When her back touched the cold wall of the cooking island she realized she'd scooted backwards across the floor.

Every breath Jake took seemed labored. "I don't know. She wants marriage. I don't, never did. But I think that was her plan all along." He paused. "I don't remember any time we didn't use double birth control." He sat very still, one hand gripping the other wrist, as if he had to hold himself together. "At least, no time that I know of."

Kira wanted to think anger made her clench her fists, but it was more to fight the image of Jake and Darcy in bed. Or maybe to brace herself against the sensation of dreams slipping away. Again.

"So you think she got pregnant, what, as an insurance policy in case you didn't want to marry her?"

Suddenly Jake lurched to his feet and began circling the room. "Yeah, something like that. You saw her at your party. She likes to schmooze. She thinks she's good at it."

"Then let *her* run for mayor." Kira got to her feet and faced Jake, though that was difficult since he wouldn't stand still. "Let her schmooze on her own behalf. Why does she have to ruin your life to get what she wants?"

He stopped moving. "She wants me, Kira. She's been hinting at marriage for weeks. She mentioned it on the phone just now. God knows why she wants a guy who doesn't want her." He slumped against the island and covered his eyes with one hand. "God, Kira. I'm going to be a father."

Despite the pain, Kira almost smiled. "You know you'll be a great one." She stepped closer. He took her hand loosely in his, and the connection intensified the pain in her chest. She had to ask, even if it was more selfishness.

"What does this mean for us?"

She watched him swallow. He kept his head down, and she knew he was going to avoid it. They still wouldn't have a candid discussion of "them." Not that Kira could blame him. Another woman was going to have his child.

His child.

Her heart iced over permanently.

"Our friendship is more important to me than Darcy's wishes," he finally said, his hand tightening around hers. "I can't give you more than that, but I won't give you less."

Kira fought against the war raging inside her, the need to scream that Jake was hers and Darcy be damned. It was exactly how she'd acted all their lives.

But she knew he was wrong. If he gave in to Darcy, their friendship was over.

"I understand," she whispered. *Too much*. He pulled her into his arms and she fought tears. "I love you, Jake."

"I love you, too, Kira."

She still didn't know what that meant.

*   *   *

At home later that night, Kira sat on her bed making a tiny hole in her comforter larger and contemplating her options. She could go back to Boston. She *should* go back to Boston. She needed to touch some bases, check her mail, see what was happening work-wise. She'd obtained the instructions for the Brook Hollow School District networking project, and would put together a proposal.

Restless, she lurched off the bed and straightened the crooked window shade. The mess on her dresser caught her attention, and she began tossing hair clips and change into separate porcelain boxes.

She didn't want to put together a proposal. She didn't want to live for two years in this town with Jake and the mother of his baby. It would kill her to watch them together, however they were together, and know Jake had chosen Darcy over her.

On the other hand, if she stayed in town, she could fight for her man.

Her image in the mirror over the dresser lifted her lips in an ironic smile. *Her man*. Jake had always been her man, and she hadn't noticed.

Now he wasn't, and she didn't want to let him go.

She was an idiot.

* * *

Jake's instinct was to avoid Darcy as long as he could. But that was not only a foolish delaying tactic, it would just make things harder when she came after him. Who knew what she was capable of?

He spent hours debating with himself. Pre-commitment babies no longer required weddings. They could make legal custodial arrangements. Jake could offer some financial support, though on his now-adequate income maintaining two households would be difficult at best.

There were three other things wrong with that scenario. One was the damage it would do to his standing in the community, to his campaign for mayor. He was unopposed *now*, but there was plenty of time for that to change.

The second problem was Darcy. She'd made it clear she wanted marriage, which still didn't make sense to Jake. He'd never understand a woman determined to get a man who didn't want her.

The other problem, the one he couldn't rationalize, was the baby. His son. Or daughter. Custodial arrangements on paper made everything all black and white, logical, workable. But kids weren't black and white. They operated on emotion, and this kid would wonder why Daddy didn't live with them. Why Daddy didn't love Mommy.

Actually, they'd wonder that no matter what choice Jake made.

He really did not want to marry Darcy. If she was beginning to irritate him before this, he couldn't stand her now. The thought of living with her, even unmarried, even for the sake of their child, gave him an ulcer.

Weariness began to plague Jake as he plodded through the next few weeks. He could go to bed at eight o'clock, sleep twelve hours, and still have trouble lifting his feet to walk across the room.

The marina was closed, of course, and the shop wouldn't be profitable if he kept it open. This was his time of year for repairs and maintenance and planning for the next season. He considered new boats, prepared old ones for sale or scrap. Painted walls and replaced rotted boards. Pulled docks from the lake and scraped hulls. But not even physical labor could take him away from his problem.

She followed him.

The only good thing about his headaches, Jake decided one frigid

January day, was that the pain almost drowned out Darcy. He was replacing boards over his boathouse windows after a whipping storm. Darcy huddled under a giant down coat and crouched on a sawed-off log. She had to be uncomfortable, but she didn't give in.

"What names have you come up with?" Her question managed to penetrate his fog. He shouldn't have taken the pain medication an hour ago. Of course, he'd been hoping she wouldn't show today, but he should have known how faint that hope was.

"I haven't," he said, not even regretting his abruptness.

"I like Shawna for a girl, and David for a boy. They're traditional without being boring." She yammered on in counterpoint to Jake's hammer blows until he couldn't stand it anymore.

"I'm done." He interrupted her monologue and gathered his tools. Darcy didn't pause as she followed him inside, but she did change her tone.

"I did some shopping yesterday."

Jake pretended she hadn't switched to enticement mode and concentrated on digging in a drawer for masking tape. He didn't know why he needed masking tape, but suddenly he was desperate for it.

"Wanna see what I bought?"

Out of the corner of his eye he saw her coat drop to the floor. She stood in a classic seduction pose. He groaned and wished he could crawl into the drawer. Darcy wouldn't be able to follow him, and maybe he could find the damned masking tape.

"Jake?"

He could tell her fingers were unbuttoning her sweater. He didn't want her to unbutton her sweater, but suddenly speech was beyond him. He sank onto a plastic tub that usually held bait and gripped his head in both hands.

"Jake, honey, what's wrong?" Her concern sounded sincere, and her hand was cool on the back of his neck when she sat next to him.

"I have a blistering headache," he admitted through his teeth.

"Poor baby. You have too much on your mind." She shifted so her breasts pressed against his shoulder. Her smooth fingers began stroking his temples. "I can help you, sweetheart. Just relax. Lean against me."

Against his will, Jake did so. He didn't have the energy to resist her pressing hands. Her breasts slid upward until his head was resting on them. He was glad nothing on his body stirred. Almost equally glad that the pain in his head was beginning to slide away. He moaned in relief.

"That's it, baby."

Darcy's voice had grown husky. Jake thought maybe he should do something about that, but he didn't have the energy. He just wanted to sleep.

"Lie down," he muttered, wondering why his mouth was full of sweater fuzz.

"Yes." Darcy maneuvered them to the floor so Jake's head was in her lap. Her fingers kept stroking his scalp, massaging his neck and shoulders, gliding around his ears and across his face. "Yes, Jake, let's lie down."

He didn't know how she did it, but suddenly Darcy was next to him, one arm supporting his head, the other hand pressing his own against her breast. Alertness sprang on him like a tiger on prey.

"No!"

He hadn't meant to shout it, though it did have the desired effect of startling Darcy away from him. She looked angry and chased him across the floor as he backed up. He struggled to sit before she landed on him.

"No what, baby? No, not here? No, not now? I can't wait. I've been wanting you for weeks." Despite his attempts to avoid her, she got in his face, her lips near his, her body half across him. "Your parents have got to go. Or you need to come live with me, like I asked you to." Her mouth nipped his. "Now, Jake. I want you now." She tugged at his jeans.

"I said no!" Jake managed to get to his feet. "Doesn't no mean no anymore?" Sheesh, he sounded like a movie of the week.

He turned and walked away from the devil-woman still on the floor, saying nothing until the counter was between them. When he looked up, she still sprawled where he'd left her, strategically allowing him full view of her cleavage through the gap in her sweater.

"Darcy, I told you before. We're over. Our baby is the extent of our relationship."

Darcy came gracefully to her feet and buttoned her sweater. "So you'll marry me and never have sex with me?"

With Kira it had been making love. Even on the desk at the country club, as carnal as that had been, it had been because of love. He'd never had that with Darcy. Never would, no matter what choices they made.

"We may not have to worry about that," he said, waiting for the explosion. But Darcy studied him impassively, as if trying to choose her next tactic.

"So now you're not gonna marry me?"

Jake found the masking tape on the far end of the counter and began wrapping the crumbling handle of his hammer. "I never told you I was."

"But how—"

Jake interrupted her. "I will take responsibility for the baby, Darcy. And I'll be a good father, somehow. But there are few advantages to trying to make this a marriage."

Darcy's face turned purple. "What are you going to do, be an absentee father?"

Jake felt a calm invade him in the face of Darcy's ferocity. "Darcy, this is Brook Hollow. Unless you move away, we can live next door to each other. This kid can have it all."

"What about the campaign?" Her voice had turned deadly and the hand braced on her hip was white as she apparently tried to keep her control.

Regret shoved aside the calm. Jake closed his eyes and felt his dreams begin to crumble like the handle of his overused hammer. "What about it?"

"You think you'll be elected to run this town when you can't manage your own affairs?" She looked pleased with her double entendre.

Jake managed to keep his motions smooth and his eyes on what he was doing. He didn't want to give Darcy ammunition.

"The baby's more important than a job, Darcy."

That silenced her for a minute. "You still contend that it's just a job?"

"Yep."

"And this baby is important to you?"

Jake didn't hesitate. "Of course." He wished they hadn't created it, but it had to be important to him.

"Well, I don't believe you." Darcy leaned forward. "I think 'the job' means more than you're letting on. And if you care about the baby, and being mayor, you'll see you have no choice but to marry me."

She tossed her head triumphantly and swept out the door.

Thank God.

* * *

Brrrriiinnnngg.

Kira ignored the noise and tried to latch onto the key piece missing from her networking proposal.

Brrriiinnnngg.

The elusive solution slid away. "Damn." She banged a fist on her desk and snatched up the phone. "Hello!"

"Kira."

For years, when she answered the phone and heard her name in Jake's familiar chocolaty voice, pleasure had filled her and made the day one of her best.

Tonight, what filled her was so chock-full of conflicting emotions Kira only wanted to hang up.

"Hi, Jake."

Habit and loyalty sent her to curl up in her favorite spot on the couch. She geared up to listen, commiserate, and be a good friend. Because that was all she could be, and she wasn't willing to give it up.

"How're things going?" she asked. Her finger started to ache and she realized she'd twisted the phone cord around it, turning it purple. She let the cord unwind and tried not to fiddle with it.

"All right. Darcy picked names."

"Already?" Envy gained a foothold on the mountain of her emotions. She wanted to be the one to pick names. She wanted to be the one with life growing inside her.

But she wasn't. *Deal with reality, Kira, not fantasy.*

"How is she feeling? Any morning sickness?"

"No. Not that she's complained of, anyway."

"Have you heard the baby's heartbeat?" Kira should have changed the subject by now, but she had a morbid need to know everything. To gather ammunition to punish herself with later.

"No," Jake said again. Kira could almost hear him frowning. "As a matter of fact, I haven't been to any appointments. I'm not sure she's had one yet."

"She hasn't seen a doctor?" She looked at the calendar on the wall next to her desk. "Jake, she should have seen one twice by now."

"She must have. I don't know why she hasn't told me about it. She tells me everything else," he grumbled. When Kira didn't answer, he cleared his throat. "We had a go-around today. She's still pushing for marriage."

Hope flared in Kira. "And?"

"And I don't want to marry her. But she's using my sense of responsibility and my desire to be mayor against me."

Kira heard his frustration though he tried to sound matter-of-fact.

"So she's trying to convince you it's best for the baby if you get married?" The bitch.

"Something like that."

"And?"

Silence.

"How's work?"

Kira sighed. Obviously, this was as far as Jake wanted to go on that topic. She didn't push him. He was being pushed enough. "Good," she said. "I have a few small jobs. Some upgrades. Enough to keep the wolves at bay."

"Enough to last until the BHSD job?"

Kira hadn't yet submitted her proposal for the Brook Hollow School District project. It was complete, and could win the bid, she was sure. But she hadn't been able to make herself send it in.

"I guess," she told him.

"Do you want it?"

Her real answer was too complex to voice, and it would just add to Jake's difficulty.

"I guess."

"If you get it, and take it, will you be my campaign manager?"

That was the last request Kira expected. "What—why? I mean, sure, but why do you need one? You've got the whole town in the palm of your hand."

Jake snorted. "I did, until word got out about my *indiscretions*. Fritz subtly threatened to withdraw his backing. Darcy keeps schmoozing every business owner in town, not realizing it only highlights my moral problems. All she cares about is convincing me to marry her."

"But Jake, it doesn't matter," she argued, desperate to convince him this was not a smart thing to do. She had enough doubts about her ability to live in the same town and not tear Darcy's hair out, then claim Jake as her own, without forcing them to see each other regularly. "You're unopposed."

"I was."

Stunned, Kira fell silent. Even with "indiscretions" she couldn't imagine who would be... whatever enough to run against Brook Hollow's favorite son. "Who is it? Who dares to run against you?"

"Karen Plummer."

It took Kira a minute to make the connection. "The bookshop owner? The one with the cigarette butts?"

"That's the one."

Kira chuckled. "Don't tell me, you voted against her in the great parking lot issue."

She felt his shrug. "We had evidence."

Now she laughed, an overabundance of emotion making her ridiculous. "You had evidence. This big crime. Cigarette butts in the parking lot. What, you instituted surveillance? McGarvey actually bent to pick something up? Or you saw patrons of the bookstore toss their own butts?"

"Come on, Kira, this is serious. She's running on a moral ticket. She already did an interview with the paper and an ad on the radio telling people to elect the upright citizen with traditional family values. I need you."

"It's not like you're different from any other politician."

"Thanks."

Kira winced at the hurt in his voice.

"You really want me to come back?" Unspoken was the deeper question, did he really want to be around her? And did she want to be around him? *Could* she?

She missed Jake like crazy. She missed her family and Maggie, too, but felt Jake's absence in her life like a gaping hole. And he deserved to win this election, to be mayor of the town he loved.

A devil got into her, made her want to test him. "You know, Jake, you could solve a lot of the issues by just marrying Darcy." What would she do if he gave in?

"Are you nuts?"

Suddenly Kira was angry at Jake, angry that he had been careless with Darcy—regardless of how she may have tricked him—angry that he couldn't just blow Darcy off, tell her he was in love with Kira.

The anger hid the fear that maybe he'd decided he *wasn't* in love with her anymore. Or never had been.

"I'll think about it," she told him.

But she knew that in three weeks, despite the anger, despite the fear, she'd be back in Brook Hollow. Working for the man she loved, and hating every minute of it.

CHAPTER 14

"Congratulations, sweetheart!"

Kira welcomed her mother's hug and tried to smile at her father, who'd carried her bags inside. "Thanks, Mom."

"I know it's not a big deal to you, darling." Elyse pulled back and squeezed her daughter's arms just above the elbows. "But it is for us. You're home for at least two years!"

The hiss of water hitting a hot burner saved Kira from having to respond. She unzipped her parka and hung it in the back foyer while her mother rescued the pan on the stove.

"I'm just making a simple dinner," her mother told her, draining the pasta into a colander in the sink. "I have a ton of packing left to do."

Kira moved closer to see if she could help, but her mother seemed to have everything under control. She'd snitched a cucumber slice from the salad and taken a bite before her mother's words penetrated.

"Packing? For what?"

"My trip. Didn't your sister tell you?" She bustled from stove to sink to table to counter, clearly jazzed by something. "The Christmas present."

"Oh." Kira supposed Sophie had said something, now that she thought about it. "The Christmas trip. You guys are going to Vegas after all?"

"No, dear. I told you, I don't want to go to Vegas. I'm going on my own trip."

"And leaving Daddy?" Kira looked at her silent father as they all moved to the table and sat. Misery was clear in the dullness of his eyes and the extra lines on his face.

Elyse sighed and folded her hands in front of her plate. "Yes, dear, I'm leaving Daddy." Her tone was of a teacher to a kindergartener. "He's staying home. I'm going on a trip. After nearly thirty years I'm entitled to some time to myself, don't you think? Duncan, say grace please."

Her husband dutifully murmured the prayer, then reached for the serving dishes. He still hadn't said anything about the trip.

"Mom, I understand, but what will Daddy do while you're gone?" Kira didn't really want to talk in front of her father, but she felt so confused she couldn't stop herself.

"Same as always." Elyse's tone was brisk, and Kira knew she was losing patience. "He'll go plumb some houses, watch sports on TV, go to the pub once a week."

"What about meals?"

"I'm not helpless, lass." For the first time, he spoke. And though he still looked dejected, a little pride had relit the sparkle in his eyes. "I can cook and clean. Your mother never had the full burden of that."

"See? He'll be fine." Elyse forked up her last mouthful and stood. "My flight leaves at six tomorrow. Kira, can you take me to the airport? Thanks, sweetie." She kissed her daughter on top of the head and bustled out of the room.

"A.M?" Kira didn't want to know the answer. It would undoubtedly be as bad as all the rest of them.

* * *

Jake knew he was dreaming. Even a deep subconscious state couldn't fool his mind into thinking he'd have put flowers in his bedroom. Their scent was almost overwhelming, making him want to sink even deeper into sleep to escape.

"Jacob. Jaaaa-cob."

Except a deeper sleep might bring him out of his dream. And it was starting to get to be a good one. Warmth seeped into him, the kind of warmth that signaled "woman." He wanted it to signal "Kira," but for some reason his brain resisted. Hands were roaming his skin, though, and lips sucked at his neck, his nipple. If Kira were in the bed with him, he'd roll right over and drive into her, ease the ache he'd had at every thought of her. Do something with the hard-on he'd gotten during every phone conversation. God, he wanted it. His heart beat faster, his hands clenched the bedsheets.

But something was wrong. He couldn't make the woman in his dream-bed be Kira. Which was stupid. It was his dream. He could make love to Kira if he wanted to.

"Come on, baby. You're not helping me out here."

A hand closed over his penis and he jerked awake. Instantly he became aware of Darcy next to him, her cloying perfume making it hard to breathe. She wore a silky negligee and nothing underneath. He could tell because it had dropped to her waist.

He pulled away so fast he fell off the bed. Pain speared his groin because she hadn't let go when he moved. He buried his face in the side of the bed.

"Dammit, Darcy."

"What?" She leaned over next to him. Despite his pain he jumped up and grabbed his robe from the chair at the foot of the bed.

"What the hell are you doing here?" Panic seemed to claw at his throat. He tied his belt in a double knot.

Darcy ignored his anger and rose to her knees on the bed. Jake had fallen off on the narrow side, near the wall, so she was only two feet away. Her hand came up and rested on his chest.

"I wanted you, baby."

Jake felt pinned to the wall. A wall his parents slept directly behind.

"You know my parents are here. Are you crazy? Stupid? What?" The panic had fed his anger until it became fury. He kept his voice down to not wake his parents, but the strength of his feelings frightened him. He had to get away from her.

"I just want you, that's all. You *are* going to be my husband."

Jake rounded the bed and put as much distance between them as possible. Plus a chair and a pillow that he'd grabbed on his way by.

He couldn't believe the woman's gall. "How much plainer can I make it, Darcy? I don't want you. I will not have you. If you keep pursuing me, I won't work with you. I'll sue for custody if I have to, but I'll have nothing to do with you. And that won't get you much power, will it?"

His chest heaved as he watched her stare at him. He regretted the words as soon as he said them. A custody battle certainly wasn't the answer. He waited for Darcy's annoyance, anger, disgust, even pouting. He hadn't expected to see desperation in her face. Suddenly, he wasn't so angry. Suddenly, it seemed much more prudent—not to mention mature—to be friends with the mother of his child.

He sat on the bed. She sat next to him, crossing her arms over her chest.

"Jake, I just don't know what to do. I'm...I'm lonely." She seemed to like that tactic. Seemed to sense the softening in him. "I'm scared. I want to feel like we're going to be a family, and the only way I know how to start is to go to bed with you."

Jake sighed. They could keep on like this, battling each other, setting up a horrible environment for a child to grow up in. Or, he could be a bigger person. Assume this situation wasn't Darcy's fault any more than it was his. Maybe she hadn't intended to get pregnant. Maybe she hadn't sensed he was going to break up with her. Maybe she was a woman stuck in circumstances she didn't want. Just like him.

Or maybe he was just a sucker for the "I'm lonely" bit.

"Darcy, I'm sorry." He put his hand on her knee. She leaned her head on his shoulder. He didn't pull away, and felt something inside begin to heal.

"Can we start over, please, Jake? I don't want to fight you," she said, this time with a sniffle.

Jake thought of Kira, coming home that very night. Of how hard it would be to see her, want her. Longing took his breath away, and he knew how much stronger it would be when they were together. He didn't know how he could build a new relationship with Kira parallel to the one he had to build with his baby's mother. But he knew he had to do both.

"Okay, Darcy. We can try."

*   *   *

Kira stared into the gleaming white bowl and waited. She didn't fight it, because she'd learned in the last three days that fighting it only prolonged the inevitable. Soon she was rewarded—if that were the proper term—with a gush of water and half a dozen dry heaves.

When her stomach stopped trying to empty itself of nothing she flushed the toilet, rinsed her mouth, and continued with her morning routine.

She'd learned to get up half an hour earlier each day to accommodate the bout of queasiness. She still hadn't determined whether she kept eating something that didn't agree with her or if she had an allergy to something at the school. She refused to consider the obvious.

She grabbed her folio and purse and headed downstairs for a

breakfast of grapefruit and toast. Dry toast. Her father had already left, apparently to an early call. Kira didn't mind the time alone. In fact, she was beginning to crave it.

The networking job was going smoothly so far. She'd spent many days evaluating the current system, interviewing the people who'd be using it to determine their needs, and researching available equipment. She'd developed a system within their budget and ordered the equipment. Now she had a bit of down time until it all arrived.

Which gave her plenty of time to work on Jake's campaign. Karen Plummer had plastered the town with signs and fliers and banners, proclaiming herself "the moral candidate." As far as Kira could tell, the woman was getting more of a reputation for being holier-than-thou, but she knew better than to count her out. She was being interviewed on the local lunchtime radio program and Kira wanted to be in Galloway's restaurant to gauge the town's reaction to it. She had some software to check out, first, though, so she finished her meager breakfast and headed for the school.

The software turned out to be a dud, which was a good thing because for some reason today was the staff's day for voicing concerns.

"Kira?" The secretary of the high school, where Kira had been given a temporary work station, knocked on her door shortly after she arrived. "Got a minute?"

"Sure, Hester." Kira rubbed her eyes. "What's up?"

"I just wanted to ask if we were getting Macs or PCs when all the new stuff comes."

"Macs. We're moving to an all-Mac platform."

Hester was already shaking her head. "That won't do. I've been using a PC for six years. The same one, if you can believe it." She chuckled but looked intent on convincing Kira. "I'm nearing sixty years old, Kira, and I'll never learn the new computer. They'll let me go if I can't do my job—"

"Hester." Kira leaned forward and patted the edge of her desk in front of the only other chair in the closet-turned-office. "Sit, please."

Hester sat, looking dejected. "It's probably too late, isn't it? You've already ordered me a Mac."

"Well, yes, but it's more than that. The district had already purchased a dozen new iMacs. In order to gain the efficiency and productivity that's our goal, we have to be able to run the network from one server, which means all the computers have to be the same."

She squeezed Hester's hand. "But you don't have to worry. First, the computer I've ordered for you is very much like what you're already used to. We can program your word processor and spreadsheet to work just like the one you have. And I'll be holding training classes so you won't fall behind when it comes. I promise, everything will be fine."

Hester looked at her for a minute, and finally sighed. "If you say so. I don't guess I have a choice."

"Unfortunately, no." Kira smiled and waited for the woman to leave. To her surprise, she lingered, though she didn't say anything right away.

"Karen Plummer is in my quilting circle," she finally said. "She says that Jake McKenna is loose."

Kira swallowed a giggle at the old-fashioned term. She'd never heard it used to describe a man before. "I've never known him to be, ma'am."

"Hm." She pressed her lips together. "Me, neither." She stood, then sighed. "Thank you, dear."

"You're welcome."

The secretary had barely cleared the doorway when Kira's phone rang.

"Is it true we're changing all our software? How stupid is that! What about all our old documents?"

"Wait, slow down, Aggie. That's not true. Upgrading isn't changing and doesn't affect the old documents...."

By the time Kira eased the fears of office worker number three, she was almost too late to get to Galloway's before the radio show. The interviewer was introducing his guest when Wilma showed Kira to her seat.

"Just a cup of onion soup," Kira whispered to the waitress, who nodded and swept silently off to the kitchen.

The restaurant was crowded, but eerily silent. Nearly everyone was listening to the radio being broadcast through overhead speakers.

"...Ms. Plummer is an upstanding business owner in this town, and has been a presence in local politics on a minor basis for the past three years."

That was news to Kira. She pulled her pad and pen out and began jotting notes. She had some more research to do.

"A wife and mother of three teenaged children, Karen understands the trials and tribulations that befall our local parents. She has successfully navigated the dangers and is prepared to help us do the same. May I welcome—Karen Plummer."

Kira frowned and took more notes. The interviewer was clearly biased, which meant it wouldn't be very smart to get Jake on her program at a later date. They'd be better off with the morning show or drive time, or even the late evening DJ, if she could convince the program manager to cut into his precious Top Forty time.

Teenagers were a potential hot button, too. Karen may claim she'd been successful, but few parents knew everything their teenagers were into. Kira didn't want to hurt the kids, but if they had any vandalism or poor academic records or something that could discredit Karen, it could help.

She grimaced. She hated smear campaigns. Better to stick to Jake's positives than Karen's negatives.

She tuned into the interview, which had finally progressed beyond chitchat.

"Jake McKenna has been Brook Hollow's favored son for many, many years," the interviewer was saying. For the life of her, Kira couldn't remember his name. It wasn't someone she remembered. "What made you decide to take him on?"

"Well, Bob, it wasn't an easy decision. But I love this town as much as anyone, and it hurts me to see it declining. And frankly, the actions Mr. McKenna has taken on the town council have only helped that decline. I couldn't sit by and wring my hands. If you're not part of the solution, you're part of the problem."

Kira rolled her eyes. How eighties. But she could see some heads nodding around the room and reminded herself that she was not in Boston. Cutting-edge was about six years old, and ten years old was comfortable.

"So tell us how you plan to be part of the solution?"

"Brook Hollow has a beautiful downtown. We have dynamic businesses, bustling retail—and a litter problem. We need to allocate resources to give smokers somewhere to dispose of their refuse. More noticeable, attractive receptacles for candy wrappers and coffee cups. Newspaper containers for recycling."

Kira listened to her drone on and looked out the window at the yellow and green trash can right in front of her. The sand-filled top contained a few cigarette butts, and a separate pocket on the side was half-stuffed with newspapers. "Please recycle" was clearly scripted across the side. Kira laughed under her breath. This woman did not know how to pick her battles.

"Another issue sweeping the nation as well as the town is morality," the interviewer said. "Whether America—and Brook Hollow—are losing our moral compass. Teen pregnancy rates, crime rates, drunk driving, drugs—where do you see these issues as they affect Brook Hollow?"

"To be honest, Tom—"

Tom? Kira thought she'd called him Bob a minute ago.

"—Brook Hollow is poised on the brink. Of course we have crime, and teen sex, and drinking. No one avoids that. But I believe we need to take the reins firmly in hand before our young people head in the wrong direction. And frankly, Jake McKenna is the wrong person to do that."

"Why? Jake has been a positive role model in this town for a long time."

Hm. Maybe Bob-Tom wasn't as biased as Kira had thought.

"He is involved in many organizations that deal with today's youth, and works with them one on one as well. No one has ever accused him of immorality."

"Actions speak louder than words, Bob. It's a 'do as I say, not as I do,' kind of thing. Sure, Jake may pay lip service to groups that advocate abstinence—"

Kira didn't even know of such a group, unless it was a student group, and Jake definitely was not involved in one. His time was spent with athletic and career organizations to help kids figure out what they wanted to do with their lives and how they could get there. He didn't preach to anyone.

"But we've all heard the rumors about him."

"What rumors would those be?"

Bob sounded like he was trying to goad Karen. This was the part Kira had been worried about.

There was actual dead air for several seconds. The advertisers weren't going to like that.

"Well," Bob began, but was interrupted by Karen, who finally seemed to have gotten her courage up.

"The rumors, Tom, that Jake McKenna is promiscuous."

She said it in a rush, using the wrong name again. Kira didn't know whether to groan or chuckle. She studied the faces around her. None seemed shocked or appalled. A few looked amused, one or two frowned, but for what reason Kira couldn't tell.

"That's a rumor I hadn't heard, Karen."

"Yes, it's been circulating since the holidays. Now, I don't give credence to the truth of rumors," she asserted.

"No?"

"Of course not. But the rumors themselves do damage. Whether Mr. McKenna sleeps around or not is meaningless. The *belief* that he does makes it okay to the young people of this town who look up to him. In fact, there's even been talk that he's…"

CHAPTER 15

"We need to take a quick break, so hold that thought, Karen. Ladies and gentlemen, we'll find out what meaningful allegation Karen Plummer, candidate for mayor, will make right after this word from your favorite local restaurant."

The theme music for Galloway's rang over the speakers and the volume in the room rose suddenly. Wilma appeared at Kira's side with her soup.

"Sorry, hon, I got so caught up in that interview I forgot your soup. Everyone else had been served." A couple of patrons waved at the waitress now, but she didn't look up. "What're you gonna do about this?" she asked Kira.

Kira rubbed dread-induced goosebumps through her thin sweater. She hoped Karen wasn't going to say what Kira thought she was going to say. "About what?" she responded to Wilma's question.

Wilma gave her a shrewd look as she dug in her apron pocket. "That's right, you ignore that junk. Jakey's been our golden boy forever. She's got no right to take that away from us."

"Don't let her, Will. Vote McKenna in November." She grinned as the waitress hurried away with a wink, but the grin faded quickly. November was a hell of a long way away. Eight months away. A lot could happen between now and then.

Suddenly Kira's attention was drawn by a figure crossing the restaurant toward her. Her heart rate increased with each step he took. Tall, blond, rugged in a sheepskin-lined denim jacket and cowboy boots...

Cowboy boots?

"Since when do you wear cowboy boots?" she asked Jake when he slipped into the booth across from her.

He grimaced as he slid off his jacket. "Since Darcy gave them to me." He held a finger to his lips and pointed to the speaker above them. The interview was coming back on.

Kira half listened to the introduction and recap of the first half of the show. Jake looked terrible. Dark circles made his eyes appear sunken. The lines around his mouth and eyes had deepened, aging him at least seven years.

"Before the break, Ms. Plummer, you were about to make an allegation about your opposition."

"Excuse me?"

"Er, you were about to voice a rumor about Jake McKenna's romantic life."

"I don't think so."

Kira straightened. Had the woman gotten cold feet? Advice from her lawyer about slander?

"I think what I was going to say is that a big fear we as business people and citizens of Brook Hollow are facing is the commercialization of this town."

Wow. Quite an about-face. Quite an escape on their part. She heaved a sigh of relief, then listened as the woman found her groove and gave a five minute monologue about the dangers of Wal-Mart, Barnes & Noble, Home Depot, and McDonald's, none of which had found their way to their town yet.

When the interview was over Rhonda, the owner, turned the music down to a background level. Kira sat silently watching the crowd, picking up bits of conversation as groups passed, gauging attitudes as people stopped to talk to Jake. The support was clearly on his side.

"Well, what do you think?" Jake asked after Kira had paid her bill and they were outside.

"I'm not sure. She lost her nerve, I think. Or maybe she decided it was too early. But I don't think she gave a favorable impression. Especially since she kept calling the interviewer by the wrong name."

"Yeah, I'm sure that solidified his support of her." Jake studied his feet as they walked. "He'd been leaning in her direction until now."

"I could tell by his introduction. But he said some things that sounded like he was on your side."

Jake lifted his head again and squinted against the bright sun. "Could have just been playing both sides. Aiming for some kind of impartiality."

"Well, we don't have to worry yet, I don't think," Kira concluded. "She didn't do much damage. Her biggest issue was superstores, but we don't have any looking our way, do we?"

"Darcy wants to open a McDonald's," he admitted.

"What?" Kira stared at him. "Are you kidding? There are three diners that could threaten."

He shook his head, looking more depressed than Kira had ever seen him. "She mentioned it the night of the ball, but she'd drunk too much so I ignored it. She told me the other night that she has started investigating the franchise procedure. She knows of a piece of land on the outskirts of town she thinks would pull people from the highway."

Kira snorted. "That would go over real well after Karen's speech just now."

"I can try to talk her out of it, but I don't have much power over her at the moment."

He sounded so dejected Kira worried briefly about his mental health. She pulled her hand out of her pocket and slid her fingers through his. "What's going on, Jake?"

He squeezed her hand once, then let go and put his own back in his jacket pocket. "Nothing new. She keeps trying to sleep with me, I keep saying no, she cries, I feel bad, she buys me boots, then tries to get in my bed again."

Kira didn't want to hear about this. Her heart throbbed around the thorn in it every time she thought of Jake with another woman. He should be with *her*, damn it!

"So why are you wearing the boots?" she asked, half afraid she'd cursed out loud.

He bared his teeth in nothing resembling a smile. "If I wear the boots, she'll stay out of my house tonight."

"Oh, Jake." The thorn twisted. Her resentment of Darcy increased.

"Forget about me. We always talk about my problems. How are you doing?"

"Fine." She latched onto the change of subject. "The equipment is ordered, only one major component is on backorder, I'm slowly getting people to stop resisting the idea...."

"No, I mean how are *you* doing?"

Kira studied the sky as they crossed the street near the school. "I don't know what you mean."

"Brianna says you're sick."

She stared at him in shock. "What? How does she know that?" She cursed inwardly. "I'm not sick."

"You're father says you are. You're throwing up all the time, and you're too pale—which I can see for myself—and you've lost weight."

"Yeah, like my father would notice that I've lost weight."

Jake leaned against the low stone wall surrounding the campus. "I notice." His voice was low, caring, too close to the danger zone they'd been avoiding with bare success. Neither seemed to want to approach the subject of "them" until Jake straightened out his situation with Darcy.

"I'm fine, Jake, just a flu. I'll get over it. It's going around." Not that she'd noticed, but she hoped he took her word for it. She didn't want him jumping to conclusions.

"See a doctor, Kira," he urged. Panic blocked her throat at the thought. Her subconscious knew what was wrong and her conscious mind was fighting it for all she was worth. She hunched her shoulders against the sudden wind. Nearly March, but feeling like the dead of winter.

"I gotta go back to work. See ya." She buried her face in the collar of her jacket and hurried up the walk. She could feel Jake watching her as she went.

* * *

That Sunday found her trying to help her father prepare a "traditional" Sunday dinner. Sophie was coming from Boston and Brianna would be over. Duncan was determined to prove to them that he was fine without his wife.

Sophie had called every day, Kira knew, and Brianna stopped either at the house after work or at whatever job their father was on that day. Kira herself hadn't had the energy or appetite to make meals for him, but she made sure he wasn't starving. She was the only one not worried about her old man.

"No, Dad, don't pour the marinade over the roast. It's contaminated. Raw meat. Toss it. You made extra, remember?"

"Oh, that's right." He snapped his fingers and pulled the bowl from the refrigerator. "I heard from your mother, today," he said casually while he fought with the plastic wrap covering the bowl.

"You did?" Kira jumped off the stool where she was grating carrots and circled the center island. "Where is she? When is she coming home?"

He shook his head and concentrated on pouring half the marinade over the meat. "She didn't say. She sounds great, though. Relaxed, having fun. She met some other women there and they've been seeing the sights and stuff. She really needed this trip," he told her. Instead of sounding surprised, he sounded like he was trying to reassure her.

"I know, Dad. She kept telling us so." Her tone was wry, but she sat back on her stool. She added the carrots to the top of the salad and set it aside, then pulled a bag of potatoes closer to her. "Mashed potatoes tonight, right?"

"Right. Well, if you know, why are you having such a hard time with it?" He slid the meat into the oven and set the timer. "Two hours, should be finished just as your sister gets here. And you girls thought I couldn't cook."

"I'm not having a hard time with it, Dad. Really."

He gave her a look that said he clearly didn't believe her.

"Why don't you help me peel these potatoes?" She nudged a paring knife closer to him.

He pulled a spud out of the bag and began cutting a long, curling strip of peel. "Kira, it's no threat to your future that your mother and I are spending time apart."

"I know, Dad. I don't even live at home anymore. I'm a grown woman. I'm not threatened by my parents' happiness. Or lack thereof."

Instead of protesting that they were still happy, her father kept silent for a few moments. Then he said, with more insight than he'd ever shown regarding any of his daughters in twenty-eight years, "You think this situation is proving what you've always thought. That familiarity breeds boredom."

She didn't bother to protest. "Well, it sure seems evidence of it." Not that it mattered. The longer she and Jake went without the opportunity to prove her wrong, the less likely it seemed possible they'd get a chance to try.

"Well, with the situation you're all in now, it seems you have a long way to go before you have to worry about boredom again, lass."

Kira frowned at him. "What do you mean?" She began digging eyes out of the freshly peeled potato in her hands. "What situation?"

"Jake loving you. Darcy wanting Jake. Darcy being pregnant." His voice lowered. "You being pregnant."

To Kira's complete amazement she burst into tears. She'd intended calm denial, maybe a bit of true amusement. Instead, all the pain and fear of the past few weeks crashed in on her, leaving her sobbing and sniffing and soaking a dish towel.

That was, of course, the moment her sisters walked in the back door.

"You're early," she accused when they immediately descended on her.

"What did you do to her, Daddy?" demanded Sophie. Brianna had been around her sister more recently, however, and she simply wrapped an arm around her shoulders and let her get it out.

"Why do you think that?" Kira finally asked her father. "I don't have any evidence of it."

"I have three children, lass." He hadn't moved from his position, hands braced on the island. His eyes held compassion and love and a fierce protectiveness that would have had Kira fearing for Jake's life if the situation were any less bizarre. "I knew before your mother did, after the first time."

Brianna stroked her hair back from her face. "Are you sure?" she asked Kira quietly.

"Not at all. I didn't even have suspicions until Daddy blurted it out."

"I knew it." Sophie jammed her fists onto her hips. "You *did* do this, Daddy. Blurted what out?"

"It's not for me to say," he demurred, going back to his potato.

Kira snuffled and accepted the tissue Brie handed her. She studied the meager pile of potatoes on the counter and inhaled the succulent odor of the roasting beef. "We need to get a move on. That roast is cooking fast."

"You're not changing the subject that quickly," Sophie protested, but her father stopped her with a hand on her arm.

"I'm afraid she is. I invited Jake to dinner, and he's coming up the walk."

The panic on Kira's face, the chastisement on Brie's, and the sheepishness on Duncan's clued Sophie in immediately. "Oh. My. God!"

The door opened. "Am I too early?" Jake asked as he walked through.

Sophie didn't even seem to notice him.

"You're pregnant!" she shouted.

CHAPTER 16

The kitchen looked like one of those living mannequin windows the department store did at Christmas time. Everyone froze. Kira's father looked embarrassed enough to crumple right to the floor. Sophie stared at her, open mouthed, her hands on her hips again, seemingly unaware of what she had just done. Brianna stood by her, strong, supportive—out of character—staring Jake down as if daring him to say the wrong thing.

Jake looked the funniest of all. His hair seemed to have somehow stood on end at the outburst. His mouth, like Sophie's, hung open. He stood frozen just inside the door, one hand still on the knob, his foot behind him as he'd stopped midstride.

The emotions in his eyes were anything but funny. Kira tried to swallow but couldn't. She had seen unmitigated joy in his first reaction. But it was immediately tempered by confusion, then despair so deep she didn't think he'd ever climb out of it. Her only thought was to spare him more misery.

Only an instant had flashed by, though it seemed much longer. Kira drew on reserves she didn't know she had when she laughed in her sister's face.

"God, no, Sophie! Why on earth would you think that? It's the flu."

"You saw the doctor, then?" Brianna asked.

Kira almost kissed her for playing along, but kept her attention on the potato eyes she continued to dig out.

"Yeah, there's a strain of Asian flu that's milder but hangs on for a long time. I'll kick it eventually."

Jake finally came the rest of the way through the door and closed it.

"Brr!" Sophie seemed to finally catch on and shook off her amazement. "Trying to make us ice cubes, Jake?"

"You bet!" He put his hands on the back of her neck and she squealed, trying to get away.

Kira smiled, relieved that everyone had taken her at her word. The roughhousing continued, and it felt like old times.

Then she caught a glimpse of Jake's grin and her heart flipped over.

Well, not quite old times.

* * *

Jake had thought dinner at the Macgregors would take his mind off his problems. They'd reminisce, tease each other, act like they were ten. Elyse would mother him, he and Duncan would watch basketball, and the girls would paint their nails or something girly like that.

The afternoon was nothing like he'd envisioned. He'd forgotten that Elyse was on a trip. The idea of her going somewhere on her own was so odd he kept looking for her by the sink or in the laundry room.

The basketball game, a rout by one team he hated over another team he really didn't like, failed to hold his or Duncan's interest. The older man wandered to the basement to reorganize his work bench and didn't invite Jake along. He didn't know why that made him feel so rejected.

Kira and Brie holed up in the bedroom, doing God knew what, and Jake wondered if they were avoiding him. When he found himself alone in the living room, he knew he had to either leave or make himself at home.

He'd never failed to make himself at home.

He followed a curse that drifted from the laundry room. Sophie was trying to match her father's socks, which were scattered all over the floor. She looked up at him and growled.

"The man can't have one kind of sock. No, he has to have eighteen pairs of different socks. Six different lengths, four different patterns, some with a gold toe, some with a gray heel. How the hell does my mother put up with this?"

Jake chuckled and squatted, matching like socks and folding them into the laundry basket next to him. "I think we've figured out why your mother needed a vacation."

"If this is what life with him is like, I think she needs more than a vacation."

"Why are you doing this, anyway?" Jake asked her, plucking the lone black dress sock from its spot between the washer and dryer. "You don't live here."

"So? I didn't want the burden of taking care of him to fall on Keer and Brie. They say they're not doing much, but I still feel guilty being in the city."

They finished matching socks and moved on to folding undershirts.

"How's work going?"

Sophie shrugged. "It's going. I hate it. But I don't know what else I want to do, so I'm stuck for now. How's yours?"

"You have no idea." He thought about the radio show earlier in the week and his stomach began to churn.

"I have some idea. Kira told me about the campaign. You're in for a long one, friend. It's barely March!"

The churning picked up its pace. Jake grabbed a hanger and hung up a work shirt he'd pulled from the dryer. "Maybe she'll burn herself out. It's been known to happen."

"Maybe."

They hung and folded in silence for a few minutes. Jake debated whether or not to try prying information out of Sophie. If she had it, she might not give it to him. She usually didn't care about discretion, but Kira *was* her sister.

"Soph, what was going on in here when I came in?"

A red flush washed over Sophie's cheeks and she turned away from him. "I don't know."

It was better than "nothing."

"Well, you must have some idea."

"Not really."

"Sophie, come on. I'm worried about Kira. She's been sick, and has lost weight, and she won't talk to me."

"She says she's had the flu."

"For three weeks?"

The memory of Kira's avoidance every time he tried to talk about important things tormented him. Like the memory of her in his arms tormented him, like her kisses and voice and scent and the feel of her hair on his hands tormented him. What had he done to deserve this hell?

"Well, it must have been pretty bad," Sophie remarked. "You *look* like hell."

Jake jerked his head up. "Did I say that out loud?"

"You sure did." Sophie had finished the clean laundry and was now perched on top of the dryer, leaning on her hands. "What's going on, Jake?"

Jake hopped up onto the washing machine beside her and lightly banged his sneakers on the metal side. "You really care, or you just want to make sure you know everything?"

She looked insulted. "Both, of course."

He laughed. "Do you know what's going on with Darcy?"

"Only that she wants to get into more than your bed."

"She's pregnant."

She whistled. "I guess she's gotten what she wants."

"She's trying to. She claims she'll settle for no less than marriage, but I don't know why she's so desperate for a guy who doesn't want her. Plus she'll be showing soon, and my campaign will be completely derailed if I'm the father of an illegitimate child." He sighed. "I still haven't figured out what to do."

Sophie frowned. "This happened before Christmas?"

Jake nodded.

"When's her due date?"

Jake realized he didn't know. He wasn't sure if she'd told him and he'd ignored it, not wanting to retain any detail that made his situation more concrete. "Why?"

"I saw her at the grocery store today when I stopped to get rolls for dinner." Her frown deepened. "I'm not sure, but with her figure, I'd expect her to be looking different by now. More voluptuous, a rounded belly. Is she sick? Tired?"

He thought about her figure. "She looks the same to me as she always has. She hasn't said she has morning sickness, and if she's tired, it doesn't show." He told her about Darcy's non-stop chatter, glad-handing about town, and midnight forays into his bedroom.

"Well, this explains a lot. Don't worry about Kira."

"I can't help worrying about Kira." It was part of his job description.

"Jake, Kira's...well, she was crying tonight. I thought Dad had done it, or maybe Mom being gone, but now I think I know why."

It didn't take a nuclear physicist to figure out. "Darcy?"

Sophie nodded and jumped down. She folded her arms and studied him, her head tilted to one side. "I'll tell you a secret, big brother. I've always expected you and Kira to get together. You'd have a big flashy wedding, full of sappy stuff about love and fate, and you would finally be my real brother, there to protect me and comfort me and kick guys' butts."

Jake lifted one side of his mouth and smoothed a finger over her cheek. "I am your big brother, Sophie. I don't have to marry Kira to protect you. Or love you."

She smiled, but the look in her eyes was so serious, it almost scared him. He'd never seen that look on her before.

"The point is, we've all thought you and Kira were *it*. We were just waiting for her to figure it out. I think maybe she finally has. But you can't make my dreams come true, Jake, brother or not. You can't make anyone's dreams come true. Maybe not even yours."

He thought of the shrill, demanding woman who'd probably be on his doorstep when he got home. The dirty battle he faced for mayor. And the woman upstairs who was the other half of his soul.

Somehow, his dreams had become nightmare.

* * *

A week later Kira couldn't deny it any longer. Not to herself, anyway. She didn't need a drugstore kit to tell her what her tender breasts, heaving stomach, and overwhelming fatigue had already forced into her head.

She was pregnant.

She curled around her extra pillow and pulled the covers over her head. The school could do without her for one day. The shipment she expected to arrive today was simple, and the office could handle signing for it. She couldn't focus on anything beyond the cool sheet beneath her cheek, the throbbing awareness in her head, and the overwhelming feeling of fragility that permeated her entire being.

She was pregnant.

Anger. Fear. Horror. Resignation. Any of those emotions would be justified. Expected. Normal, even. But she couldn't summon any of them. When she prodded, when she imagined this baby, Jake's baby, she felt only one thing.

Relief.

Now wasn't *that* ridiculous? She shifted a little to a cooler spot on the pillow. Her stomach was starting to calm. Maybe she'd be okay today. Okay enough to get confirmation, anyway.

Relief.

There was only one reason she could figure for feeling this way. Competition. Being pregnant put her on level ground with Darcy. She had an equal claim to Jake's attentions. In fact, she had an edge. He could only marry one of them. He loved her, even if only as his best friend. Who else would he marry? Not the woman who annoyed him every minute.

Relief turned to bitterness, then Kira felt self-disgust take over. She didn't want to win Jake that way. She didn't want to play "make him choose." He'd hate both of them for it. The children—both of them—would suffer. And he'd never become mayor.

She was a comet, she reminded herself, reaching for the water on her bedside table. She raised her head enough to take a sip, grimacing at the gurgle when it hit her stomach. She waited, but it stayed calm. She laid her head back down and pressed a hand to her abdomen.

What was she going to do? She couldn't let Jake know about this baby. The rumors of one baby were doing enough damage to his campaign. He'd be forced to drop out of the race if there were *two*. She had to go back to Boston before he saw. That gave her only about three months before it would be too obvious to hide under the right clothes.

What would she do about the contract? She was locked in, but nothing said she couldn't subcontract it. She'd set up as much as she could, then hire someone to do the final configuring and handle the maintenance for the first year, at least.

Jake's campaign.

She groaned. Nothing had happened since the radio show, but in three months or so the heavy campaigning would start. The schmoozing, the speeches, the debates. The ads, the appearances. Jake needed a campaign manager, someone to take the stress off him.

Sophie. She could do it. She was sick of her job, and Kira knew her sister had enough socked away to give her a few months off. Jake would pay her, she was sure. It wouldn't be much, but enough to put food on the table. Mom would be ecstatic to have her middle daughter back home again.

Mom.

Kira groaned and dragged herself out of bed. She'd be better off going to the school to accept the shipment. The last thing she wanted to think about was telling her parents. Ugh.

* * *

Jake dug in his desk for the folder he needed for tonight's council meeting. He heard Darcy enter the room but didn't look up. She'd made them dinner tonight and had been the sweetest, most deferential, doting wife-wanna-be he'd ever seen. But he needed to find the file and get out of there or he'd be late.

He saw it sticking out from under a box of boat number labels and started to round the desk. He stopped short when he saw Darcy standing in front of him.

The "old" Darcy. The Darcy of last year. Ice fishing Darcy.

Funny how all he could think about was ice fishing. His eyes wouldn't budge from the woman propped against the doorjamb.

She was dressed collar bone to ankle in leather. Skin tight, shiny, unzipped-to-there-but-it-didn't-matter-he-could-see-her-nipples-through-the-leather leather.

"How the hell did you get into that?" he croaked. The clock chimed. He was late.

"It wasn't easy." She grinned a sexy, conspiratorial grin and stroked her hand over her chest and flat stomach. "But I remembered our conversation a few months ago. I thought you'd like it."

It was sexy, he couldn't deny it. But he also couldn't deny that it did nothing for him. If Kira had been wearing it, that would have been a different story. But she wasn't. The only woman he had a right to was here in front of him, offering herself to him quite blatantly—as she pulled the front zipper even lower—and he didn't want her.

"Darcy, I have a meeting."

"So? Haven't you ever missed a meeting before?"

"Not for this."

She pouted. Her breasts were all but falling out of the jumpsuit now, and the zipper was low enough that he could tell she wasn't wearing underwear. She slid away from the doorjamb and began to slither across the floor to him.

"No, Darcy," he tried to say, but she made a move worthy of any NFL linebacker and brought him down onto an overstuffed chair.

She didn't bother saying anything this time, trying to convince him with words. She must have figured her body was enough. But the smell of the leather made him feel sick to his stomach, and the weight of her breasts on his face suffocated him.

He decided not to struggle. If he stayed passive, maybe she'd get the picture faster. But it soon became clear that she was doing this, with or without his cooperation.

Something began to clang in the back of his brain when he finally dropped the folder and briefcase he'd been holding and levered her away from him. He stood and dropped her into the chair, picked up his stuff, and walked out, leaving her screeching behind him.

The alarm continued to clang, and her threats had escalated past the point of legality by the time he went out the front door. But he relegated them both to the bottom of his priority list as he headed for the council meeting. There was plenty of time to deal with Darcy.

* * *

"The spring banners are missing, I tell you." The indignant little woman standing in front of the council seemed to think the misplacement of the light post decorations was the worst crime their town had seen in a decade. Jake heard the grumblings around him but didn't join in. He couldn't afford to show his boredom or annoyance at every petty issue brought before them. He was running for mayor.

"Do you know who was responsible for putting them away, Mrs. Pettigrew?" he asked in as conciliatory a tone as he could manage.

"Karen Plummer. She was the head of the beautification committee last year."

Karen Plummer. Great.

"Mrs. Pettigrew, if you can wait until we're finished, I will go downstairs with you this evening and we will look."

The woman beamed at him. "Thank you, dear. I knew you'd come through for the town."

If only finding light pole banners were the worst of his worries.

He had a hell of a time keeping his mind on the night's agenda. It kept zipping back to the image of Darcy leaning against the doorjamb, displaying her flat belly, her unchanged breasts. Then to Sophie's questions about Darcy's symptoms. Her apparent lack of them. And the knowledge that most women, as far as he could tell, felt lousy enough in the first trimester to want nothing to do with sex, yet Darcy was desperate to get into his bed.

He was working hard to keep his suspicions under control. He couldn't go off half-cocked and make accusations that would cause his situation to worsen. Even more, he couldn't afford to let hope get a toehold in his heart.

"What's next?" Fritz asked, making a note. Jake hoped no one else wanted to speak, but Gladys Featherington stood. She squared her shoulders under the polka-dot dress, her matching handbag hanging over her forearm. She nearly clicked her heels when she stood at the microphone.

"The square is in dire need of painting. The parking spaces are indistinct. The curbs are faded. People cannot tell where their side of the road ends. Accidents have occurred, and the sidewalks will be damaged if people keep driving their cars into the curb."

Fritz rubbed his eyes with his left hand. His right tapped the pencil against his pad. "Gladys, painting can't be done in the winter."

"And why not?" Her chin came up and she clasped her hands.

"It's too cold, the road is too icy or snowy or slushy, we can't get the cinders and gravel out of the way...." The mayor waved his hand in a circle. "Things like that. Rest assured that it will be taken care of as soon as weather permits. Just like every year."

Gladys offered a prim "thank you" accompanied by a sniff of dissatisfaction and returned to her seat. A tall, harried-looking young woman with lank hair that hung in her eyes hopped up and immediately took her place.

"Mr. Mayor, council members, I'm concerned about the light at Fifth Street. Every day at midnight it flashes yellow. Isn't that dangerous?"

The mayor was massaging his temples now, so Jake answered this one. "Ma'am, the light flashes intentionally. Traffic is too light at that time of night to require a regular cycle. Few people are on the road at that time and are not likely to cause an accident. It flashes red on Maple," he added when his explanation didn't ease the worry on her face. "People traveling down Maple have to stop. If no one is coming, they can proceed."

Her face cleared. "Oh! Oh, I never noticed that. Thank you."

Hank Potter, next to him, leaned close. "If she's out there at midnight, why can't she see the red glow of the light?" Jake shrugged and shook his head. Hank smirked. "Are you sure you want to be in charge of this stuff?"

Fritz was making his last call for new business. Finally, a few minutes later, the meeting adjourned. Mrs. Pettigrew pounced on Jake before he'd even stood.

"I'm ready when you are, dear."

"Just let me gather my papers, Mrs. Pettigrew." He tried to be patient, but this petty baloney was really getting on his nerves. He was starting to dread anything to do with the town council, which didn't bode well for his tolerance for the mayorship.

He held out an elbow for the little old lady and let her lead him down the hall to the stairs. The door creaked as they entered the dark stairwell.

"You'd better wait while I get the lights," Jake said, but the woman was already descending the steps. He hurried after her.

"The switch is right here," she said, and suddenly he could see where he was going. He frowned.

"Isn't there a switch at the top?"

"Of course, but it's at the end of the hall." Her shadowy form disappeared around a corner. Jake followed and walked right into a spider web.

"Pttp. Ptttthhpt. Don't we have a custodian?" he grumbled, wiping fine strands out of his hair and pulling them off his eyelashes.

Mrs. Pettigrew was fitting a key into the lock of a storage room door. "It's hard to keep up with cobwebs at this time of year," she explained. "It gets a bit warm outside, then cold again, and they come inside. I once cleared one from my foyer and before I returned from putting the broom away, it was back. If you can believe it."

Jake murmured something polite and glanced around the crowded room they'd just entered. "What color are the banners?" he asked, hoping to get this done quickly.

"Blue. They were right here." She waved vaguely at a shelf. "Or, were supposed to be. But they're not now."

Jake stepped closer to the ceiling-high set of shelves and squinted in the pinkish light from the bare bulb overhead. He saw a roll of nylon with something stitched onto it, and pulled it off the shelf. He unrolled it a bit.

"Life is Beautiful in Brook Hollow," he read. A picture of a basket of flowers adorned the center, made from stitched-on pieces of brightly colored fabric. "Are these what you were looking for?" He tried to hide his amusement and exasperation.

"No, those are the ones we used last year."

He stared at her. "Isn't that what you wanted?"

She shook her head. "You asked who put them away last year. I told you. You didn't ask when I saw them last."

Jake dropped his chin to his chest. "Why don't we use the same ones?"

Now *she* stared at *him*. "What on earth would we do that for?"

Forget it. "What do the ones we're looking for look like?"

"Like that." She pointed at the banners in Jake's hands. "Only with bunnies on them."

"Oh, with *bunnies*. Oh, well, that makes all the difference." He thrust the flower banners back onto the shelf. Luckily, Mrs. Pettigrew didn't seem to notice his sarcasm. Jake shifted a few items, but Mrs. Pettigrew kept telling him she'd looked there. And there. And there. They weren't in here.

Then what was he doing in here? This stupid search seemed as futile as the rest of his life.

Finally he spotted a large box that was definitely too heavy for the older woman to have moved. He shoved it to the side and a roll of blue banners displaying white cotton-tailed bunnies fell to the floor with a thud.

"Oh, thank you!" The woman snatched them up and patted Jake enthusiastically on the arm. "You're a miracle worker."

He wished.

CHAPTER 17

To Jake's immense relief, Darcy was not at his house when he got home. Neither were his parents, a rare occasion he decided to take advantage of. He got a beer and a bag of tortilla chips, grabbed the salsa his mother had made the day before, and headed for the television. He was going to veg.

First, though, he had to set some wheels in motion. He settled in his recliner, arranged his snack and the remote, and picked up the phone. He'd never gotten around to removing Darcy's number from his speed dial.

She picked up on the first ring.

"Hi, Darce. How are you feeling?"

"Um, fine. Why?"

"Just wondering. I know you're not quite into the second trimester, and this is usually when women feel crummiest."

She didn't say anything at first, then, "I've been lucky, I guess."

"Good. Hey, when's your next doctor's appointment?"

"Why?"

Hm. Interesting response. Definitely a little suspicion in there. The flicker of hope he'd been trying to squash flared a little higher. He ruthlessly stomped it down. He'd shown little interest in the pregnancy before now. His sudden questions could be why she was suspicious.

"I'd like to go. I haven't been very involved with this pregnancy, and I realized I'm missing stuff." He could almost hear her mind racing, trying to figure out where this was coming from. "I don't want to miss stuff. This is my baby. So, when is your next appointment?"

Her breathing sounded nervous in his ear. "I don't remember. I'll have to check and get back to you."

"Okay." He played agreeable. He was going to be nice to her if it killed him. Whatever he had to do to prove her deception.

If it was a deception, he cautioned himself.

"Can you call me back tonight?"

"I'll try."

But she didn't call. Jake slept well for the first time in two months.

* * *

Two days later, at their monthly planning meeting in Kira's tiny office, Kira watched Jake but tried not to let him know she was doing it. She didn't know what was going on with him. He was humming as he skimmed the list of speeches and appearances she'd given him. Humming. The circles had disappeared from under his eyes. Nothing had changed that she knew of. So why was he so happy?

He crossed off a speech scheduled the next week.

"I can't do the Rotary Club luncheon. Reschedule for next month."

"Why can't you?" She made a note on her to do list. "When I asked, you said the date was fine."

"I'm going to Darcy's OB appointment that day."

He sounded so cheerful Kira's stomach cramped. He was adjusting, she realized. Getting used to the idea. Getting used to Darcy. The thought added a crack to her battered heart, but she forced a smile.

"That's great. I hope you hear the heartbeat."

Jake smiled a smug little smile. "Me, too."

Kira fought a sudden wave of nausea. It must have shown on her face because Jake jumped up and pulled her into his arms as if to support her.

"What is it? Kira? Are you all right? Do you need a doctor?"

She swallowed hard and it receded. "Of course not. It's just a remnant of the flu. Certain odors make me feel queasy." It would have been a good explanation if there had been any odors in the room.

Jake smoothed her hair back. The curls didn't behave, so he anchored them with his palm on the side of her head. His thumb rested on her jaw just below her ear.

Kira knew her heart was on her face, knew he could read it. But she couldn't hide it. The pressure in her chest was overwhelming, trying to force her to *tell him*. The three words whispered in her mind. Her tongue trembled. Her lips parted. Her throat closed before she could say it.

"Kira."

The whisper caressed her mouth and drifted away. His lips dropped to hers, the kiss tender enough to bring tears to her eyes. It lasted only a moment, enough to bring conflict to Jake's face.

"I gotta go to the marina." He picked up his files and fled.

Kira touched her lips, and made a decision. She pulled out her organizer and found her gynecologist's card. She made an appointment for the following week, then called Maggie.

"I need a favor."

* * *

The day of Kira's appointment was another brilliantly sunny day. Abby slept in her car seat strapped into the back of the 4Runner and Maggie sighed after turning to check on her.

"She's such a good baby, Kira. Always happy or sleeping. She's getting close to sitting up, did I tell you?"

Kira grinned. "And showed me."

"Sorry."

"Don't be, it's wonderful." And before too long she'd be doing the same thing. The thought sobered her quickly. "How's John?"

"Great. His counselor said he's making great progress. He's planning to move in at the end of the month."

Kira didn't want to poke at her friend's bubble, but couldn't help but ask, "Aren't you scared?"

Maggie looked at her ruefully. "Terrified. That's why I'm seeing the counselor, too. I didn't realize it, just kept making excuses for why John wasn't ready to come back. I go once a week, and we have a joint session every two weeks. It's working well."

"How? I mean, what is the counselor doing that's helping you, besides asking you questions?"

"He's giving us trust exercises, things we can do at home to stretch the boundaries of that trust, enlarge our comfort zone. It's funny, I'm not even physically afraid of John. It's emotionally. I don't ever want to feel that way again."

They were nearly to Boston before Maggie finally began grilling Kira on her appointment. Kira had only told her she was afraid she was pregnant and wanted moral support when she found out.

"Do you really think you are?"

"Yeah."

"Did you take a home test?"

"No. I tried, but every time I went to buy one, someone I knew was near or at the counter and I didn't want anyone to see it."

"The curse of a small town," Maggie said.

"One of them."

"Is it Jake?" Maggie asked quietly.

"Is who Jake?"

"Stop it." Maggie turned sideways in her seat so she could see Kira's face. "Is Jake the father of this baby?"

Kira fought tears. They were coming into the city and the construction made everything very confusing. Split-second decisions had to be made, and tears would cause them to end up in Lexington.

"If I am pregnant, the baby would have to be Jake's," she admitted in a voice just above a whisper. Maggie seemed to know Kira didn't need a response. She simply reached over and squeezed Kira' arm.

Maggie waited in the waiting area just outside the exam room. Kira talked to the doctor in his office, answered his questions about her cycle and symptoms, and let him take her blood pressure.

"When was the first day of your last period?" he asked, pulling out a cardboard slider. Kira told him, and he calculated. "Well, it would be September fifteenth, assuming you're correct. You're thirteen weeks. Quite far along to be coming for your first visit." He gave her a stern look over his reading glasses.

Kira apologized. "I didn't suspect until a couple of weeks ago, and I didn't want to admit…." She trailed off and the doctor nodded.

"Circumstances aren't the best?" he asked kindly.

She shrugged. When she didn't elaborate, he closed her file and stood, walking to the door.

"Well, let's go check you out." He motioned her to precede him into the hall. Her eyes caught Maggie's questioning ones. The other woman was discreetly nursing her daughter, and Kira felt a tug of yearning, much like she had before. Soon she could be doing that, she thought. She realized the doctor was still talking.

"We'll proceed as if you are—ah, there's Debbie with the results of your dip." The nurse nodded. "Okay, then, it appears you are pregnant!"

Tears pricked the backs of Kira's eyelids. She blinked them back as the nurse led her into the exam room and instructed her on donning the gown. Once she was changed, Debbie came back in and drew blood, then took her vitals and had her sign some forms.

"Your first?" she asked.

Kira responded, though it was clear the woman was only making conversation. Soon the doctor returned, performed the complete exam, and smiled at her.

"Well, Kira, every indication is that you are definitely pregnant. Let's take a listen, shall we?" He dried the hands he'd just washed and squirted gel from a plastic bottle onto her abdomen.

"It's warm!" she said, thankful for small comforts.

"We have it in a warmer." He placed a wand in the pile of gel and smeared it around, then moved it more purposefully. Through the static on the loudspeaker next to Kira's head came a gurgling groan. "That was lunch." He shifted the wand, still staring into space. They could hear a slow, steady heartbeat. "That's yours." Silence except for the sounds of the wand sliding across her skin. Suddenly a "wow-wow-wow-wow-wow-wow" came through, incredibly fast. The doctor smiled in satisfaction. "That's it." He studied his watch while they listened. "Good beat. Nice and strong." He removed the wand and wiped her off with a towel, then helped her sit up.

"Now, I noticed you listed Brook Hollow as your residence. That's quite a distance."

Kira nodded. "I have a temporary job there."

"That's your home town?"

"Yes."

"You should consider transferring to a physician there. I can recommend an excellent obstetrician. We went to medical school together." He pulled a card from his pocket and wrote a name before Kira could stop him.

"I'll probably be returning to Boston before the baby's born," she told him. He looked up.

"Oh. Well, take this anyway." He handed her the card. "I'll be happy to treat you, but if you stay in Brook Hollow things will be much smoother and safer if there are complications. You'll feel better if you can't get to Boston and know the doctor in town."

Kira thanked him and took her time getting dressed after he left. She had so much to think about, her mind was blank.

She talked little on the way back, though Maggie bugged her halfway for details. She couldn't bring herself to admit how stupid she was being, nor could she tell Maggie before she told Jake.

And she *had* decided to tell Jake. She wasn't being noble, keeping secrets from him. She was being stupid by not allowing him to make a choice. So she'd give him one.

She gripped the steering wheel tightly as she watched Maggie carry her own baby into her house. Then she turned the car around and headed for Jake's.

*   *   *

Darcy kept uncharacteristically silent as she and Jake made their way into Dr. Gettle's office. The waiting room wasn't crowded, and Jake didn't think they'd be kept waiting long. Except when Darcy returned from the reception window, she held a clipboard with a blank patient form that she began to complete.

"Didn't you already do that?" Jake asked.

"I changed doctors," she said. "This is my first appointment here."

Oh, really? Jake hid his glee. Hopefully, by the time this visit was over, he'd have the answers he needed and have half of his miserable life back to normal.

The nurse called Darcy after only ten minutes or so. Jake followed her and didn't respond to the questioning look the nurse gave him.

They were shown into a doctor's office. "Dr. Gettle will be right with you."

Dr. Gettle was a slight woman with a sleek hairdo and refined demeanor. She shook both their hands, then sat and opened the file on the desk.

"What are we here for, today?"

Darcy twisted her hands in her lap. "Prenatal care. I've changed doctors." She seemed about to say more, but stopped herself.

"I don't see any records from the previous physician."

"No, they haven't arrived yet. Everything has been normal."

"How far along are you, Darcy?"

"About three months."

"You don't know exactly?"

There was a painful silence while the doctor waited. Jake stared at Darcy, whose face was beat red.

"Seventeen weeks."

The doctor nodded and made a note in the chart. "Morning sickness?"

"No."

"Spotting?"

"No."

"Frequent urination, headaches, cramping?"

"No."

Dr. Gettle looked up. "No cramping? You should be feeling some stretching in the ligaments by now."

"Maybe a little. It's mild."

"Okay."

The doctor asked a few more questions and seemed to take everything Darcy said at face value. Jake began to get frustrated when nothing else Darcy said seemed to be a lie. Then the doctor stood.

"Since this is your first visit with me, I'd like to do a full exam. Mr. McKenna, you can sit outside the examining room until we're done. You can return to hear the heartbeat."

Yes. That would be it. There wouldn't be a heartbeat, if he was lucky. *Please, God, let him be lucky.* He waited impatiently outside to be called back in. Five minutes went by. Ten. Fifteen. Suddenly the door opened and the doctor walked by without looking at him. She went into her office and sat at her desk. A minute later the door opened again and Darcy, fully dressed, emerged. She went into the doctor's office and shut the door. Jake didn't know whether to be angry or elated. Something unexpected had happened in there. The nurse went back into the exam room and began cleaning up. He wanted to ask her what had happened, but doubted she'd tell him. Another ten minutes later the doctor's office door opened and Darcy emerged, now white-faced. The doctor didn't look up from her paperwork.

"We can go," Darcy told him. She didn't meet his eyes.

Jake stood. "What about the heartbeat? I wanted to hear it."

"Not today. She said it wouldn't be strong enough. To hear. It's too...early."

Jake *knew* that was a lie. He'd read some articles on the Internet after his suspicions had been aroused, and they would have been able to hear it several weeks ago.

"What did the doctor want to talk to you about?" Jake asked. Darcy strode past the appointment desk. "Wait, don't you have to make your next appointment?"

She didn't answer. He hurried to catch up. "What did you talk about after the exam? Is everything okay?" Darcy kept quiet. By the time they got to the car, she'd started to cry. Jake figured they were either fake tears, or generated because she didn't know how to dig herself out.

He decided to let her sweat a bit. They'd see what story she came up with when they got home.

* * *

Of course, Jake wasn't home when Kira got there. She drove to the marina, then slowly through town, looking for his car. Where the hell was he?

Her secret burned in her chest, intensified by impatience. It was so hot, she took an antacid. She drove past Jake's again. Still no car. Completely at loose ends, she decided to go to work and took the turn that would bring her to the high school. Half a mile from her destination, she finally spotted his car.

In the obstetrician's parking lot.

Confused, Kira pulled to the curb. Was it really his car? Yes, she knew the license plate, and the shallow dent in front of the gas cover where some chick had bumped him in July Fourth traffic several years before. What was he doing here? At the OB Kira's own doctor had recommended only a few hours ago?

As she sat trying to sort it out, Jake and Darcy emerged from the building. Darcy was crying, and Jake looked angry. Kira didn't know what interpretation to put on the scene.

Now, more than ever, she had to talk to Jake. But she wasn't going to follow them home and confront him while Darcy watched. She'd wait. Even if it killed her, she'd wait.

* * *

It should have been easy. Jake had *expected* it to be easy. He'd watch carefully, catch Darcy in a lie, confront her, and they'd be done with it. But when they'd returned to the condo after that odd doctor's appointment, the story Darcy had come up with had been weak but not enough to call her a liar.

"So," Jake demanded when they walked in the front door, "what happened? Why didn't I get to hear the heartbeat?"

Darcy kept her red-rimmed eyes lowered. "I'm embarrassed, Jake."

"Tell me." He tried to be coaxing rather than harsh. He stepped over to her and lifted her chin with a finger. The perfume she wore gagged him, but he breathed through his mouth and didn't move away. "What happened?"

Tears filled her eyes. "I have an infection," she said, and Jake flinched. This was stuff guys did *not* want to hear about. "A bad one. I was so upset I forgot to have them call you in. The doctor gave me a prescription and it will be cleared up in a few days, but she scolded me for not getting it treated sooner, and I was embarrassed."

Uncomfortable with the topic, Jake walked away into the kitchen. "Why didn't you make another appointment?"

"I'll call to make one." She slid onto a bar stool and Jake noticed she didn't directly answer his question.

He gave her a bottle of fruit juice and yanked the cap off his beer. He watched her as he took a swallow. He'd have to find some other way to catch her up.

On the plus side, whether or not she really had an infection, she wouldn't expect him to want to sleep with her.

* * *

As soon as Darcy left Jake tried to call Kira. He couldn't wait to tell her his suspicions. But she didn't answer the phone at home and her parents hadn't seen her. He tried Brianna next. "Have you seen your sister?"

"Not really. She's been working twelve hours a day on this network." She sounded distracted, so Jake hung up and tried to think how else to find Kira. He remembered Maggie and looked up her phone number on his old employee list.

She answered right away, but seemed unusually reserved. She claimed not to know where Kira was but, like Brianna had, mentioned how many hours she'd been working.

"No wonder she's sick," Jake growled. "Has she seen a doctor?"

Maggie's answer was only some kind of choked snargle.

"What was that?"

"Nothing. I don't know if she's seen a doctor for the flu."

The way she said that made Jake suspicious. "Has she seen a doctor for anything else?"

She didn't answer. Alarm flared. "Is she sick? Really sick? Maggie, come on, you've got to tell me."

"I don't have to tell you anything!" She gentled her tone. "You have to talk to Kira."

"I'm trying!" He sighed. "God, this is hard."

"Yeah, you are in a difficult situation."

"Any idea how I can get out of it?" he half-joked. There was silence for a minute. When Maggie spoke again, her reserve seemed to drop away.

"The Baby Shop—you know, on Maple, off the square? They have the neatest amplifier. You wear headphones and hold it up against the pregnant woman's belly to hear the heartbeat. Wouldn't that be a cool thing to do?"

Jake's heart leapt. "Maggie, I love you." He dropped the phone into the cradle and grabbed his leather jacket. The Baby Shop had better be open.

That was his mantra all the way across town. He'd chosen the wrong focus for that mental energy, however. They were open, but the monitors were out of stock.

"I'm sorry, sir." Luckily, the clerk didn't know him. "We expect another shipment in a couple of weeks."

"I can't wait."

She pulled a magazine across the counter. "There could be...." She flipped through the back pages, then paused, smiling. "Here it is. Mail order. Says allow four to six weeks, but they have a web site. I bet you could order it overnight or at least two-day mail."

"Fabulous!" Jake scribbled down the web site, then raced to the office and booted up his computer. His heart rate hadn't slowed since Maggie had told him her idea. He swallowed hard as the page loaded. The amplifier was advertised right on the home page. He followed the instructions to order it. If he was lucky, he'd have gotten rid of Darcy by the weekend.

He couldn't stand to be alone in his present state, so he grabbed his jacket again and headed to the elementary school. Kira was likely still there, judging by the hours Brianna had said she'd been working. Adrenaline made him jittery as he circled the school, looking for a way in or the room where Kira was. The office and all the classrooms were dark. He got back in his car and tried the middle school. Same thing. At the high school, however, there was a light on in the main office and the hallway, and one of the side doors was unlocked.

He whistled as he headed toward the office door. Kira suddenly appeared in the open doorway, a screwdriver in her right hand, her left pushing back a hank of hair that had pulled out of her clip. One strap of her overalls was hanging. Her cropped sweater showed a scrumptious strip of skin where her raised arm had lifted it.

"What are you doing here?" Her eyes were unfocused, as if still considering the guts of the machine visible on a desk behind her.

"I wanted to see you."

"Okay." She shrugged and turned back into the room. "Come on in. I have a lot to finish in here, so I hope you don't mind my working."

"Of course not."

"So what's up?" Kira's voice was muffled. Jake raised his a bit, guessing she couldn't hear very well under there.

"I've missed you. You haven't been around."

"Been busy." Kira backed out and stood, pressing the round power button on the keyboard of the white iMac. Her mind raced, trying to figure out how to ask Jake about what she'd seen. How to tell him she was pregnant.

How to add to his problems.

She kept her gaze on the computer screen, acutely aware of the man behind her. She knew if she backed up two steps, she'd be in his lap. For more than one reason, she almost did it.

But it wouldn't resolve things. So she sighed and turned to face him. She took a deep breath, opened her mouth—

"I don't think Darcy's pregnant."

Jake's sudden announcement froze Kira with her mouth wide open. The words she'd been about to say stuck in her brain, effectively blocking all thought.

Finally, she recovered enough to ask why he thought that. He explained Sophie's suspicions, confirmed the night of the council meeting. He told her his plan to trip her up at the doctor's office.

"So that's what you were doing there!"

Jake frowned at her.

"I wasn't spying on you. I just happened to see you leaving the building. It was odd—" She faltered, remembering part of why it had seemed odd. "Well, did it work?"

"No." Frustration carved lines in his forehead. "She managed to play it to her advantage. But Maggie gave me an idea." The lines smoothed. "I called her looking for you. She told me about this *in utero* baby monitor." He explained his plans and Kira couldn't dampen the hope that filled her.

What if it were true? If Darcy really wasn't pregnant, and she and Jake could be together? A family, with their baby....

She took another deep breath. She was going too fast. After all that had happened, Jake might not want her anymore. That fear had her taking one thing at a time.

"I hope it works," she said, moving closer and squeezing his hand. "Everything will be back to normal if it does."

He snorted. "I don't know what normal is." He looked up at her and tried to pull her closer. "I don't want normal."

Kira resisted both the tug of his hand and the lure of his gaze. *One thing at a time.* She could still tell him about the baby today. It would likely make him more eager than ever to expose Darcy. But how much sweeter it would be to tell him later, when he was free. Free of Darcy, free to love Kira, free to live his dreams.

One thing at a time.

CHAPTER 18

The amplifier took way too long to arrive. Jake spent three weeks on tenterhooks, checking the mail six times a day. The package was finally delivered the day before Kira had to go back to Boston to work for a few days. Jake wanted some kind of resolution before she left. Part of him was afraid she wouldn't come back.

Jake opened the box, tested the machine, and immediately called Darcy.

"Darce, why don't you come over for lunch today?" He tried to sound neutral enough that she wouldn't think he was ready to go to bed with her. "I got something in the mail I want to show you."

She hesitated, then agreed. "Make the meal kind of bland, though. I haven't been handling strong odors well."

"Since when?" he couldn't help asking. The lack of morning sickness was one of the things that had made Jake suspicious.

"Just recently."

"Hm. Usually that starts in the first trimester and ends in the second. Did you tell the doctor?"

"Of course. She said not to worry."

Something in the way she rushed to assure him rang false. But that could be because he wanted it to. They hung up, and Jake began preparing a suitable meal, though he doubted they'd eat it.

As soon as Darcy arrived, Jake hustled her into the living room.

"Look what I got." He pulled out the monitor. "It'll let us hear the heartbeat. Since I missed it at the appointment."

Panic flashed in Darcy's eyes and she crossed her arms over her stomach.

"It's too soon," she said, hunching her shoulders protectively.

Jake shook his head. "I read the instructions. It's just the right time." He hooked the headphones into his ears and held out the amplifier. "You don't have to lift up your shirt. It'll hear through it."

As soon as he got close, Darcy jumped off the couch and darted across the room.

Jake stayed where he was, kneeling in front of the couch. "What's the matter?"

She stammered something incomprehensible.

"Darcy." He stood and pulled the earphones from his ears. He crossed the room and placed his hands gently on her shoulders. "You're not pregnant, are you?"

He'd said it as gently as he could, but she still reacted violently, jerking to get out of his grasp, tears pouring down her cheeks.

He held her until she quieted, pulling her tight to his chest and actually feeling sorry for her, for the desperation that had led them to this.

"I know you're not," he said finally, sensing that her mind was trying to come up with a counter to his statement. "You can't convince me you are."

This time when she wrenched herself from his grasp he let her go. The look she threw at him was pure hatred.

"You won't get away with this, you bastard. We're not over. Not by a long shot."

"Get away with what?" he yelled, astounded at how she tried to turn this back at him. "You're the one who tried to scam me into marrying you. Who damaged my chances for being elected mayor. I could sue you, you know."

It was the wrong thing to say. Darcy shrugged on her coat and slung her purse over her shoulder, then turned on him, poking him in the chest with a sharp fingernail. "You think I damaged your chances? You ain't seen nothing yet, buster."

She slammed out of the house, but Jake didn't think about her threat. He grabbed his own coat and headed for his car. His only thought was that he was free, and he had to get to Kira before she left.

* * *

Kira shoved another box into the back of her truck and stretched the tight muscles in her back. An old client was having problems with their network and a new one promised big bucks if she did a rush job for them. Conscious of her uncertain future, Kira had accepted the short-term assignment and was killing two birds with one stone, bringing some of Sophie's things to her. Their mother was a tornado since her return from her trip, determined to clean out the entire house. "Out with the old, in with the new," she kept saying, though Kira couldn't figure out what was new except her mother. She'd gone white water rafting and hiking in West Virginia, despite the unpredictable early spring weather, then touristing in Washington, D.C. She'd even made Kira hook up a computer so she could keep up with all her new friends.

Kira sat on the tailgate, resting a minute before being put to work again when she went back into the house. She was feeling better, but was still a little weak and easily fatigued. It didn't help that she hadn't told her parents yet about the baby, and couldn't come up with a valid excuse to avoid physical labor.

She'd just stood and reached for the hatch when a car squealed around the corner and screeched to a stop in her parents' driveway. Jake leaped out and ran up the walk, apparently without seeing her standing there. Kira followed him.

"Where's the fire?" she asked from behind him. He whirled. She had never seen such excitement on his face.

"Kira, it worked. It's over. She's gone. Out of my life." He swept his hand in a wide arc. "Can you believe it? The nightmare is finally over!"

Kira let him sweep her up in an exuberant hug, but for some reason she didn't share his excitement. She only felt numb, and skeptical.

"She let you go that easily?" she asked when he finally released her.

He snorted. "Hardly easy. She wouldn't let me use the amplifier. Burst into tears and fought me when I accused her of lying. Told me I wouldn't get away with this and threatened my campaign. But she didn't deny it."

Fear followed a familiar path down Kira's spine. "She threatened your campaign?"

"Kind of. When I said she'd hurt my chances for election, she said I hadn't seen anything yet. But what can she do now?"

Kira didn't bother to list the ways. But neither did she take Darcy's threats as casually as Jake had. When he left a few minutes later, late for a planned campaign event, she hadn't told him he was still going to be a father before Election Day. She watched him drive away and tried to figure out what to do.

"Why didn't you tell him?" Sophie asked from behind her.

Kira sighed. "Why aren't you in Boston?" she countered.

"I had a dentist appointment this afternoon."

Kira walked into the house. "You need to get a Boston dentist."

Sophie shrugged. "It's too much hassle. Besides, it gives me an excuse to come home for the weekend."

"It's Thursday."

"Okay, a long weekend."

Irritated, Kira glared at her sister. "I just loaded six boxes of your junk into my truck. You owe me."

"Fine, I owe you." She grabbed Kira's hand and yanked her down onto the couch. "Why didn't you tell him?"

"Tell him what?"

"That you're pregnant."

Kira gave up the idea that she could deny it to anyone anymore. "I can't."

"Of course you can."

"I will. Just not yet. I want it to be a happy thing, not clouded by whatever doom Darcy tries to spread." Her voice grew hoarser as emotion constricted her throat. "I've done so much damage to him already. I don't want this to do more."

Sophie grunted unsympathetically. "Not telling him is doing more damage than telling him."

Kira figured Sophie was probably right, but she couldn't be sure. She had to see what Darcy was going to do first.

What happened in the next few days proved her instincts correct.

The client with the problem network was a small business halfway between Boston and Brook Hollow. Kira was in the main office trying to coax some cooperation from the seven-year-old computer when a voice on the radio caught her attention. It was Bob/Tom, the noontime DJ who had interviewed Karen Plummer. Kira felt her heart sink when she heard Darcy's voice.

"So, Darcy, tell us why you think Jake McKenna isn't the right man to be our mayor? Until recently you couldn't say enough about him. You schmoozed every business owner and half the property owners in town."

"A few weeks ago Jake McKenna was my fiancé," Darcy replied with just the right blend of earnestness, innocence, and bitterness in her voice. "Now, I'm a pregnant single woman jilted by a man everyone else thinks is sliced bread."

"Pregnant! Whoa, that's news!" Bob exclaimed. "Who's the father?"

Kira almost laughed. She didn't know if he was dumb, playing dumb, or just wanted to make Darcy say it.

Interestingly, she avoided the question. "That's between me and him," she said so matter-of-factly Bob didn't pursue it. "The point is, Jake tossed me out on my ear without so much as a dime."

Kira growled low in her throat, startling the accounts payable clerk, and rushed to complete her work. She sent up a quick prayer that the solution was a simple software upgrade, fixed the problem, and quickly left the building.

Luckily, she'd been listening to the Brook Hollow station on the drive down and it came right in.

"...not quite penniless," Darcy was saying. "After all, I am a successful real estate agent. I'm just saying after a relationship as long as ours, he owes me."

"You've gotta be kidding me," Kira grumbled. She strapped on her seatbelt and started the engine.

There was a rustle of papers on the air. "You moved to town in October, right?"

"Um, right."

"So you were dating Jake McKenna for less than six months before he broke up with you?"

She didn't reply.

"Sounds a bit like sour grapes. Let's get some caller's opinions—"

Darcy jumped in before he could open a phone line. "That's not the only reason he's not fit to be mayor!"

"Oh?"

Bob had obviously learned the fine art of a well-placed silence. Kira could almost see Darcy chewing her lip. What stupid, untrue, easily-proven-false accusation would she try next?

"Jake has leanings," she finally burst out.

"Leanings?" Bob sounded incredulous. "What, like he invites a bunch of people over to lean against the wall?"

"No!" She didn't say "stupid," but the word was implied. Kira doubted Bob liked that very much. "He has...sexual...leanings." Kira could picture Darcy making a limp wrist motion.

Bob seemed to suppress a chuckle, then said, "Well, that's all the time we have today."

Kira looked at the clock on the dash. One o'clock. Saved by advertising. But not completely saved. Jake was going to have to do lots of explaining and tap dancing to get through the crap this interview had kicked up.

Kira pulled out of the parking space and headed back to Sophie's, where she was staying for the short time she was in the city. She'd prefer the privacy of her condo—her little sister was a bit too judgmental these days—but the people she'd sublet it to were still there.

Her mind whirled with things Jake could do to discredit Darcy. To pay her back. She knew Jake wouldn't go for that, though. He hated dirty pool. He'd rather rebuild his own reputation than tear down someone else's. Even Darcy.

When she got to Sophie's, she found a message from Jake on the answering machine.

"Kira, please call me. Darcy did a radio interview. It was disastrous. I need your help." His recorded voice sent a shiver down her spine and a buzz through her veins.

She called him back right away. "Hi," she said when he answered on the first ring. She shrugged out of her coat and scribbled a few notes for her invoice. "I heard the interview."

"How?"

"I was in Mainlow on a job. What are you going to do?"

Jake snorted. "You're my campaign manager, you tell me."

"You could go on Bob's show yourself and explain. Give some dirt on Darcy. Discredit her by telling them she's not pregnant. Challenging her to prove it and bring forward the father, because you certainly aren't it."

She could sense him shaking his head. "No. I'm sick of this pregnancy thing. I want to address the issue."

"Jake, the issue *is* the pregnancy! Unless they decide they'd rather chew on the gay implication."

"They already chose that. I've had three calls already, and it's only been an hour since the show."

"Who called?" Kira grabbed a pencil. It always helped plan a strategy when you knew who had to be convinced first.

"My mom, first, to beg me to tell her I'm not gay. She wants grandchildren, she said. Then she asked about Darcy, and I told her the truth. She gave a huge sigh of relief. 'I never liked her, Jake.'" He raised his tone to nearly match his mother's. "'I wouldn't say so, of course, but I am glad you got rid of her.'"

"Then was the next call *my* mother?"

"No, it was Fritz. Your mom was third. Fritz said he'd warned me about scandal. Didn't let me talk, just complained about his endorsement and roared about getting married."

"Okay, he's first on the list, then." Kira scribbled ideas. "Take him to lunch tomorrow. The most popular place in town. Let a crowd see you. Explain you're not gay, that Darcy is desperately angry because you broke up with her. Point out what good you've done lately for the town. He'll come around."

"Except there isn't much good I've done lately for the town." For the first time in this conversation, he sounded discouraged, beaten.

"What do you mean?" Kira asked, worried now.

"Darcy's distracted me for too long," he admitted, sounding even more frustrated. "I missed town council meetings, even when I was there. Too much on my mind. Karen Plummer is telling everyone how little I care about Brook Hollow.

"I've been hiding, Kira, and letting everything happen to me. I need to take some control. Help me."

"Okay, calm down." She thought quickly, jotting notes and advising him on his next actions. They brainstormed for an hour and a half, until they finally had a workable plan and Jake sounded more optimistic.

"I miss you," he murmured. "When are you coming back?"

"Early next week." As soon as she possibly could. The promise in Jake's voice gave her hope, despite her anxiety about telling him *she* was pregnant. She missed Jake, missed him like she'd miss an eye or her tongue. She could live without them, but they were indispensable.

"Hurry," Jake murmured. "We have things to do."

She didn't think he meant the campaign.

* * *

"Well, it's very exciting, you know. Jake is just everywhere, glad-handing everyone with that sexy smile of his. He went with Michael James, the police officer, to a DARE event at the elementary school." Elyse rattled on and on. Kira was glad she had a headphone attachment for the telephone, or her ear would burn for a week.

"Darcy is all over town, too, being snide and spreading more rumors."

"What's the latest?" Kira asked, trying to pack the stuff she'd scattered throughout Sophie's guest room over the past week and a half. She'd been delayed by the "quickie" job for the new client, but was finally going to be able to go home tomorrow.

"Well, she had to admit she wasn't pregnant, but tried to imply she lost the baby. Some reporter proved there were no hospital records. Dr. Gettle apparently wasn't too impressed with her, either, because she told someone she'd never been a maternity patient."

The woman never takes a breath, Kira admired silently. She had to be silent. She couldn't get a word in edgewise.

"Now Darcy's saying Jake has bigger aspirations, that he won't be a life-term mayor like Fritz. He'll be moving on to the Senate or something." Her tone was indignant. Kira had to smile. "Well, so what if he does? He's talented. Honest. He'd be a great Senator."

"They'd eat him alive," Kira interjected. She closed the suitcase and wrapped up the conversation.

"When will you be home, again?" Elyse asked.

"Tomorrow, Mom. Late afternoon." After her doctor's appointment. Kira couldn't believe it had been a month already. The changes in her body made her nervous. She had to tell Jake before someone else did.

The appointment went smoothly, but the doctor again encouraged Kira to see his colleague in Brook Hollow. Kira assured him she would, certain now that she wasn't moving back to the city.

Nearly two hours later, she wished she'd made that decision sooner. The water she'd been pouring down her throat all morning—at her doctor's orders—clamored to be released. Not able to wait ten more minutes, she wheeled into Brook Hollow's main gas station and danced across the macadam to the ladies' room.

Her relief was short-lived.

As she walked back to her car, she caught sight of Darcy's Miata at the gas pumps. Darcy, standing next to her car, stared so hard at Kira she could feel it through the woman's sunglasses.

She became suddenly conscious of her knit top and elastic-waist pants that did nothing to conceal the slight bulge of her belly. The hard, definitely-not-diet-failure belly. The belly that would have been invisible without the stiff spring breeze that molded her clothes to her.

CHAPTER 19

Jake was finally beginning to feel optimistic. Kira's suggestions plus hours and hours of publicity work—both scheduled events and impromptu activities—were paying off. The town liked him again. Public opinion was definitely swinging back his way. Fritz was on his side, even though he never stopped mentioning marriage. And Darcy had seemed to run out of things to say.

Or so he thought.

To celebrate spring, the Brook Hollow rec department sponsored a mini-carnival at Hollow Park. Jake volunteered for the pie booth and ended up going home immediately after to shower the whipped cream out of his hair. Consequently, he missed the first part of Darcy's speech.

Lance and Sue met him at the parking lot and began hustling him across the grass.

"You gotta be there, man. She's going too far this time. You've got to defend yourself."

Jake looked at Lance, too confused to pull his arms away. "What are you talking about?"

"I'm so sorry, Jake." Sue's face was pinched and worried. "I didn't know she could be so malicious."

They reached the side of the park that held a hand-hewn log-built stage. Karaoke was supposed to be going on now, but somehow Darcy had gotten a hold of the microphone.

"...despite his apparent good intentions when we thought I was pregnant," she was saying. The sun shone directly on her to good effect, making her look pure in her white sundress, her hair pulled softly back at the sides. Jake's stomach churned, from anger or fear he didn't know.

"I know Jake has rebuilt his image in this community recently. I hate to destroy all that hard work."

Yeah. Sure she did.

"But I have some information that will drastically change your view of Jake McKenna's moral character. Some ironic information, actually." The small smile on her mouth displayed triumph, and without knowing what she was going to say Jake wanted to wipe it permanently off her lips. He clenched his fists, trying to retain some control.

"Kira Macgregor is another native of this town, one most of you know. Most of you also know she has made it disdainfully clear, time and again, that she prefers Boston over boring little Brook Hollow."

This was a new tack, bringing Kira into things. Jake wondered what she could possibly have to say about Kira that was damaging to him. Unless she'd found out about their tryst at the ball.

"I have very good evidence—my own eyes—that Kira Macgregor is pregnant."

Jake reeled. "No way," he whispered, his clenched fists tightening. Darcy was lying again.

But a voice in his head—not Darcy's—generated doubt. The desk in the country club office flashed into his mind. Then Sophie's exclamation that Sunday before dinner. Kira had been sick for a long time. She'd avoided him as much as possible when she thought he owed Darcy. He couldn't believe it, but he couldn't not.

Kira was pregnant.

Was it his?

He cursed himself immediately. Of course it was his. She wouldn't have slept with anyone else. She couldn't have.

"The irony," Darcy continued over the murmur of the crowd. Jake heard a lot of "so whats" but they quieted as Darcy went on.

"The irony is that Jake McKenna created this pregnancy—with his best friend, no less—while he believed I was pregnant with his child. While he was engaged to another woman."

Now the murmur was angrier. Jake couldn't tell through his own fury whether the crowd's anger was directed at him or at Darcy or at Kira. His first instinct was to storm the stage and counter Darcy's lies.

Even if Kira *was* pregnant, even if he was the father, it had happened at the ball, before Darcy told him she was pregnant. And they were *never* engaged.

It still didn't look good, though. He'd cheated on Darcy. He'd known he was going to break up with her, but *she* hadn't known. She'd been at the party getting drunk.

He realized he'd moved closer to the stage. He turned and zigzagged through the crowd, not wanting Darcy to see him and make him a real target. He stopped when Maggie appeared in front of him. She, too, looked worried.

"Jake, what are you going to do?"

The fact that she didn't start by denying Kira's pregnancy turned his blood to ice. Joy and anger and exasperation warred in him. Hope turned its back. Things between him and Kira had been down more than up, and he couldn't, even with this news, see a happy ending.

"Is she coming home today?" he demanded. "Elyse said she might be home today."

Maggie gave a little shrug. "I don't know."

He pushed past her and kept going down the street until he got to the Macgregors' house. Brianna opened the door before he knocked.

"Jake, hi!" The smile on her face slid away. She stepped back quickly when he stomped into the house.

"Is Kira coming home today?" he rounded on her. Her eyes widened. "How long have you known?" he barked, not waiting for an answer to his first question.

"Known what?"

He growled. "That she's pregnant."

The air seemed to go out of Brianna. "What happened?"

Not, "How did you find out?" Jake noticed. Brie was good at keeping secrets, but he could see the truth in her eyes.

"Just tell me if Kira is coming home."

"She's here," Brie told him quietly. "Upstairs. But go easy on her," She stopped him before he took a step. "She had her reasons for keeping quiet."

Jake took the stairs two at a time, his mind and heart racing. He could just imagine what those reasons were. Kira *knew* how he felt about her. The only reason she hadn't told him was that she still had doubts about *her* feelings for *him*. About her ability to build a life in boring little Brook Hollow.

He deliberately fed the fury to cover the pain.

Kira's bedroom door was open. She was unpacking a small suitcase, but when she looked up, he could tell she'd been expecting him.

"We have to talk." He shut her door behind him.

* * *

Kira kept her gaze on Jake, who looked more thunderous than Hurricane Alexander, as she shoved the suitcase aside and sat on the bed. He knew. She didn't have to guess how.

"Darcy's at it again," he declared. Her heart sank. He waited. She shrugged. She had to know what the woman had done before she could defend herself.

"She's telling the whole town that you're pregnant. That it's mine. That I got you pregnant while engaged to *another* woman I got pregnant."

"That's not true!" Annoyance and agitation made her bounce to her feet. "She didn't claim to be pregnant until after...after we...."

"I know. And she wasn't pregnant, and we were never engaged. Somehow, though, this one thing seems to be the *only* thing she said that's not a lie. What I don't know is why you didn't tell me."

Kira jumped to her feet. "Because of this." She opened her arms. "Because of what the community will think. Because you deserve to be mayor more than you deserve to be held back by me."

"How noble."

His tone was so cold, Kira shivered. "I was going to tell you," she whispered. "As soon as I saw you. But Darcy saw me first."

His anger suddenly seemed to disappear, leaving only the hurt it had been hiding. "I have tried, Kira, so many times to show you that we belong together. That I have something to offer you. That Brook Hollow has something to offer you. You just can't see it."

"I *can* see it, Jake." She rushed on. "When I was in Boston, I couldn't wait to get back here, to tell you." Her hand rested automatically on her belly and his eyes followed.

Jake shook his head. "Having you and our child would have been more important to me, more rewarding than any political office ever could have been. But you didn't give me a chance to tell you that, did you? You made decisions we should have made together."

"I was trying not to be a comet!" she shouted, swiping at the tears running down her cheeks.

Jake sighed and rubbed his hand over his face. "I need a break. I don't want to fight anymore. Not anyone." He looked so defeated Kira didn't stop him as he went out the door.

She didn't know what to do next. She'd made such a mess, piling bad decision on top of stupid action, hurting the one person who'd supported her her whole life.

Her first instinct was to run right back to Boston. Get away, stay away, let everyone get on with their lives. But she knew that wasn't realistic. So she took a deep breath, steeled her backbone, and headed for the kitchen. Straightening out three lives was going to require fortification.

* * *

Kira wanted to take care of Darcy first, fix things so she would stay out of their lives for good. But she wasn't sure of the best approach. Confrontation would surely push her in the direction she was already heading. Befriending her was too much for Kira to stomach. She wasn't sneaky or mean enough to beat her at her own game. She solicited her family's advice at the dinner her mother wouldn't let her out of.

"Kneecap her," was Sophie's less than helpful choice.

"Bury her in the woods," Brie offered, getting right into the spirit of things.

"Give her a ticket to Vegas," Kira's father said, winking. Kira raised her eyebrows when her mother gave her father a come-hither look.

"I guess you two are working it out, huh?" Kira forced herself to take a bite of chicken. Her anxiety made the morning sickness feel like a party. But she had to eat.

"My trip did exactly what it was supposed to," Elyse said, placing her hand over her husband's. "But we don't need to talk about that tonight. Why do you need to do *anything* about Darcy, dear? Just make things right with Jake."

Kira groaned. "I don't think things can ever be right with Jake. I've made such a mess. But maybe things can be better if I can stop Darcy."

"Sweetheart, you didn't start Darcy, you can't stop her. Going to her or trying to beat her or teach her a lesson won't work. You need to ignore her and fix you and Jake."

Kira stared at her still-full plate. Her mother was right. Nothing Kira or Jake had ever done had stopped Darcy.

"Okay, then, what do I do with Jake? How do I convince him I've changed?"

"*Have* you changed?" Brianna asked, her mouth full of rice. She swallowed and explained, "Are you sure you don't want to stay in Boston? Can you settle down here and raise a family in Jake's town?"

Kira had hated the last two weeks in Boston. Her job—she couldn't call it a career anymore—didn't satisfy her. She wasn't sure what would. But motherhood had a pretty good chance.

Would she hate Brook Hollow? *No.* She'd never hated it. Been bored, yes, but when had she tried not to be? She'd rushed out when she was eighteen and never looked back. Since the holidays, nothing had pulled her more than the camaraderie and charm of her hometown.

"Yes, I can."

"Do you love Jake?" her mother asked, her voice soft, her gaze direct.

Kira kept eye contact and said again, with no need to soul-search, "Yes."

"Then just go to him. Tell him. Stay there and convince him. It will work out," Elyse assured her. She picked up her glass of milk. "Go now, hon. You know what to do."

Kira jumped up and tossed her napkin to the table. She did know what to do. She'd go to Jake. But she had one stop to make first.

* * *

Jake couldn't stop pacing. The anger had morphed to frustration, the same old frustration he'd felt whenever he considered telling Kira he loved her and she'd done or said something that made it plain she could never return his feelings. It was still plain, because if she could love him as much as he loved her, the stupid election and the stupid town wouldn't matter. All that would matter would be him.

He couldn't stop listening for the phone or the door, either. Because that frustration had always been coupled with hope. "Someday" hope, that "someday" things would change, that Kira would see him differently and they'd live happily ever after.

But he knew there was no ever after. He'd seen glimpses of it every so often, but the problem was getting there. A new obstacle popped up every time a person got close. So hope was pointless.

The doorbell rang.

He whirled and stared at the door. His fevered imagination, no doubt. But he waited, frozen.

"Jake?"

His breath whooshed out and he was at the door, pulling it open before he realized the hope had overtaken the frustration.

"Kira?"

She smiled tremulously. He almost didn't let her in. He didn't want to set himself up for another "I love you but." Something told him this time was different, though, and he stepped back.

He just hoped the something wasn't wishful thinking.

Kira walked to the living room and stood by the couch. "Are your parents home?"

"No, they're out for dinner and a movie. Date night."

"Good." She kept turning something over and over in her hands. It looked like a black jewelry box.

She held it out. Jake stepped forward and took it, scrutinizing her face but finding no clues. He lifted the lid and removed the flip box, opening that slowly. Inside was a stone, a large piece of what looked like broken cement.

"It's not very pretty, but I was in too much of a hurry to go down to the lake for something more appropriate." It wasn't much of an explanation.

"I don't get it."

Kira began to pace. "You said a few months ago that I was a comet."

"Yeah, and I'm your anchor." He couldn't keep the bitterness out of his voice.

"Well, I was wrong. You aren't my anchor, Jake. You're my rock. Solid, strong, but changeable, too. A part of the landscape, but also of the foundation.

"And I'm not a comet." He started to argue, but she put a finger over his lips and he couldn't remember what he'd been about to say. It had been ages since she'd touched him.

"I *was* a comet. I'm not anymore. You know what a comet is when it burns out?" She lifted the cement from its bed. "It's a rock."

Jake was silent for way too long. Kira's breathing got shallower and shallower and she was afraid she'd hyperventilate before he responded. Finally, he dropped the ring box he'd been clutching and wrapped his arms around her.

Home. It had never felt so right to Kira. Nothing had ever fit as perfectly as this embrace. It wasn't even heated. His lips weren't on hers. His arms were wrapped so far around her his hands were on his own elbows.

But she was home.

Tears spilled down her face again, soaking immediately into the sweater he pressed her into. This time, they were happy tears.

Jake pulled back. "You don't want to go back to Boston?"

She shook her head. "There's nothing there for me. I've outgrown it. Home is here." She hoped.

"What will you do here?" He still sounded a bit skeptical. Kira didn't know how to reassure him.

"I'll finish my contract with the school while I practice being a wife and mother." She held her breath. Jake frowned.

"I've never proposed to you."

"No, I'm proposing to you."

He studied her. The frown deepened, then lifted. "Okay."

This time the embrace included a kiss. Kira reveled in the tenderness they hadn't ever had time for. But before they got too deep, she pushed against his biceps and leaned back.

"What are we going to do about the election?"

Jake shook his head. "I'm withdrawing."

"You can't!"

"Yes, I can. I told you, Kira, you and this baby," he pressed his hand to the swell sheltering his child, "are more important to me than a job. Even one I've wanted half my life."

The tears welled again when Jake lifted her chin and she saw all the love in his eyes.

"I've wanted you *all* my life."

EPILOGUE

Kira gently laid a blanket over her sleeping son and made sure the hood of the bassinet blocked any light from the other side of the living room. She crossed to the couch and snuggled next to her husband, who'd just flicked on the TV.

Jake had muted the sound, but they didn't need it to see they were almost ready to announce the election results. A commercial popped on and Kira looked up at Jake.

"How are you doing?" He'd handled the last few months remarkably well, considering how often people cursed him or cajoled him or begged him or insulted him about dropping out of the mayoral race. Fritz Kleinfelter had spent hours restating his support of Jake, no matter how many times Jake told him he wasn't running.

Besides that, Kira had been incredibly happy. They'd bought a house—not through Darcy—and married in the church where they'd been baptized. Kira had had a smooth pregnancy and relatively easy delivery of a healthy baby boy, whom they'd named Joseph. She couldn't ask for anything else.

Except for her husband to have achieved his dream.

"I'm fine," Jake assured her.

And he was. He rested his head against his wife's wild mane, and smiled across the room where their child's matching curls were just visible over the top of the lacey bassinet. Joey was the light of his life, and he couldn't believe he'd almost lost the chance at this incredible family. Not just because of Kira's stubbornness, but his own, as well.

They'd come a long way.

"This is it." Kira aimed the remote at the television and turned the volume up just enough to hear the location reporter.

"...results are just astonishing. This campaign for mayor has been a historical one, the first between two women, the first in Brook Hollow to mirror the mud-slinging of many national campaigns." She reiterated Darcy's rumor-mongering before Jake dropped out of the race, and described some of the woman's more distasteful actions since she'd entered the race.

"Miss Langlais's opponent, Karen Plummer, a woman we all know as the sweet, cheerful bookstore owner, held her own and managed to place some well-aimed shots at Ms. Langlais."

The woman glanced down, a half-smile playing about her lips.

"I wish she'd stop playing around and announce the winner, already." Jake shoved his hand through his hair and wondered if Kira would let him shut off the TV.

"Shh."

"The townspeople apparently do not, however, mimic the country when it comes to dirty campaigns. In many national and state elections, the winner has been the candidate who can make his—or her—opponent look the worst. Brook Hollow, apparently, prefers the silent type."

She looked straight into the camera, and with a huge grin, said, "The winner of the election for mayor of Brook Hollow is Jacob Macgregor."

NATALIE J. DAMSCHRODER

Natalie J. Damschroder became a writer the hard way—by avoiding it. Though she wrote her first book at age five (appropriately titled, *My Very First Book*) and received accolades for her academic writing (Ruth Davies Award for Excellence in Writing for a paper on deforestation her senior year in college), she hated doing it. Colonial food and the habits of the European Starling just weren't her thing.

Shortly after graduating from college, however, she found her niche—romantic fiction. After an internship with the National Geographic Society, customer service for a phone company just wasn't that exciting. So she began learning how to write the books she'd loved to read all her life. Four books and six years later, she finally sold. Now she struggles to balance her frenetic writing life (how else can she get all the stories in her head on paper?) with her family, the most supportive husband in the world and two beautiful, intelligent, stubborn, independent daughters (one of whom has already declared her desire to be a writer, too). She somehow also fits in a day job and various volunteer positions in and out of the writing industry.

More can be found at www.nataliedamschroder.com.

AMBER QUILL PRESS, LLC
THE GOLD STANDARD IN PUBLISHING

QUALITY BOOKS
IN BOTH PRINT AND ELECTRONIC FORMATS

ACTION/ADVENTURE	SUSPENSE/THRILLER
SCIENCE FICTION	PARANORMAL
MAINSTREAM	MYSTERY
FANTASY	EROTICA
ROMANCE	HORROR
HISTORICAL	WESTERN
YOUNG ADULT	NON-FICTION

AMBER QUILL PRESS, LLC
http://www.amberquill.com